LIFE AND TIMES
OF
SCRUFFY LOMAX

LIFE AND TIMES
OF
SCRUFFY LOMAX

DENNIS MCKAY

iUniverse®

LIFE AND TIMES OF SCRUFFY LOMAX

iUniverse books may be ordered through booksellers or by contacting:

iUniverse
1663 Liberty Drive
Bloomington, IN 47403
www.iuniverse.com
844-349-9409

Because of the dynamic nature of the Internet, any web addresses or links contained in this book may have changed since publication and may no longer be valid. The views expressed in this work are solely those of the author and do not necessarily reflect the views of the publisher, and the publisher hereby disclaims any responsibility for them.

Any people depicted in stock imagery provided by Getty Images are models, and such images are being used for illustrative purposes only.
Certain stock imagery © Getty Images.

Book cover design by Megan Belford

ISBN: 978-1-6632-1311-2 (sc)
ISBN: 978-1-6632-1312-9 (e)

Library of Congress Control Number: 2020922369

Print information available on the last page.

iUniverse rev. date: 11/06/2020

The proper function of man is to live, not to exist.

—Jack London

PART I

CHAPTER 1

September 1922, Yakima, Washington

IN THE DARK OF NIGHT, Scruffy Lomax hid in a cluster of scrub trees a hundred yards up the rails from the Yakima, Washington, train station. As the freight, right on schedule, rolled by, slowly picking up speed, Scruffy tossed his bedroll and a burlap sack—or bindle, in hobo lingo—packed with enough food, he hoped, to last the journey into an open freight car, and hopped up. This is the moment he had been waiting for since back in ninth grade when he read a book of a hobo's account of riding the Northern Pacific to Minnesota, and then the Great Western Railway to Chicago.

There was something appealing about hopping a freight train and seeing this great land of America. From the book, he had learned that along with the adventure there was danger, with some rough characters riding the rails, as well as the private police—or bulls, as they were called in the book—who enjoyed nothing more than "busting" hobos. *So let the adventure begin.*

Two days in, Scruffy had ridden alone, hour after boring hour, stopping occasionally at a train yard, the steam engine announcing its whistling entry into a station, the rolling, rollicking clang and bang and rumble of a chugging train sounding as the vessel groaned to a stop to take on water for the steam engine or change engineers. Where were the hobos? Where were the bulls? Part of him was fine with riding alone, but another part had been anticipating the challenge of the unknown.

In the middle of the night of the third day, the train made its fifth stop, which he knew the location of from the schedule he had memorized, and he confirmed this when a sign on the side of the rails came into view: "Northern Pacific Railroad Depot, Missoula Montana."

As the train groaned to a stop, the only sound he heard was that of two watchmen arguing about the World Series between the New York Giants and the New York Yankees. Scruffy was scrunched away in the corner of his boxcar, beginning to wonder why boredom had never been mentioned in the hobo book he'd read.

This was not what he had expected. He expected hobos to ride along with him, old wise men telling stories about adventures of the road and rail; not solitary rides where time seemed to stop, especially at night, when he was too jacked up to sleep while remaining vigilant for a railroad bull to toss him out in the middle of nowhere.

As the train chugged ever so slowly out of the Missoula station and down past the depot, a satchel was tossed into the car, startling the life out of Scruffy.

A man climbed the ladder, entered, and looked around, not seeing Scruffy.

The man turned back and took a baby from a woman jogging alongside the car, who then climbed up. This had not been in the book. There had been no mention of women, and especially not babies. But at least he had company.

"Howdy," Scruffy said.

The man pivoted around in Scruffy's direction.

"I am hitching a free ride just like you," Scruffy said as he gestured for them to sit.

"I hear the bell ringer on this route is a furious sort," the man said as he took the baby from the woman, who sat against the back wall.

"That might explain why you are my first company," Scruffy said.

The man handed the baby back to the woman and then sat next to Scruffy, who said, "I am riding to Brainerd and then on to Chicago to find work. How about you?"

"We departed Big Bear, Alaska, where I prospected for two years with no luck, got hit with worse luck, and then good fortune when I struck gold meeting Attu," he said offering a hand toward the woman, who looked somewhat Yakama, though her features were broader, with a flat nose and heavy brow. Her hair was black and straight, and her skin brown like an Indian's—Eskimo most likely.

"Ran out of money," the man said, "and we are heading back to my folks' farm in Kenosha, Wisconsin."

"I am Scruffy Lomax."

"Robert Logan, here, and my wife, Attu, and our son, Robert Junior."

"Now is that not something," Scruffy said. "My proper name is Logan Lomax Junior, but everyone calls me Scruffy." He made a face. *How about that.*

They exchanged looks for a beat before Scruffy said, "Alaska, you say."

"Yes," Robert replied, "Big Bear is halfway between Valdez and Fairbanks. I mostly panned for gold. Struck it rich once but was robbed and pistol-whipped on my way to the assay office."

"Really?" Scruffy said in a tone that said, *Tell me more.*

"Well, it was not all bad," Robert said with affirming glance at Attu, who had begun to breastfeed the baby, covering herself and the child with a blanket. "Attu's father, who was a trapper, found me left for dead in a culvert. Strapped me over his mule and took me back to his cabin, where Attu nursed me back to health."

"That sounds like something out of the Wild West," Scruffy said as he noted the baby pulling its head back from feeding, as though not hungry.

"Indeed," Robert said. "There is a saloon in Big Bear called the Long Branch that is right out of those days."

"Saloon?" Scruffy said. "How is that possible with Prohibition?"

"Up there in the wilderness, it is a neglected territory." Robert went on to mention that Alaska had a bone-dry law enacted a couple of years before Prohibition, but that with Alaska being a territory and not a state, it was barely enforced.

"Sounds mighty interesting," Scruffy said.

"What about you, Scruffy?" Robert asked. "What got you to riding the rails?"

"Wanderlust," Scruffy said with a shrug. "Never been more than twenty outside my hometown—Yakima, Washington—and want to see what is out there."

The baby let out a whimpering wail and a sickly cough, gasping for air as though having trouble breathing. Attu tucked the blanket under his chin.

Scruffy lifted a concerned brow to Robert.

Robert glanced at his son, who could not have been more than six months. "We need to find a doctor but don't have any money left. Hope to get to Kenosha and the family doc."

Scruffy had learned last spring in his senior year of high school about a diphtheria outbreak spreading across the country—a bacterial infection that could be deadly if not tended to quickly. "Don't mean to stick my nose in where …"

Scruffy cast a hesitant look at Robert, whose eyes said, "Please continue."

"*I* think you'd better find a doctor right quick."

Robert was a medium-sized fellow with a thrash of curly hair and big brown eyes that now had an out-of-his-element look.

Scruffy said, "Next stop is Billings." He pulled up the cuff on his trousers and removed a wad of money from a pocket he had sewn on the inside of his pants leg—his life savings, save five dollars he kept in his regular pocket in case he was robbed; that way he would not lose it all and would appease the robber—a trick he'd learned from the hobo book. He peeled off a ten-dollar bill that had taken a lot of picked apples to earn and handed it to Robert. "Get off in Billings and find a doctor."

He handed Robert another ten-dollar bill and said, "And then purchase fare to Kenosha."

Robert looked at the money in his hand and then at Attu as if seeking her approval.

"Thank you," Attu said to Scruffy as she held the baby in close to her chest. "Thank you very much."

"If you are ever in Kenosha, Wisconsin, Scruffy Lomax," Robert said with conviction, "there is a place for you."

By the time the train had reached its final destination in Brainerd, Minnesota, Scruffy was ready for a break from riding the rails for four days straight, his only company the Logan family. By midafternoon he walked out of the rail yard, creaky and sore from sitting for so long, and walked up a dirt road that led to another dirt road that ran through the town of Brainerd. There were some clapboard buildings on both sides of the main street, and at the end of town was a grassy area with a gazebo in the middle and a smattering of benches—a rural version of a park.

Entering the park, Scruffy came upon two men sitting on a bench. '*Bos*, he thought.

"You might walk into town with that bindle, short stuff, but I damn sure bet you will not walk out with it. Haa … haa … haaaaa!" said an unshaven, unkempt heavyset man.

These two men fit the description of a tramp given in the hobo book that Scruffy had read and reread and reread. He knew that book inside out. He knew the hobo lingo, what to watch out for, and what to look for.

Scruffy walked over to the bench. "Jungle near here?"

The burly hobo raised his eyebrows, feigning amazement. "Well what have we here," he said in a low rumbly voice. He looked off with a touch of dramatic flair. "Sonny boy," he said, "you best head on back from wherever you come from—am I not right, Ecto?" He leaned his head toward his companion.

The brown-skinned man, haggard and gaunt, the ridges of his cheekbones set above an unkempt beard, lifted his hand in the direction Scruffy had come from. "Cross Front Street, back over the tracks, beyond a thicket of trees is a small clearing." He nodded at Scruffy in a not unkind manner.

"We not running no orphanage for bow-legged runaway runts," the big hobo said.

Scruffy felt the hair on the back of his neck rise, but he held his poise, keeping his gaze on the gaunt man called Ecto. "Thank you," he said and turned and headed toward the hobo camp site—or jungle, as it was called in the book.

CHAPTER 2

THE LONG TRAIN RIDE HAD depleted Scruffy's supply of food. His burlap sack was now empty, save one can of beans. His stash of money—fifty dollars, now reduced to thirty—was safely ensconced in his hidden pocket, save a few bucks in his pants pocket. At the edge of town was a white clapboard building with "Johnson's Groceries" scrolled in black across a storefront window.

On display in the front window with a blue-and-white-striped awing were three rows of shelves. The top held jars of candy; the second, loaves of bread; and the bottom, baskets of apples and smaller ones of cherries. Scruffy thought it possible the fruit had come from a Yakima orchard, and possibly, though not probably, he might have picked them.

At the front counter, a big-boned woman wearing bib overalls and a plaid flannel shirt greeted Scruffy with a hard look of appraisal.

Her stark blonde hair, contained by pigtails, ran nearly to her waist; her icy blue eyes had a look of one who had endured many difficulties in life: someone familiar with work—someone capable and also intimidating.

The woman lifted her brow to Scruffy as if saying, "And what might you want?"

"Howdy," Scruffy said in his friendly voice—a voice that had gotten him off on the right foot on many an occasion.

"Don't give handouts and don't need any chores done," the blonde woman said.

"Fair enough. Might I have two loaves of your bread in the window and"—he focused on a sign on a shelf behind the woman reading "1 lb. can of beans 5 ₡"—"That special you are running on canned beans."

He lifted his finger in the direction of the sign and gave her his Scruffy smile: eyes widened, lips parted to reveal his strong white teeth, and a pair of cheeky dimples.

The blonde woman cocked her fist against her side, appraising from across the counter this unusual specimen of boy-man in front of her. "You have money?"

Scruffy reached into his pocket, pulled out a dollar bill, and placed it on the counter.

Scruffy heard the rumbly murmur of voices before he saw the hobo camp. He was in a thicket of trees, in search of the clearing, his bedroll across his shoulder and his bindle with his purchase in his left hand. The voices were low and masculine, with an undercurrent of camaraderie. At the edge of the thicket, he came to the clearing, where a dozen or so men were sitting around in three clusters, each with a pot over a campfire.

They were a scroungy collection dressed in raggedy clothes—old threadbare suit jackets that were too big or too small, and baggy, worn trousers. All had growth on their faces ranging from five-o'clock shadow to long whiskers. The men were conversing quietly as though not wanting to be overheard.

Scruffy took a here-goes breath and entered the camp. The conversations stopped as all eyes landed on the newcomer. "Friend or foe?" an older 'bo said.

"Friend," Scruffy replied as he removed one of the loaves of bread from his burlap bag.

"I say so," the old 'bo said. "Come on over and join us."

Scruffy nodded okay, tore the loaf of bread in two, put it back in the bag, and did the same with the other loaf. He then handed out a section of bread to each group before sitting down at his interlocutor's fire.

Tin plates and utensils were handed out, and the lids were removed from the pots. "Mulligan stew," another 'bo at Scruffy's fire said to him.

"Thank you," Scruffy said as the man ladled his plate. The air was heavy with the rank odor of unbathed men, and Scruffy wondered if he also did not stink, having not bathed for days.

There was little conversation during the meal. The men were

obviously hungry, but none gobbled their food down. No, quite the opposite, they savored it, eating in slow, thoughtful chews.

There were bits of tomato, corn, and carrots, and a chunk or two of some sort of meat. Scruffy thought it right tasty, and even more, he thought it amazing that his wanderlust had plunked him right down in the outskirts of Brainerd, Minnesota, where he was sitting at a hobo campfire, sharing Mulligan stew with the fellas. *Wow!*

But Scruffy's momentary bliss was short-lived, as the two hobos from the park soon entered camp. "I thought I made it clear—no boy runts," the burly 'bo said as he came up to Scruffy's fire.

"Hold on, BoJack," the old 'bo said. "This here young fella done passed out bread."

"You do say, Stick Man," BoJack replied. He reached into the inside pocket of his jacket, revealing a whiskey flask. He took a short swig and let out an "Aahhh." He then walked up behind Scruffy and kicked his plate of food out of his hands.

The 'bos stopped eating, nary a sound could be heard. Scruffy had read that when challenged, a newcomer had to stand his ground to let one and all know that he would not be abused. He thought back to school, when the class bully had called him a Redskin and a fight had ensued. Scruffy had delivered a good thrashing to his taunter. Since then, no one had much bothered Scruffy, who was known in Yakima for his prowess as a picker and his physical strength, which was displayed each harvest by the ease with which he could lift bushel after bushel of fruit onto a truck without a hint of muscle fatigue.

But now he was outside familiar turf. He was an unknown in this new setting, and he was aware he had to let them know who he was.

"All righty, then," Scruffy said, standing and peering up at his tormentor, whose dark, stubbly face was marked by red scratches on his forehead and chin.

BoJack was a beastly-looking man standing a good six feet tall and having broad shoulders and a thick neck that bore a pulsing vein. "Let's settle it now," Scruffy said as he rolled up the sleeve of his flannel shirt, keeping a watchful eye on the big 'bo before him.

"Look at you, runt-boy," BoJack said. He cocked his fist and lifted his chin, indicating for Scruffy to skedaddle.

"Name is Scruffy Lomax," Scruffy said, just as calm as could be, "and I am not going anywhere." He spread his fingers before balling his large hand into a fist. "Bring it on."

A 'bo at another campfire stood. He was taller than BoJack and had the appearance of a well-to-do person who had fallen on hard times. "Leave the boy be." His voice had a ring of authority.

Stick Man said, "You either act proper or leave the site, BoJack."

A concurring murmur came from the other 'bos.

Ecto came up to BoJack's side and put his hand over his balled-up fist.

BoJack jerked his hand away and snarled, revealing dark-stained teeth.

He was an ugly, uncouth man who appeared to have nary a redeeming social quality. *Why do the 'bos put up with this thuggish man?*

BoJack sat at the fire farthest from Scruffy's while Ecto took a seat next to Scruffy. Stick Man ladled Scruffy a refill of stew and then gave some to Ecto. Scruffy tore his remaining bread in half and offered it to Ecto.

Ecto took the bread. "Much appreciated, Scruffy Lomax." He said the name with a tone of approval—a tone that said, *You are an okay fella.*

After the meal was finished and Scruffy pitched in to clean the pots and utensils, some of the men read newspapers, and others began conversations about a range of subjects, including a derailment over in Aberdeen that "kilt twenty 'bos" and the Mineral Leasing Act. Discussion of the latter led to a heated conversation about the Teapot Dome Scandal.

Some of these men were well informed—especially the tall man who had stood up for Scruffy earlier. "Warren Harding is a dishonest, ignorant, unsophisticated nincompoop. Mark my words, gentlemen, he will go down in history as one of the worst—if not *the* worst— presidents in our history."

"Now wait a minute, Harvard," another 'bo said, pointing a finger. "President Harding is a right good fella, and my pap went to school with him back in Ohio." The 'bo brought his knees to his chest and placed his hands on his kneecaps. "Why, I was a delivery boy for the newspaper he owned. One Christmas he gave me a silver dollar."

Harvard nodded as though considering the man's words. He had a long face with chestnut eyes and a matching shelf of long hair that fell across a wide and high forehead. Beneath his hobo exterior—stubbly beard, once expensive-looking tweed jacket with holes in the elbows—was the air of education, with clear diction and an accent Scruffy had never quite heard the likes of before. The closest was his elementary school teacher, Mr. Magister, but Harvard's voice had an intriguing resonance almost like an echo—a clear and distinct echo.

"I dispute nothing you have said," Harvard said with a lift in his voice, "but that does not change the fact that as president he is a failure of the highest order."

Some of the other 'bos entered into the conversation. Some were pro-Harding, others not; but what was apparent was that these were not stupid men.

At dusk, Stick Man gave out the order to douse the fires. "Overheard a couple of men in town talking about an attack on a girl—course we gonna get blamed." He surveyed the camp with a jut-jawed grimace. "So let's sleep with one eye open, and best skedaddle in the morn."

CHAPTER 3

A CACOPHONY OF LOUD VOICES STIRRED Scruffy from a deep sleep. He had been dreaming that he had married a girl he had spent time with back in Yakama—the daughter of the owner of the apple orchard—and they had a newborn son named Logan Lomax III. It all should have been wonderful, with security, a loving wife, and a son; but in the dream, Scruffy had been trapped with no escape. He had responsibility, meaning he was never to ride the rails, see the good old USA, and live the hobo experience.

The impact of something hard into his side brought Scruffy wide awake as a surge of pain shot through his ribs. Surrounding the camp with powerful flashlights were men—big men, farmers most likely—in flannel shirts and hunting jackets, armed with shotguns and pipes. "Nobody move," said a man wearing a campaign hat.

The 'bos were now all sitting up, eyes on the good citizens of Brainerd, Minnesota.

"All right," the man continued as he lowered the wide brim of his hat as though to make a point, "which one of you did it?"

An uneasy silence ensued as the 'bos looked around at each other.

"Fourteen-year-old girl fought off a tramp in the barn on the Spruill place," the man said. "Even you lowlifes have some sense of decency." He looked over the 'bos, who squinted as the flashlights' beams went from face to face.

"All right then," he said in a creepy tone that matched his creepy eyes, which seemed ready to spring from their sockets, "we can do it the hard way." He jabbed his finger at a gnarly willow tree at the edge of the thicket. A farmer who walked with a limp tossed a thick-plaited rope with a noose over a branch ten feet above the ground.

The 'bo from Ohio stood and said, "This is America, you cannot do this."

A farmer walked over and smashed an iron pipe into the side of Ohio's head. He fell in a heap to the ground—out cold.

The man in charge grabbed Scruffy from behind by the collar of his shirt and directed him over to the tree and the noose.

Scruffy had an urge to run but held up. He would wait until they attempted to put the noose around his neck—if it got that far—and when he had no other choice, he would make a run for it through the cover of the trees.

"Wait a minute, now, Swenson," one of the farmers, a man with a thicket of red hair said. "We cannot hang this boy."

"Like hell," Swenson said as he gripped Scruffy's collar so tightly Scruffy thought he might choke to death.

Scruffy fought the urge to run as the possibility arose that this could be the end of an adventure that had just begun—of a life that had just begun.

"May I speak," Harvard said.

The farmers looked to find the voice that had spoken: a voice of reason, a voice of education—a voice that said, *Let's work this out.*

"No," Swenson said.

"Yes he can," the red-headed man said. "It was my daughter that was attacked. I should have the final say on this."

Harvard stood and raised his hands, palms up, toward the father of the girl. "Mr. Spruill," he said in a tone that seemed to confirm his deduction as to the man's identity, "let us see if we cannot resolve this."

"Goddamn," Swenson said as he spat into the ground while jerking Scruffy for good measure.

"Continue," Spruill said.

"Did you daughter get a look at her attacker?"

No, he sneaked up behind her in the barn. She said she fought him like a wildcat before getting away," Spruill said.

"Did she say anything else?"

"Said he smelled like rotten whiskey."

"Did she mention how she fought him off?"

"She was pretty upset, I didn't want to push her."

"You said she fought like a wildcat?"

"Yes," Spruill said as his eyes glinted. "Said she scratched him but good. That is when he let her go enough that she broke free."

"So," Harvard said with finger raised. "The attacker should have some sort of marks on his face."

BoJack took off running toward the thicket of trees, but he did not get far, as a swarm of farmers, including Swenson, converged on him and pummeled him to the ground. Now free, Scruffy eyed his gear just a few steps away. He sensed that this was all coming to a head—that he needed to act decisively.

"String him up," Swenson said in a maniacal, crazed voice.

A melee broke out. Pipes were swung, and 'bos were going down, blood leaking from body parts. It was gruesome. Scruffy took two steps, bent down, and grabbed his gear before scurrying into the thicket and running for his life. He gave one last look over his shoulder as a swarm of farmers held a flailing BoJack as they attempted to fit a noose around his neck.

Scrambling out of the thicket while trying his best to avoid briar patches and low-hanging limbs, Scruffy felt the blast of a shotgun register in his core like a peal of thunder, encouraging him to move quicker, briars be damned.

Veering away from town on the side of a dirt road, Scruffy was not sure where he was heading. It was pitch dark outside, save a glimmer of moonlight. After a couple of hours, tired and thirsty, he walked into a small copse of trees and took a seat on a rotting log.

This was not the romantic adventure Scruffy had expected. No sir, this was real life with deadly consequences, with firsthand violence and hatred that he had read about in school, but to witness it in person was sickening. He was no longer living in a community of folks that knew and trusted him. He was outside his safety net, and if he was going to continue to seek adventure, he needed to be vigilant.

Not more than five minutes later, a shadowy figure approached along the side of the road. It was a tall man with a bedroll strung over his shoulder and a sack in one hand, moving with long strides and glancing over his back.

"Psst, Harvard," Scruffy said. "Over here." A sense of relief washed over Scruffy as he lifted his hand to the person who may well have saved his life: this man who had the gift of gab—a man whose company would provide security.

Harvard stopped in his tracks. He looked over, still not seeing where the voice was coming from.

"It is me—Scruffy," he said with a wave of his hand.

"Of course it is," Harvard said with a wave back as he made his way over.

Harvard took a seat next to Scruffy and let out a long stream of air. "We witnessed firsthand mankind at its worst." He went on to tell Scruffy that BoJack fought with furious vigor, but he added, "The farmer with the limp shot-gunned him right in his neck, blood splattering all around—dead before he hit the ground."

He went on to say that Ecto yelled out, "Murderers!" After that, everyone ran, farmers included. "'Bos were scattering every which way."

"What now?" Scruffy said.

"Well," Harvard said, squinting, as the first glimmer of dawn peeked over a line of dark hills. "Let us rest a spell and then head up the road and see what the day may bring."

Harvard dug into his knapsack and removed a kidney-shaped leather bag with a nozzle. "Thirsty?" he said as he handed the bag to Scruffy.

Scruffy took a swallow and wiped his mouth with the back of his hand. The water was warm, but it sent a river of relief down his parched throat.

"Go ahead," Harvard said with a confirming nod. "Take another swig."

"Thank you," Scruffy said as he took a short swallow of water.

"What is this called?" Scruffy said, as he handed the leather bag back.

"Bota bag. I picked it up in Holland during the war."

"You fought in the Great War?"

"Survived is more like it." Harvard went on to tell of enlisting in England in 1915 and serving in the British Army and being captured by the Germans at the Battle of the Somme. "Spent three miserable bone-chilling months as a prisoner in a camp in Lower Saxony before I and three chaps tunneled our way out and ended up in Holland." Harvard lifted his hand as though he preferred not to talk further about the war.

"You are not a regular 'bo," Scruffy said.

Harvard lifted his gaze toward the road, where in the distance the sun rose through the morning mist, casting a shadowy glow across the hills. "Nor are you, my friend."

Scruffy reached into his pack, removed a can of beans, and was about to slice it open with his pocket knife when Harvard said, "Try this."

He handed Scruffy a device with two arms attached to a closed end with a circular blade on one side and a handle on the other.

Scruffy placed the blade on the rim of the can and closed the handles. He looked at Harvard, who nodded for him to continue. Scruffy turned the handle, and the device rotated around the rim of the can. "How about that," Scruffy said.

Harvard smiled his approval. "Figured right out how to use a can opener."

"Can opener, huh," Scruffy said. "Good tool."

As they sat eating beans and sipping water from the bota bag, Scruffy said, "I am a quarter Yakama Indian." He made a face. *How do you like that.* "My mother grew up on the reservation and met my father picking apples on the land I grew up on."

"Your father a white man?" Harvard said, more as a fact than as a question.

"Yeah," Scruffy said. "He died the day I was born—bad fall during harvest. My mother named me after my father—Logan Lomax."

"Life has a way of presenting one with the utmost irony," Harvard said as he scrapped the side of the can, collecting a stray bean.

Harvard asked Scruffy what had made him take on the 'bo's life.

"Never been outside of Yakima and the orchards—only life I knew." He wiped his mouth with the heel of his hand. "Had to see what this great country I have read about in school is all about." He slid a look over at Harvard. "I am guessing you attended college at Harvard?—my civics teacher in high school said it is the best college in the land."

"Yes, I graduated from Harvard with a degree in English literature and went on to law school. My name is Winthrop Cornwall Emerson the third." A smile seemed to come to his eyes. "I went by Winnie until I hit the road."

They exchanged looks for a beat before Harvard said, "I imagine you are wondering how a Harvard-educated fellow with a law degree ends up in a hobo camp."

"I imagine irony had something to do with it."

They sat in silence for a while before Harvard asked Scruffy his destination.

"Chicago for a while. After that not sure, other than away from Yakima." Scruffy looked at Harvard, his eyes saying, "You?"

"Back East. Been on the road for a year." Harvard went on to say that after the war, he took a job at a law firm in Boston, "But it all seemed so"—he balled his hand into a fist and settled it under his chin—"unimportant. I had an urge to travel without privilege—to understand what it was like to be poor and powerless."

"Anything stand out to you?" Scruffy asked.

"Yes," Harvard said. "I learned that America is more than a country. It is an idea." He paused. "And we need good and honorable men in positions of authority to protect that idea."

Back on the road, Harvard said that they were heading to St. Cloud and from there could catch a freight train to St. Paul, and then Chicago. "But we will need to hitch a ride, since it is over fifty miles to St. Cloud."

After an hour on the road, they had passed a cherry orchard and a field of wheat stubble, and now they came upon a pasture of cattle.

Scruffy said, "Haven't seen a living soul since we hit the road."

"To the Hindu people of India," Harvard said with a lift of his chin toward a bull chewing a cud, watching the passersby, "they are regarded as sacred souls."

"Sacred?"

Their attention was diverted by the sound of an engine coming from their rear. They turned to see a stake truck approaching.

Instinctively, Scruffy started to run for cover, but Harvard said, "Hold up." He raised his hand for the truck to stop.

The truck was a Ford Model TT—one that Scruffy was familiar with, since the owner of the orchard, Mr. Pinchwell, had purchased one that Scruffy had learned to drive in half an hour. He would haul a truckload of apples from the orchard up to the holding barn, where he would unload the haul.

The truck came to a stop. The driver was an older man in bib overalls, and riding next to him was a boy of about ten years old.

Harvard leaned into the passenger window and said, "We could use a lift if you are so inclined." He offered his hand to the empty flatbed.

The old man leaned his head over, inspecting Harvard and Scruffy. "Tramps?" He was heavyset, with a massive head atop which sat a head of white hair.

"We are adventurers on an adventure, you might say," Harvard said, his upper-class voice belying his appearance.

The boy was staring at the two men before him. He had big, wondering eyes and dark hair with a sideways cowlick in the back.

"Well ..." the old man said, "I guess that would be all right. We are heading to St. Cloud—if that helps you."

CHAPTER 4

CRUFFY AND HARVARD SAT IN the back of the flatbed, rattling along a country road. Distancing himself from Brainerd brought Scruffy a great sense of relief. The incident at the hobo camp had left an indelible mark—an understanding of the whims of life. He had seen how one minute a person could be happy-go-lucky and the next fleeing the scene of the murder of a man—a bad man for sure, but BoJack did not to deserve to die that way without a fair trial. It was the first of many life lessons the road would provide.

They passed an apple orchard, the twenty-foot-high trees lined in straight rows, bursting with fat apples.

"Grand Alexanders," Scruffy said with a wave of his hand toward the orchard. "Picked a few of those," he said as he splayed his hands in front of himself.

"Scruffy—" They hit a bump in the road, lifting both up and then down.

"Sorry 'bout that fellas," the driver said, leaning his head out the window.

"Not a problem, good sir," Harvard said over his shoulder.

He returned his attention to Scruffy. "As I was saying, you have an impressive pair of hands—or, as the Dutch would say, *grote haden*."

"They come in handing for picking—that is for sure."

The orchard faded as they descended a hill, and Scruffy said, "I am guessing when you get back home you are going to use your lawyer skills to help those less fortunate."

Harvard turned his gaze on Scruffy, his eyes holding a gleam of appreciation. "I see your hands are not your only asset."

Scruffy and Harvard were let out in the middle of town in front of stately-looking red brick building with two-story columns and a cupola on the roof.

The old man and boy got out of the cab and approached the sidewalk. "That would be the St. Cloud courthouse," the old man said with a lift of his chin toward the building. He looked up the street lined with two- and three-story buildings as an electric streetcar—with a trolley pole connected to an overhead wire—came into view, clanging along on wrought-iron tracks down the middle of the street. The *ding-ding* of a bell announced its arrival as it came to a stop in front of the courthouse.

"Wow," Scruffy said as he eyed the handsomely finished hardwood sides and the metal plate in the front with "Sauk Rapids/ St. Cloud" painted on. It was beautiful, with seven windows to a side.

A conductor got off the car and helped a woman exit. He was wearing a conductor's hat with a hard black brim and a flat black crown, a starched white shirt, a bow tie, and a vest adorned with a pocket watch chain leading to a pocket. Everything appeared so civil and civilized and orderly.

"That car is headed to the train yard," the old man said.

"Shall we do it?" Scruffy said.

"Break the hobo code?" Harvard said through a toothy grin.

"I will buy," Scruffy said.

With that, Harvard lifted a hand to the old man. "Much appreciate your kindness, sir."

"Hope your fellas find what you are looking fer," the old man said as he put his hand on the boy's shoulder.

"Grandpa ..." the boy said in a wistful tone, "someday I would like to take an adventure."

Scruffy sat next to the window, Harvard next to him. Scruffy had ridden in the trolley a few times back in Yakima, but riding in this car held a whole new level of interest, with the sights of the magnificent buildings with tall pillars and detailed scrollwork, the automobiles rumbling to and fro, and the people on the sidewalk walking with a determined purpose. Scruffy pointed to a vertical sign attached to the corner of a four--story building with "Emporium" written out in capital letters from the top to the bottom. "Is that not something, Harvard."

"Welcome to the world, young man. Welcome."

Scruffy flashed a grin at Harvard and then returned his attention to the window. The trolley came to a stop at a corner. The building before them had a huge billboard on the roof with a man in a white chef's hat holding a loaf of bread. Above his head was scrolled in dark letters, "Double Wrapped."

People departed the car, and others got on and took seats, and the trolley proceeded around the corner. Up ahead was a sight that held Scruffy like nothing before in his life. They approached a bridge passing over a river, and the trolley was going to cross it. "That the Mississippi?"

"In all her glory," Harvard said as he leaned into Scruffy to get a better view. "That is a four-span high deck pin-connected truss bridge."

"Huh," Scruffy said. "How do you know that?"

"My grandfather was an engineer on the erection of the Brooklyn Bridge back in the old century. I know my bridges."

They were now entering onto the bridge. Down below rolled the mighty Mississippi, and Harvard was right—she was there in all her glory. The water was a rich, dark blue, its current rippling downstream. Beautiful it was, with trees lining the banks. At the end of a small dock, two boys were fishing, one boy casting his fishing line.

Scruffy thought of *The Adventures of Tom Sawyer* as he imaged those two boys living similar lives as that irascible pair, Tom and Huck— maybe swimming in the Mississippi, rafting downriver to a deserted island, or just fishing off the dock. One of the boys was netting in a large silvery fish. Scruffy had not a clue what type it was. He had fished in the Yakima River from time to time, catching mostly catfish and steelheads, but nothing this long and big, nor anything with a row of dorsal fins like little humps.

As the trolley rattled across the bridge, Scruffy imagined himself unattached to the land and water, instead an agent of the sky, floating overhead—the rattling *clang* of the wheels and *whir* of the motor whisked from his conscious mind—as he crossed this great body of water, as free as the wind in this great land of the free. What Scruffy had learned in school about his country could not compare to actually seeing and living the American experience.

As they departed the bridge, Scruffy said to Harvard, "I will never forget this for as long as I live."

CHAPTER 5

E XITING THE TROLLEY AT THE train station, Scruffy was taken hold of by a surge of regret. Riding on the trolley as a paying customer had given him a sense of worth, as though he was paying his fair share. He'd felt he had a right to enjoy the view, to wonder with real curiosity what it would have been like to have been one of those boys fishing in the Mississippi. But now he was back to sneaking a ride on a freight train.

Part of him wanted to buy a ticket to St. Paul for him and Harvard, but another part—a stronger part—said no. He felt he needed to see this great land from inside a freight car, to converse with the 'bos and tramps along the way, to understand the perspective of the downtrodden and lost. Why that was, he was not sure, but it was deep inside him that this was the way to go. And besides, if he was going to see America, he could not afford to purchase fares, for he would run out of money. That he was sure of.

At the sound of a train whistle in the distance, Harvard led Scruffy down the tracks and past a water tank mounted on stilts, to a cluster of gnarly bramble off to the side of the rails. As an engine came to a halt just past the water tower, a worker climbed a ladder on the tower and filled the train's tender, situated behind the engine, with a water spout attached to the tower.

"That freight would be heading to St. Paul," Harvard said.

"You sure?"

"Trust me," Harvard said with a wink. "It is heading east, and east is where St. Paul is."

Scruffy was fortunate to have met Harvard. The young 'bo was now under the guidance of the wise Ivy Leaguer, who provided knowledge of the road and life, and along with it a sense of safety in his presence.

He wondered if Harvard was the only man with an Ivy League education to tramp—probably not. And he guessed the others did so under worse circumstances than those of Harvard, who would be returning to his previous life with a year of riding the rails under his belt. It was an experience that would serve him well as he advanced in his life. He imagined Harvard sitting around the family dinner table, recounting tales to his grandchildren about events back in the day—the characters he met and the experiences he had. Would he ever mention a young lad by the name of Scruffy Lomax?

And how would it all end up for Scruffy? He had no Ivy League education to fall back on. His life journey would present more challenges, but with them came an opportunity to really experience the different parts of a life, and to live free and unencumbered. At least, that is what he told himself, but deep down he sensed that there was always the chance of a turn of events—some unforeseen calamity or an opportunity that might be hard to say no to.

The daydream was broken by a tall, lean man in a dark blue high-necked uniform jacket and matching trouser, white shirt, and tie clutching a night stick as he inspected the empty freight cars.

A badge on the lapel of the uniform glinted in the sunlight. "That be a bull?"

"Yup," Harvard said. "He looks like a mean one."

"What's the plan?"

"Wait until the train starts moving, and we make our move."

"What if," Scruffy said as he watched the bull continue down the line of cars, boarding some and giving others a quick check, "he spots us?"

"The idea is to not let that occur," Harvard said as the water spout was removed from the tender and the train began to chug forward, its different parts—the wheels, couplings, springs, axles—cranking and creaking an array of metallic sounds.

The bull boarded the caboose, but not before giving one final look.

"Now?" Scruffy said.

"Wait."

As the train was groaning and straining forward, a figure darted out from a covey of scrubby trees and headed down toward the end of the train. He hopped up on a boxcar ladder two cars down from the caboose and swung himself into the open car.

The bull hopped off the rear of the caboose, gun drawn, and moved in long strides to the open car. "Come on out of there," he demanded as he strode along the moving train.

Silence.

"If I have to get up in there, your sorry ass will regret it." He lifted his pistol overhead and fired a warning shot.

A 'bo appeared at the edge of the open door. It was Ecto, BoJack's comrade. He appeared even more emaciated now, a bag of bones in a raggedy coat and threadbare trousers.

"Get off," the bull demanded, with his gun pointed at Ecto as he strode along beside the car that was ever so slowly picking up speed.

Ecto reached for the ladder, and the bull grabbed him by his shirt and jerked him down, letting go as Ecto fell awkwardly, his arms and legs going every which way. He landed headfirst and rolled over on his back, out cold.

The bull looked down toward the station, which had nary a person in view. Without a word, he pointed his pistol at the prone 'bo and fired a round into his skull. Ecto's body twitched as though he had been shocked, and then he was still.

"That son of a bitch," Scruffy said as he started to stand, but Harvard grabbed his arm.

"You will only get us killed too."

The bull looked furtively up and down the tracks and over at the bramble. He then hoisted the lifeless body over his shoulder and scrambled over to the rear platform of the caboose and stepped up and into the car.

"Come on," Harvard said as they made a run for the car that Ecto had just departed.

They sat against the back wall, with the car door open, the countryside blurring by—scrubby landscape of cheaply-made box houses, and then the farms, some with irrigation ditches that brought memories of digging them for the orchards. How long ago Yakima now seemed. Scruffy had been away for less than a week, and it seemed as though it had been a previous life.

Still shaken at witnessing the murder of Ecto, Scruffy ran over and over in his mind the thoughtless cruelty of the bull—the taking of a man's life as though it were no more than throwing out the garbage.

Harvard said that the bull would probably toss the body off "in the middle of nowhere."

"Somebody will see it at some point," Scruffy said, more as a question than a statement.

"Eventually," Harvard said. "But there will be no investigation—just a luckless 'bo who will get buried in the potter's field ... if he is lucky."

"What if we report it in St. Paul? It could be your first case defending the downtrodden."

Harvard narrowed his gaze. "I would need to look presentable, and I only have six bits to my name."

Scruffy reached into his hidden pocket in his pants leg and removed his stash. "I have nearly thirty dollars. What say we get ourselves cleaned up and buy some *presentable* attire?"

Around a bend, the St. Paul rail yard came into view. The train was inching to a stop, and Harvard said, "Let's get off here."

They jumped off and scurried into a copse of trees and then made a beeline for the station.

Inside the depot, Harvard went over to an elderly gentleman sitting on a bench with a leather suitcase at his feet. "Professor Willis," Harvard said as he approached the man.

The gentleman looked up from reading a book, his gaze uncertain as he eyed the tall man with a scraggly beard, wearing a worn jacket, beneath which was a frayed denim shirt.

"I am Winthrop Emerson. I took your ethics and constitutional law classes back in oh-nine and ten."

Professor Willis was wearing a three-piece suit with a starched white shirt and bow tie. He wore pointed brown shoes with detailed stitching. He looked like a professor at an exclusive college, such as Harvard. "Mr. Emerson?" The professor said with a tone of disbelief—a tone that said, *What in the world happened to you?*

"After the war, I had some issues to sort," Harvard said with a shrug. "This is my friend Scruffy Lomax."

Scruffy nodded a hello as the professor gave him the once-over.

Harvard went on to explain his last year traveling the country and his plan to represent those less fortunate back in Boston.

"Very worthy," the professor said.

"But," Harvard said, "before I return, I have a matter here in St. Paul I need to address." He went on to tell of the murder of Ecto. "Scruffy and I witnessed it. I would like to make a complaint to the authorities."

"I have spent the last three years vacationing on a nearby lake with a colleague and his family," the professor said before his attention was diverted by a raised voice at the ticket window.

"When are these damn trains going to run on time!" a man screeched in a whiney voice.

The professor made a strangled, disapproving murmur. "Hmm." He returned his attention to Harvard. "My colleague tells me that St. Paul is as crooked a city as any in the country." He went on to reveal that the police chief, John "Big Fellow" O'Connor, was in league with a powerful criminal element based in Chicago that hid out in St. Paul when the need arose. He went on to say that the Bureau of Investigation, a federal agency, had set up a field office in St. Paul to investigate.

"And if that is not enough," the professor added with a flourishing sweep of his hand, "the unofficial mayor, Dapper Dan Hogan, is in cahoots with O'Connor." He leaned forward, wiggling a finger for Harvard to come close, and whispered, "Irish thugs they are—the worst kind."

An announcement was made for a train departing for Chicago. The professor stood. "That is me," he said as picked up his suitcase. He lifted a cautionary finger and said to Harvard, "First off, if still of the mind to pursue this matter, clean yourself up"—the professor slid a look over at Scruffy—"both of you, and be careful, very careful."

With that, he lifted a hand farewell and walked toward the boarding platform.

CHAPTER 6

S T. PAUL WAS SIMILAR TO St. Cloud but bigger, with higher buildings, wider streets, bigger cars, and more people bustling about. Scruffy had purchased a flannel shirt and trousers for himself and a new suit and dress shoes for Harvard at the Milbern Clothing Company—twenty-one dollars in all. The clerk at first was hesitant at the appearance of two men in ragged, worn clothes, until Harvard spoke and his education and privileged background became evident. It seemed to Scruffy that he had brought the haughty tone up a notch.

They took their new clothes to the YMCA, where they showered and Harvard shaved.

Scruffy stood in front of a mirror in the men's room, hand-combing his thicket of dark hair and, at the same time, studying his face—an unusual face with the high cheekbones of his Yakama ancestry, the square chin and well-formed nose that his mother said were exactly like his father's, and the squinty blue eyes that were his alone. He had not seen himself since he had left Yakima, but he sensed that he had been an ungodly sight, having not bathed since his departure.

Clean and smelling fresh in his soft new clothes, Scruffy considered whether he had betrayed hobo code, regressing back to whom he was trying to get away from. But it was only to have justice done, and then he would be back on the road.

Harvard appeared to be a different man—a man of good breeding and education and with a ruddy complexion from a year of working odd jobs from New York to California. He looked as though he belonged in his gray suit with wide lapels. He appeared to be a successful man of not much more than thirty, with the aura of a bright future on his horizon. It was amazing what a shower and new clothes could do for a person.

After getting directions at the YMCA to the Bureau of Investigation, Harvard reached into his bindle and removed his can opener and handed it to Scruffy. "I will no longer need this." He dumped his hobo attire, bindle, and bedroll in a trash can in the front of the building. "I am done with the road, Scruffy," he said with a lift of his shoulders, as though the matter was out of his hands.

"I figured that," Scruffy said, gripping his bindle. "I still have more to go."

As they headed up the sidewalk, Harvard slanted a look at Scruffy. "And my good friend, I *figured* that." He raised his forefinger. "But first we have a matter to attend to before we bid each other adieu."

The tall mammoth buildings seemed to close in all around Scruffy, leaving him feeling trapped in this big town, in his clean, new clothes and scrubbed body. He yearned for the road, to head back into his adventure, but he needed to stay by Harvard and see this through.

The Bureau of Investigation office was on the first floor of a six-story building at the north end of town. The entrance was the most confounding thing Scruffy had ever seen. It consisted of three glass doors that hung on a central shaft within a cylindrical enclosure. Harvard pushed a door and stepped inside the space as the doors rotated, emptying him inside the building.

Scruffy followed what Harvard had done and was whisked around with the moving glass doors and came out inside the building. "Is that not something," he said with a shake of his head.

"You are in the twentieth century, my friend," Harvard said with a tap on Scruffy's shoulder.

In the lobby, Harvard checked an address board on the wall and then proceeded down a hallway. At a double-wide door with "Bureau of Investigation" scrolled in bold blue letters above the numeral 133, Harvard said, "Here we go."

Inside he spoke to a woman at a desk, behind which were three doors. Harvard said he wanted to speak to a federal agent about "a matter of the utmost importance."

She inquired what it was in regard to, and Harvard said, "Federal crime."

The woman, who was heavyset with plump cheeks and stark blonde hair that was tied into a bun, wore a no-frills white blouse that matched her expression of serious modesty. Scruffy figured she had grown up on a farm and was thrilled to have this position.

She studied Harvard as though to ascertain whether he had more to say. She then told him to take a seat.

They were the only visitors in the place.

Twenty minutes later, a man in a suit emerged from the middle door; other than the receptionist, this was the first person they had seen since they entered. He was of average height with light brown hair combed straight back—a solidly built gent of similar age to Harvard, with broad shoulders, thick neck, and a square-jawed face.

"Mr. Emerson," he said, as he reached for the doorknob. "Please, my office." His voice had a nasal quality similar to that of Harvard's, but with a stifling effect, as though he was trying to hide it.

Harvard stood and motioned for Scruffy to come with him.

Inside the office, which had a one-window view of a back alley, the agent asked his guests to have a seat in two straight-back chairs in front of an imposing oak desk that the agent sat behind. The space was sparse, with a metal file cabinet in a corner and nothing on the walls other than a framed diploma with a dark blue perimeter and white interior square bearing in bold lettering the phrase "Praeses Et Soch," below which was "Universitatis Yalensis," followed by three lines in Latin, and then a name, "Benjamin Franklin McGregor," which was followed by more Latin. At the bottom of the document, written in Old English font, was "Yale University."

Harvard lifted his chin toward the diploma and then turned his attention to the agent, smiling. "I see we are in the presence of an Eli."

"Frank McGregor," the agent said, holding his hand out to Harvard, who clasped it and shook firmly.

"Winthrop Emerson here." Harvard gave his head a tilt toward Scruffy. "My friend Scruffy Lomax."

McGregor nodded a hello to Scruffy and returned his attention to Harvard. "Princeton man?"

"Haar … vaard," he replied, raising his eyebrows coyly as if they were members of a secret club.

McGregor said that after obtaining his undergraduate degree, he had gone on to get his law degree from Yale. "Joined the army after passing the bar in New York, but got snatched up by the Judge Advocate General's Corps and never did get out of the States during the war." There was a trace of resignation in his voice as though he had missed a big event.

Harvard summarized his war history: "Joined up with the Brits, captured by the Krauts, escaped to Holland." He went on to tell of joining a law firm in Boston after the war. "But it was too soon," he said. He then told of riding the rails for a year. "Needed to get away for a while, and over the course of my travels I obtained a learning experience of what it was like to have not in this great land." Harvard leaned forward in his chair, his hands on his knees. "It was also a cathartic experience."

"Really," McGregor commented. "I bet you saw some things—in Europe and on the rails."

"Yes," Harvard said as he looked away for a moment and then back at McGregor. "Yesterday we witnessed a murder at the rail yard in St. Cloud by a railroad cop." He went on to give a description of the bull and his theory as to where the body might have been dumped.

While Harvard was talking, McGregor was studying his face as though an idea was formulating. "I could use a good man to assist me in investigating this ... and other cases," he said with a squinting look that brought his thick brow into a nearly straight line. "St. Paul is teeming with bad characters."

"Are you offering me a job?" Harvard asked.

"Yes," McGregor said, "that is exactly what I am doing."

The two Ivy Leaguers looked at each other. In that instant, an understanding seemed to transpire between them.

"Twenty-five dollars a week, with immediate upfront money," McGregor said as he leaned forward in his chair, hands folded on the desk. "Ten bucks to get you over the hump."

McGregor went on to say that Harvard could stay at his place until he saved money for rent and clothes.

Scruffy knew he was the odd man out. And, truth be told, he was glad of it.

He was also glad to have witnessed these two Ivy Leaguers converse with each other as though they had known each other for years, old pals back together after a few years apart, each reacquainting with the other. They both were enjoying the company of someone from their background on this stark Midwestern prairie.

After the two swished their way through the revolving front door, Harvard said to Scruffy, "I know you are anxious to hit the road. Agent McGregor and I will take it from here."

"I am anxious, and also I am confident that you and Agent McGregor will see that justice is done."

Harvard dug into his pocket and removed the ten-dollar advance from McGregor. "I want you to take this as a partial payment on the clothes."

"No can do," Scruffy said with a shake of his head. "Let's call it payment for lessons you taught me of the road. Plus"—he gave his lopsided Scruffy smile—"I still got almost a sawbuck to my name."

After they shook hands, Harvard said, "If you ever need my help, my one-of-a kind-friend, Scruffy Lomax, you most likely will find me in the years to come in Boston—in the Bureau of Investigation field office."

CHAPTER 7

SCRUFFY HEADED IN THE DIRECTION of the St. Paul train yard. He stopped at a grocery store on the way and restocked with canned goods and a half loaf of rye bread. He also filled an empty quart bottle of milk he had found in a trash can in an alley with water at the train station.

Wary of the bulls, Scruffy walked along a rise by the tracks, going far enough away from the depot that he could hop on a boxcar moving at a good clip, allowing him to be certain that the bull could not get off the caboose. According to the schedule he remembered from back in Yakima, a freight train would be arriving shortly that was heading to Chicago.

About a quarter mile from the yard, Scruffy waited in a cluster of scrubby trees. He sat with legs crossed—Indian style—and removed a can of beans from his sack. After being in the company of Harvard—or Winthrop, as he would now be called and had always been called except for his year of tramping—it was a tad lonely by himself.

As a 'bo, the name "Harvard" fit that tall, erudite man just fine; but in his gray suit and fancy-man shoes, he surely did look like a Winthrop. Hard to believe a person could change from hobo one minute to Ivy League graduate the next.

Winthrop and McGregor would be a fine team, and a strong friendship would form between them. Winthrop, Cornwall, Emerson, and Benjamin Franklin McGregor were righteous names and righteous men. A country, if it is going to be great, needs men like them, who have had all the advantages of education and social status to help those less fortunate, to strive to help their fellow man and make America an even greater place to live. He remembered Harvard's words: "I learned that America is more than a country. It is an idea. And we need good and honorable men in positions of authority to protect that idea."

At school, Mr. Magister had mentioned Teddy Roosevelt as such an example. He said something along the lines of "Teddy Roosevelt was born with a silver spoon in his mouth, but he devoted his life to public service. America needed President Roosevelt then, and we need men like him now. America will always need men who put their country ahead of their personal gains."

In high school, Scruffy had read in world history class about the cruelties of the powers that be in other countries, and though he thought the politicians in America were for the most part fair-minded, he knew that it was not a perfect situation and that many things went wrong in this democracy, such as the murders of BoJack and Ecto. He thought that Harvard had found his calling, and he would not be one bit surprised if he followed up on his desire to help those less fortunate, beginning as an employee of the federal government as a federal agent, and later on in life possibly as a private citizen using his lawyer skills. *Either way, the country wins.*

In the distance, Scruffy heard the faint whistle of a train—destination the City of the Big Shoulders. His English teacher in high school had read the poem "Chicago" by Carl Sandburg, and Scruffy found it mesmerizing. He had memorized the opening stanza:

Hog Butcher for the World,
Tool Maker, Stacker of Wheat,
Player with Railroads and the Nation's Freight Handler;
Stormy, husky, brawling,
City of the Big Shoulders:

Scruffy realized that he had been fortunate to have had an excellent teacher for elementary school, and that teacher was followed by more of the same throughout four years of high school. He learned geometry, algebra, and basic chemistry; read Shakespeare and Twain and *The Odyssey* and *The Iliad*. "Someday what you learn here will help you out," Mr. Magister, his elementary schoolteacher, had said at the beginning of every school year from first through eighth grade, pointing to the window, "out there in the real world."

And Scruffy did wonder, if not for his excellent education, whether he would be sitting here now. It was reading Mark Twain and the Greek adventures and other books with tales of derring-do that first planted the seed to see this world while he was in it.

In the fading light of dusk, Scruffy could not make out what types of cars were being pulled by the locomotive coming into the yard. Harvard had told Scruffy that Indians had given the name "iron horse" to the locomotive, and it was an apt description. *A black iron horse,* Scruffy thought. The locomotive was a beautiful piece of machinery, with its cowcatcher—a grate mounted in front to catch debris—the streamlined nose, like the prow of a ship; and the smokestack atop the cab, like the exposed blowhole on a whale.

Scruffy had gotten a book from the high school library about locomotives and learned how burning coal was converted to steam power; the fireman, or stoker, tended the fire in the cab while the engineer drove. There was a brakeman—or bull, as the 'bos called him—who inspected the trains; and the switchman attended the switch in the railroad yard, switching trains from one track to another.

It was all fascinating, and even more so were the sounds that it created: the whoosh of the steam blowing out of the cylinders when it came to a stop, the chugging rumble as it gained speed when departing a station, the hiss and screech of the brakes, and the forlorn call of its whistle in the dead of night.

The allure of the road was taking hold of Scruffy. Each sound of the train was like the sirens enticing Odysseus and his sailors—every clang, hiss, and whoosh a musical composition created by some higher power.

At the 'bo camp, Ecto had told Scruffy that once a man gets the call of the road in his bones, "It is a powerful thing to deny."

But presently something else was hard to deny; not only had the train not moved, but not a soul was about. Darkness was descending on the land, the sky fading into a grayish blanket of fading light.

Finally a man exited from the engine cab and walked along the cars, which looked like one long continuous car without enough light to make out any detail as to what type of cars they were—just a dark outline. The man walked down a ways and returned to the cab. *This must be either the engineer or the stoker, who tends the fire for the boiler. But where is the railroad cop—the bull? Do some trains not require them? If so, does that mean this train is unrideable for a freeloading 'bo?*

The locomotive began to pull out of the yard, chugging forward. By the time it passed Scruffy's location, his question was answered. The cars were all open-air hoppers, some filled with gravel, and others, coal.

Harvard had told Scruffy that some 'bos, when necessary, rode in the blind—the area between two cars—but this was dangerous, since any sudden movement could toss a man, who might fall to a gruesome death underneath the train. So Scruffy had another idea.

After checking up and down the tracks, he strung his bedroll over his shoulder and grabbed his bindle holding his supplies. He then ran for the moving train, which was now going about five miles an hour; grabbed onto a ladder with his free hand; and stepped up. At the top of the car, Scruffy tossed his gear into the bed of crushed blue stone.

As he started to swing his leg onto the mountain of stone, the train jerked forward, causing Scruffy to lose his grip on the ladder. He fell back, lunged for the ladder but missed, and landed hard on his back on the side of the tracks. A sharp pain ran from his spine down through his legs.

Scruffy tried to move, but his body did not respond. A surge of panic ran through him before his sense of feeling returned to his extremities.

He struggled to sit up, and then, with one hand on the ground, he stood. He stretched his hands over his head, told himself it was now or never, and ran stiff-legged toward … what? He no longer was sure which car he had tossed his gear into.

The train was picking up speed—no time to waste. Scruffy moved along the side of the train, trying to remember which car was his. *Was it the third back from the cab or the fourth?* He grabbed the ladder on number four, since he was unsure he could catch up to number three. At the top of the ladder, he found not gravel but coal. He realized his gear must be in number three.

He climbed into the coal car and sat atop the mountainous black chunks. It was uncomfortable sitting up high with no railing to prevent him from falling off if the train came to an abrupt stop or lurched forward. And what if, chugging around a bend, he fell off?

Lying flat on his stomach, Scruffy methodically hand-dug a pocket as the train began to gain speed. He had to stop a couple of times when the train lurched forward and press his entire body against the coal to prevent himself from sliding off the car. By the time the train was at full speed, the hole was big enough for him to scrunch on down with knees against chest, the top of his head just over the edge. It was a filthy situation to be in, but it was also much safer than sitting atop.

As the train rumbled along, Scruffy leaned back. The sky was awash in silvery stars twinkling in a blue-black sky. Floating halfway up was a shimmering half-moon. It brought to mind Scruffy's grandmother, Half Moon, who had passed nearly ten years prior, when Scruffy was only seven. He saw Half Moon only a couple of times a year, when she would depart the reservation and visit her daughter and grandson. He had little interaction with her, a quiet, solemn woman. There was a chasm of silence separating the grandmother from her grandson. These visits seemed more an obligation.

His mother, Nantes, had told Scruffy that his grandmother had been named Half Moon when she was born at night under a waxing half-moon. "It would have been an appropriate designation for me," Nantes said as she tucked her son into bed, "since I am half white and half Indian—Bois-Brulés." She stretched the word out in the tone of someone who had been dealt a bad hand in life: "Bwah—broo—ley."

"Bois-Brulés" is a term that refers to persons descended from an Indian woman by a white man. Though his mother identified as an Indian, Scruffy thought she felt incomplete, as though her white blood contaminated her. It seemed as though she were a person living between two worlds while raising a son considered white, who looked white and acted white, having grown up in a white world.

Scruffy had never given much thought to his ancestry. Other than an incident in school when the class bully had called him a redskin, and Scruffy had whupped him but good, he had never met any prejudice. And now, out in the world, he was a white man.

A wave of fatigue came over Scruffy. He had not slept in what seemed to be forever and folded his arms to his chest and fell into a deep, dark slumber.

—◄O►—

The squeal of brakes and a long and loud whistle woke a startled Scruffy. At first he was not sure where he was, and then it all came back to him. The train was coming around a bend, and up ahead in the distance were flashing red lights, the colors sharply pronounced in the dark of night.

After passing a railroad crossing at a two-lane country road, the train picked up speed for a while and then began to slow again. Shortly after, it came to a stop at a train depot—a yellow clapboard structure with a turret at the far end. It had vertical windows and a warm appeal, as though someone were inside making cookies. A sign hanging below the eaves of the vertical roof of the main body read, "Sturtevant, Wisconsin."

The map Scruffy had studied back at the St. Paul depot indicated that Sturtevant was near the Illinois border and not far from Chicago. He knew it might be now or never that he would find his gear situated in the other car. His attention was diverted by a burly man in bib overalls departing the cab. He then assisted another man, whom Scruffy had earlier seen inspecting the cars in St. Paul, down off the cab before that man collapsed in the big man's arms.

The big man picked the other man up as if he were cradling a child and carried him into the depot. Scruffy waited a while. He looked both ways down the train—nary a soul. He lifted himself from his hiding spot, staying low, emerging from the hole on his belly. At the side of the car away from the depot, Scruffy climbed down the ladder, onto the ground, and up the ladder on car number three. He lay on his stomach, inching himself forward over the carload of blue stone toward two dark objects in the front corner. There they were—his bindle and bedroll!

What a relief, he thought as he sat up for an instant, checking through his bag to make sure his supplies were still there.

"Hey there, boy!"

A light flashed in Scruffy's eyes, blinding him.

"Come on down," the voice said in a not unfriendly way.

Scruffy shielded his eyes and saw it was the big man in bib overalls, whom he figured to be the engineer. "You gonna shoot me?"

"Ha, ha, ha!" the man laughed. "How 'bout better accommodations for the remainder of the trip. Fireman took ill. I need someone to stoke my fire."

The man removed the light from Scruffy, who squinted to clear his vision. Before him stood a bear of a man smiling a gap-toothed smile.

There was something reassuring about not only the man's voice but, even in the dim depot light, also the way he held himself, standing there with his hands at his side while showing an easy-as-could-be smile that conveyed trustworthiness.

"Okay," Scruffy said. He slung his bedroll over his shoulder, grabbed his bindle, and climbed off the car.

CHAPTER 8

I AM HOPEFUL YOU ARE FAMILIAR with hard work," the engineer said to Scruffy with a look of appraisal. He then added, "By the looks of you, I would say so."

They were inside the cab, which Scruffy found amazing. There was a huge iron firebox adorned with gauges, levers, and hoses that were connected to the boiler in front of the cab. To the right of the firebox was the engineer's high seat, next to the window.

In the rear of the cab was a bin filled with coal.

"Tell me what to do," Scruffy said.

"Well, first thing," the engineer said, handing Scruffy a rag. "We need to get some of that coal dust off you."

"That is better," the engineer said as Scruffy handed him back the rag, which was now smeared black. "Now, let's get you a pair of gloves," the engineer said as he reached into a box under his seat. He handed Scruffy a pair of heavy-duty leather work gloves.

Scruffy tried to put one on, but it would not fit his hand.

"Now those are an impressive pair of mitts you got there," the engineer said. "Let's try these," he said as he reached back into the box under his seat.

"Ready," Scruffy said as stretched his hands into the tight leather.

The engineer opened the firebox door to a yellowish-red inferno of burning coal. "Grab that banjo," he said, pointing to a shovel leaning against the coal bin, "and start bailing it equally in the four corners and the middle." He gave Scruffy a conspiratorial wink and said, "I got me a locomotive to drive."

After twenty straight minutes of Scruffy loading the firebox, the engineer said, "That will be good for a while." He jerked his thumb toward the seat across the cab. "Take a break."

It was the first manual labor Scruffy had done since he left Yakima, and his body had responded with a ravenous vigor. After riding for days in a boxcar, it seemed strange to be sitting in the tall chair, facing the firebox and the gears and levers, his view on his left a fallow field.

The engineer leaned his head back out the window, his left hand on a lever that controlled the speed of the locomotive. "Check the level of the water on the water sight glass."

Scruffy scanned the instruments and pointed to a glass tube. "This?"

"Yeah. What does it read?"

"Water is less than halfway up."

"All righty, now pull that handle with the long rod—called a water injector—and stop when the water level is at three quarters."

Scruffy pulled the lever and eyed the sight glass until the level was adjusted.

"Good job," the engineer said. "John O'Hurley here, lad. What do you go by?"

"Scruffy Lomax."

O'Hurley threw a quizzical grin at Scruffy, leaned his head back out the window, and pulled a cord overhead, releasing a mighty blast of the whistle. He then winked at Scruffy accompanied by a nod of approval.

And so it went. Scruffy loaded coal into the firebox, adjusted controls, such as the atomizer and artificial draft, and got a firsthand lesson in how a steam locomotive operates. And when Scruffy was loading the firebox, O'Hurley began a conversation about his parents coming over from Ireland as teenage newlyweds during the potato famine and settling in New York City. "It was a rough go in Hell's Kitchen, but according to my Da, it was better than starving to death." O'Hurley went on to say that when he was sixteen, back in 1886, he left New York and tramped his way out west, riding the rails.

As he shoveled a load into the firebox, Scruffy said, "And you became an engineer?"

"In America, lad," O'Hurley said, "anything is possible."

Scruffy was tempted to tell O'Hurley about the murder of Ecto but thought better of it. He did not want to get him involved, and anyway, he had confidence in Harvard and McGregor.

The trip was longer than Scruffy had expected, with a stop along the way to fill the tender with water in Kenosha—where Robert Logan was from—another delay due to a signal malfunction at a small depot in Northern Illinois, and track maintenance. By the time they arrived in Chicago, it was dawn. The railyard was huge, like a city of railroad cars on lines and lines of tracks.

"What is your plan, Scruffy?" O'Hurley asked as he pulled on the brake as the train came to a halt at a loading dock near rows of warehouses.

Scruffy was sitting in the fireman's seat, staring out at the endless sea of freight cars. He turned to O'Hurley and said, "Check out Chicago, figure out how to hop a freight down south, and then head up the coast to New York."

"I got some good tips for you in that department, lad."

CHAPTER 9

C HICAGO WAS EVEN BIGGER AND bolder than Scruffy had imagined. He had walked from the railroad yard through an industrial area full of billowing smokestacks and brick warehouses.

O'Hurley had given Scruffy directions to the north end of town, "Where all the rich folks live and congregate."

Scruffy wanted to walk through the heart of the City of Big Shoulders and view Lake Michigan, which O'Hurley had said was at the north end.

"It's an easy enough city to navigate in," O'Hurley had told Scruffy. "The streets run east and west, and north and south."

After walking through a neighborhood of row houses, busy with men dressed in denim and flannel, and women in plain sack dresses, heading every which way, he turned onto a street lined with two- and three-story buildings.

Up a ways, Scruffy came upon what he had been waiting to see. Monstrous they were; some were tall spires scraping the sky, others huge masses of brick and limestone with an assortment of arches and architectural detail that bedazzled the eye. And there were other buildings under various phases of construction, and other projects with massive holes in the ground.

This is why Scruffy had left Yakima—to see such sights as this. He had wanted to walk down the streets that were like canyons, to see the red trolley cars clanging down the street, and to witness the men in their expensive business suits, striding down the boulevard.

Finally, at the end of a wide street, he came upon a park. Running down the center of the park was a path lined by well-manicured shrubs and colorful flowers. The path led to an octagonal gazebo with intricate latticework and a cupola on the roof.

At the end of the park, Scruffy came to a gravelly lane. A horse-drawn open carriage driven by a man wearing a top hat and long coat was the only vehicle; a couple being chauffeured sat within. Past the lane was a concrete promenade with people of all ages sitting on benches facing Lake Michigan, a swath of blue, its gentle waves lapping the shore.

The adults were stylishly dressed: the men in finely cut suits and wearing bowlers or fedoras, the women in long skirts and frilly blouses and bell-shaped cloches, the girls wearing straw boater hats—some with a ribbon in the back, and the boys wearing beanies or caps with short brims.

Scruffy glanced self-consciously at his recently purchased flannel shirt and cotton trousers. A film of coal dust still remained from his ride in the coal car.

Down the promenade a ways, Scruffy took a seat on a bench, removed a loaf of bread from his bindle, tore off a piece, and took a thoughtful bite. He needed to figure out a few things. If he was going to travel down to Florida and then up the East Coast, it might be a smart idea to have more money on hand. *Why not find a job right here in Chicago, save up some dough, and then ride a train down south?* He had seen a Help Wanted sign for laborers at a construction site on his way through town.

If he got the job, did he want to find a place to live or find shelter outdoors? The weather was still moderate, but it would probably not be so much longer. He decided to apply for the job and then decide.

Also, he wanted to get a sense of what life in a big city was like. What were the people like? He was not sure if he could acclimate himself to such a different environment, but he thought he at least should have the experience so he could say at some time in the future, "Yep, I lived in Chicago back in 1922 and let me tell you ..."

Hod carrying was rugged, monotonous work, but the pay was good—thirty-five cents an hour. Scruffy's job was to mix cement and carry bricks on a hod—a V-shaped open trough on a pole—to the brick masons, who worked on scaffolding, laying courses of brick for the facing of an eventual four-story building on Michigan Avenue.

The masons were Italians who spoke little English, but there was not much need for conversation, other than "Più mattoni" (More bricks) and "Più veloce amico mio" (Move faster, my friend). These men were the first Italians Scruffy had ever met, and he liked them. They were a hardworking group of dark men who took great pride in their work. They were meticulous in getting their courses straight and insisting that the mortar was mixed with a proper consistency—not too wet, not too thick.

The brick mason foreman was younger than the others and spoke English reasonably well, though his thick accent of wide vowels was sometimes hard to understand.

Scruffy had been working at the job for two weeks and had set up living quarters under a bridge two blocks from the job site. He had the spot to himself and slept tucked on a ledge at the top of a slanted support wall underneath the bridge ramp. It was noisy with the cars rumbling overhead at all hours of the night, but soon the fatigue from work and getting used to the sounds of the big city combined for a deep sleep— the best sleep he'd had since departing Yakima.

Scruffy had a routine of getting up at the crack of dawn—he was regular in awakening at that time—eating canned meat and bread, walking to work, and afterward heading to a nearby grocery store to buy any needed supplies. Three times a week, he would wash himself with a washcloth and bar of lye soap by taking off his shirt, pulling up his pant legs, and wading into Lake Michigan.

Dinner was raw vegetables and some type of meat he bought from street vendors. Hobo stew would have been grand, but he knew a fire under the bridge might draw attention.

During his lunch breaks, Scruffy would sit with the Italians on the open second story of the building. They stacked bricks for chairs and talked softly in their native tongue. One discussion grew animated, and Scruffy asked the foreman what they were talking about.

"They like America plenty good, but Prohibition they no understand." The foreman shrugged. "Me, I no drink, but my men— they not right without vino."

During a civics class in Scruffy's high school, Prohibition had been discussed, and the teacher had mentioned that there could be unforeseen consequences. "This new Eighteenth Amendment is unfair to the people in this country who like a libation from time to time," he had said with finger raised. "And where there is a will, there is a way."

Scruffy had overheard at the grocery store that there was a condemned building where bootleg whiskey and wine were being sold. He told the foreman, who lifted a thick, dark brow in a silent "Yeah?" He then said, "I knew having an Americano on the crew would help with"—he waved his hands in front of himself and smiled widely—"with ... how you say ... learning the ropes."

The next day, a mason handed Scruffy a log of Italian salami. "Grazie, Scruffy. Grazie, mio amico."

After that, Scruffy was treated like a younger brother. He began to pick up enough Italian to speak a little and understand a bit more.

After work on the third Friday of Scruffy's employment, the foreman, Francesco, invited Scruffy to dinner at his place. "My wife, she make a lasagna, and homemade bread." Francisco gave a jerk of his chin as though to say, *What do you think?* he then added, "Come. Join us."

Francisco lived in a second-story apartment in a lower-income section of town near the North Side, less than a mile from the worksite. At the top of a flight of stairs, Scruffy knocked at unit 204, and Francisco answered.

"Welcome, *mio amico*," the Italian mason said with a wave of the hand, ushering Scruffy in. Scruffy breathed in the most enticing mingling aroma of bread and what must have been lasagna. Scruffy was not even sure what lasagna was, other than some sort of Italian dish.

The apartment was basic, with a small kitchen off the living space, two casement windows, a bathroom with the door open, and another door, closed, that must have led to the bedroom. The space was sparsely furnished, with a sofa accompanied by a dinged and dented coffee table, and a couple of hardback wooden chairs. A dining table that seated four was off the kitchen and was covered by the finest thing in the apartment by far, a hand-embroidered beige tablecloth with lace inserts.

Francisco raised his chin toward the decorative table and said with a trace of pride, "We bring from Old Country, passed down from my wife's grandmother."

A ruckus of voices shouting in Italian drew Scruffy's attention to window.

"We call this Little Sicily," Francisco said with a hand toward the window.

Outside there was a whirlwind of activity that Scruffy had ventured through: street vendors hawking their wares stocked in stands or carts, food vendors shouting out specials, clusters of people bustling about, horse carts clogging the street, and residents watching from their iron-framed balconies, taking in the scene below.

The bedroom door opened, and a slim woman with dark hair that hung to her shoulders emerged. She was dressed in a white blouse that was buttoned to the neck, a dark skirt, and black shoes with short, thick heels.

"Ah," Francisco said, "Scruffy, my wife Sofia."

Sofia gave a tilt of acknowledgment toward Scruffy, her warm hazel eyes shining a smile. She said in a shy voice, "Buona sera."

Sofia spoke no English, she but listened intently from the kitchen, softly repeating a word now and then as though trying to pick up the language of her new country, as Scruffy and Francisco sat in the living room talking.

Scruffy gave a brief description of his life in Yakima—his Yakama roots, working the orchards, school, and hitting the rails.

"Tell me about your country, Francisco."

Francisco said that he and his *paisanos* from the job site were from Palermo, Sicily. "We come from generations of masons," he said with a note of pride. "That is the past." He raised his hand up as though taking an oath. "This here, America," he said with force, "is the future."

The lasagna was made of layered sheets of pasta, between which were various cheeses, creamy tomato sauce, and succulent ground beef sauce. Never in his life had Scruffy tasted anything so delicious. And the Italian bread was piping hot and slathered in butter.

At dusk, heading back to his setup at the bridge, Scruffy passed a newsboy hawking the *Chicago Tribune*. "Feds arrest murderous railroad cop," the boy said in a high-pitched voice. "Justice served in hobo slaying."

"How much?" Scruffy said.

"Two cents."

Scruffy handed the boy a nickel and told him to keep the change.

"Thank you, sir, thank you!" the boy said before turning back to the business at hand. "Extra! Extra! Read all about it! Railroad cop ..."

Scruffy stood under a street lamp and read the report. "Federal agent Frank McGregor and his assistant Winthrop Emerson arrested Northern Pacific policeman John Watson for the murder of an indigent man known only as Ecto."

Scruffy went on to read that Winthrop had witnessed the murder when working undercover. Ecto's body was recovered in a drainage ditch that ran alongside the rail line twenty miles west of St. Paul. A bullet was removed from Ecto's skull and an expert scientist had used forensics—a new scientific test in the detection of a crime—to match the bullet to Watson's gun.

Not only had Harvard assisted in the arrest, but a new type of scientific method had been critical. Scruffy's prediction that Harvard— or, more properly now, Winthrop Emerson—was on his way to helping those less fortunate had come true. Not that it helped Ecto any—dead is dead. But he knew it might help other 'bos down the way, as some of the bad-seed bulls might now think twice about cold-blooded murder.

After a month and a half of working with the Italian masons, Scruffy had accumulated a total of seventy dollars. It was now early October, and it was getting brisk sleeping outdoors, and soon it would be cold. The bridge did provide protection from the wind, and Francesco had given him a wool blanket, but it would not be long before he would wake up shivering. It was time to head south.

O'Hurley had given explicit instructions on riding the rails down south. "Lad, you want to take the ninety-six, which departs the south end of the yard every Friday at midnight, to Chattanooga, and from there take the one-ninety-three to St. Petersburg." O'Hurley had also warned what to keep an eye out for along the way. "Watch out in Atlanta for the bulls, I hear they are a bad lot."

After Scruffy's last day of work, Francesco handed him a twenty-dollar bill. He said, through a widening grin, "Your pay, plus a bonus for good work, and the bootlegger in the warehouse"—he gestured to his masons cleaning their troughs—"provide *vino rosso* for my men."

Scruffy felt rich. He had nearly one hundred dollars to his name. He did not have to catch the train to Chattanooga until midnight, so he decided to splurge a bit.

He had overheard at a newsstand two men talking about a cathouse on the south side of town, on the corner of Euclid. At first Scruffy thought they might be talking about house pets, but he soon discovered otherwise when the conversation discussed various parts of the female anatomy.

Scruffy was inexperienced in regard to women, having gone only so far as kissing a girl he dated during his senior year back in Yakima; the one time he placed a hand on her breast, he got slapped in the face.

It was too far to walk, so Scruffy took a trolley across town and caught another trolley, and then he got lost, ending up in a rough-looking neighborhood of ramshackle apartment buildings. The people on the street were all Negroes. Scruffy had seen only a couple of colored people in his entire life, both itinerant pickers from Alabama.

He approached a man on a street corner drinking wine from a bottle wrapped in a paper bag.

"Best get your white ass out of here 'fore dark, white boy." The man was tall and lean with broad shoulders. His face was as black as night, his eyes two angry slits.

As Scruffy quickened his pace, two more men came up alongside the other man, blocking Scruffy's path.

"Hey, boy," one of them said to Scruffy in a sharp, demanding tone. "Give me your money if you knows what good for yah." The man was of medium height, with a thick chest and neck, wearing a white T-shirt that showed off his bulging biceps.

The three men circled around Scruffy, who tried to run through them, but all three jumped on him, knocking him to the ground, kicking him in the ribs. Scruffy rolled over on his side and got halfway up before he felt a stinging bop on his skull. He saw stars before everything went dark.

CHAPTER 10

SCRUFFY WOKE IN AN ALLEY. The first glimmers of dawn slanted a thin ribbon of light into the narrow corridor. His head was pounding as he sat up, back against a wall, his ribs screaming with pain. His face felt swollen, as though it had been inflated. He wiped his lip, and there was blood on his fingers. Scruffy brought his hand to a lump on his cheek and another on the side of his jaw.

He imagined he looked some kind of terrible. He checked his pockets—empty. Then he felt his secret compartment—empty also!

A saying that Mr. Magister liked to quote rose in Scruffy's mind: "Adversity is a fact of life. It cannot be controlled. What we can control is how we react to it."

Well, sir, Scruffy thought as he struggled to stand, *my turn to react.* He found his bindle and bedroll. They had been ransacked, but his canned goods and can opener and a few odds and ends were left, including his pocket knife.

As he collected all his worldly possessions, each movement accompanied by a wince, he realized that he had been unconscious all night. He also realized that he was in no condition to try to ride the rails all the way to Florida. He needed someplace where he could go to recover before embarking back on his journey. His first thought was to go to Francesco's apartment, but he instinctively rejected it. He did not want to impose, and it would feel awkward.

Scruffy remembered a conversation from a while back, when he had given money to Robert Logan to tend to his sick infant. "If you are ever in Kenosha, Wisconsin, Scruffy Lomax," Robert had said with conviction, "there is a place for you."

O'Hurley's train had stopped in Kenosha to fill the tender with water. It was not far from Chicago—less than a hundred miles.

Scruffy heard the clop of horse hooves on pavement. An older man was in a horse-drawn cart with a load of rusty pipes, scraps of metal, and newspapers in the back. Scruffy raised his hand. "Can you help me?"

The man pulled on the reins, and the cart stopped under a street lamp. There was not anyone else about. The street was quiet. The old man furrowed his brow, a look of surprise glinting in his dark eyes, followed by a look that said, *What in the world have we here?*

"Boy," the old man said, drawing out the word, "you'd best get on up here."

Scruffy tried to step up into the seat, but shooting pain in his ribs brought him back down. The colored man grabbed Scruffy's wrist as he winced his way up on to the seat.

A flick of the reins and the horse began pulling the cart, clopping down the street. The old man slanted a look at Scruffy in an appraising manner. "Let me guess, you come to this side of town looking for some black top and got more than you bargained for."

"Yes, sir," Scruffy said. "That is exactly what happened."

The junk man left Scruffy out in a warehouse district less than two miles from the freight yard.

"One thing," the old man said. "There is good and bad in folks of all kinds of colors—do not go thinking we is all bad." He nodded as though to say, *You got me?*

Scruffy got off the wagon and looked up at the old man, whose expression was one of hard compassion. "Thank you for your help," he said.

"All right then," the junkman said with a final nod. He flicked his reins and headed off.

By the time Scruffy got to the rail yard, it was midmorning. Walking was a slow process. He would walk a bit and then stop to rest, as his head throbbed and his ribs ached with every step. There were tracks and freight cars everywhere. It was like a giant maze.

But O'Hurley had told Scruffy that the train to St. Paul, which went to Kenosha, departed from the same warehouse that they had arrived at. "One at noon and one at midnight."

With some time before the noon train, Scruffy hunkered down in an old empty caboose sitting across from the warehouse. The car was handsomely furnished in hardwood, equipped with lights, stove, and cushioned seats.

There was not a person around. The place looked like a graveyard for freight cars. He wondered if crews rotated from warehouse to warehouse, unloading some freight cars, while others were moved to other tracks for another leg of a journey. O'Hurley had told him that each car's load had a specific destination.

He was sitting on the floor, his back against a wall, out of view, below the car windows. Hunger gnawed at his stomach. He pulled a can of beans from his bag and thought of the wonderful dinner at Francesco's—the layered lasagna and the warm bread. *Good times and bad,* Scruffy thought as he rotated the opener around the rim of the can. *All part of the journey.*

Over the next couple of hours, Scruffy checked the window a few times but saw no sign of any activity. Then he heard the groan of a steam engine and the clatter of freight cars moving slowly from the depths of the yard toward the warehouse, where the train came to a halt.

The murmur of voices grew until there was the sound of men at work: orders being given and the clang of cars unhooking and recoupling. Scruffy stayed low as he heard footsteps outside his caboose.

Then there came a shout: "Departing for St. Paul in ten minutes!"

Thank you, Scruffy thought. *Thank you.*

Getting off the freight car in Kenosha was worse than boarding. Scruffy hurt something fierce in both sides as he swung around to the ladder and jumped off while the train was slowly approaching the depot. He lost his balance and fell over on his side, causing him to moan in pain. He lay there, unsure if he could get himself up. He rolled over, got on his hands and knees, and crawled into the cover of scrub trees and brush along the side of the tracks.

It took five minutes for the pain to be manageable before he could rise to his feet and head into town.

Kenosha was a big small town. Small, yes, but the buildings along the main street were two stories, and there was a church at the end of town with a righteous-looking steeple. There was something comforting in this town on the shore of Lake Michigan. It seemed to him as though he was safer from bodily harm here than in a big city.

Scruffy asked the proprietor at a grocery store if he knew Robert Logan. The man was around fifty, short and stout with a shiny bald head, and was wearing a white shirt with a bow tie, over which he wore a merchant's apron. He looked Scruffy over cautiously. "Who is inquiring?"

"I met Robert and Attu a while back, and he told me to look him up if I never needed help."

"Well, sir," the merchant said with a concurring nod, "You certainly look as though you could use help."

The Logan farm was three miles outside town, and Scruffy hoped he could make it. His ribs ached, and he had a terrible headache. The directions had been simple enough: "Head past the church at the west end of town, and keep going up the road until you come to a farm on your left with a white farmhouse at the end of a gravel lane."

By the time Scruffy came to a field of stubble on his left, he was having trouble breathing because of the pain in his ribs. He struggled his way up the gravel lane; a small orchard of apple trees on his right barely registered in his mind.

He stopped a couple hundred feet from the farmhouse to gather himself to make it to the front door. The house was big and impressive, including a wrap-around front porch adorned with arches and a viny trellis, gable windows on the second floor, and a turret.

Scruffy had to lift his elbow with his left hand to raise his right hand to the door knocker. Shortly after, the door opened and Attu answered, holding her baby in her arms.

She gasped at the sight before her. "Oh," she said, "come in, come in."

The inside of the house had a comfortable feel that brought a sense of relief over Scruffy as he gave a perfunctory inspection. A staircase with fancy scrollwork on the banisters led to the second floor. To his left was a spacious den with a brick fireplace, a large sofa, and inset shelves and cabinets; and across the foyer was the dining room, which housed a dinner table and cabinet, both large and both made of oak. A closed door in the back most likely led to a bedroom.

Attu led Scruffy into the den and told him to take a seat. "Are you okay?" she asked as she placed her hand on Scruffy's cheek.

"Been better," he said as his head began to spin as though the room were whirling around him. "I am feeling dizz—"

CHAPTER 11

WHEN SCRUFFY AWOKE, HE WAS lying on his back on the sofa in the den, his boots removed and a cotton patch quilt covering him. Robert sat in a chair nearby.

"Doc is on his way, Scruffy," Robert said. He leaned forward in his chair, forearms on thighs, hands folded between his knees.

Scruffy tried to sit up, but a pinging in his temple forced him back.

"Just lie still until Doc Adams arrives."

For the first time since he was attacked, Scruffy could relax. Safe and warm—and oh, so comfortable, as long as he did not make any sudden moves—he lay on the big, cushy sofa, his head resting on a pillow. "Good enough," he said with a slight nod. "One thing though," he said. "The baby is okay?"

"Yes, thanks to you. I will tell you all about it after you are feeling better."

"All right," Scruffy whispered as a warm sleep enveloped him—a hazy kind of sleep that he had never experienced before.

The murmur of voices and the closing of a door woke Scruffy. Robert came into the den accompanied by an older man with thinning gray hair and a weary demeanor. He was dressed in a white shirt and tweed suit jacket with elbow patches, and he was carrying a hefty medical bag.

Scruffy, this here is Doctor Adams," Robert said.

The doctor nodded a hello and pulled up the chair Robert had been sitting in alongside Scruffy. "I am going to check you over, son," he said as he removed his jacket and rolled his sleeves up to the elbows. He then pulled the quilt down to Scruffy's waist and unbuttoned his shirt, exposing Scruffy's torso.

Scruffy peeked down at his bare chest, discovering splotches of purples bruises on both sides of his ribs. He imagined his face had some similar coloring.

"Robert," the doctor said over his shoulder, "Get me a bowl of warm water, a bar of soap, and a washcloth."

The doctor reached into his medical bag and removed a stethoscope.

After the doctor had examined Scruffy thoroughly from head to toe, including shining a small light in both eyes, he said, "You have a concussion and bruised ribs." He gave his chin a thoughtful scratch and added, "And welts on your face and bruises atop your head." Doctor Adams sat back as though appraising the situation. He then leaned forward, a glimmer of admiration in his eyes. "I do say, you are some tough stuff. What you received would have immobilized most folks."

The doctor's expression returned to that of a concerned physician. "I am going to clean you up and then apply iodine to cuts on your lip and scalp. It might sting a little."

After the doctor cleaned dirt and grime from Scruffy's head, face, and neck, he applied iodine with a cotton swab to the patient's bottom lip, the sharp stinging sensation eliciting a grunt of pain.

When Doctor Adams had finished, Scruffy said, "Thank you, sir. I do not have any money to pay you. I did, but I was robbed."

"Not to worry, Scruffy," Robert said. "I have you covered."

Later that evening, a man came into the den as Scruffy lay resting, drifting in and out of sleep. He looked like an older version of Robert, with a similar head of curly hair that was flecked gray, deep-set brown eyes, and the thick, strong body of a man familiar with manual labor.

He approached the sofa, almost tiptoeing as though not to disturb.

Scruffy grimaced a smile.

"I am Robert's father, Edward. It is an honor to meet you, Scruffy Lomax."

"Thank you for taking me in, sir."

Edward sat in the chair and leaned forward with folded hands just as his son had done. "You do not need to thank me, but I most certainly must thank you for saving my grandson's life."

Edward went on to tell of Robert and Attu's recounting of their journey home. They had found a doctor in Billings, and Robert Junior was treated with ointments and medicine. They then they took a train back to Kenosha, and Dr. Adams continued treatment. "It was nip and tuck, but a few weeks back, Doctor Adams said my grandson was clear of the illness. Why in God's name Robert ever left for Alaska is beyond my comprehension," Edward said. "But of course, he did something right in marrying Attu and giving us a grandchild."

A woman wearing khaki trousers and a denim shirt came into the den. Scruffy figured this to be Edward's wife. She had auburn hair tied in a ponytail and was tall and angular. "Hello there, Scruffy," she said through a smile—a smile he imagined she did not shower on just any-old-body.

After a week of resting in his own bedroom and being tended to by all members of the family, Scruffy had recovered enough to volunteer to help around the farm. It was a family-run business—160 acres of predominantly corn, soybean, and potatoes, and a three-acre apple orchard worked by Edward; his wife, Eleanor; Robert, and "Local hands when the need arises," as Edward told Scruffy.

Scruffy had mentioned to Robert his experience in orchard work, and Robert asked, "Would you take a look at our apple trees? We recently harvested our second crop." Robert went on to say that the orchard had been his mother's idea. "She thought we needed to diversify."

"Let me guess," Scruffy said, "your father was not too keen on it, but at her insistence, he agreed."

Robert pointed a finger at Scruffy as though impressed by what he had just said. "Exactly," he replied. "My mother is one determined woman."

At the head of the orchard, Scruffy, Robert, and Eleanor surveyed what lay before them.

Scruffy reached down into a row amid a patch of weedy grass and picked up a handful of soil. It had a sandy, loamy quality that was appropriate for apples but also encouraged intruders. He eyed the straight line of young trees, the boughs twisted every which way in an unruly manner. "I have some suggestions," Scruffy said with a look around for confirmation.

"By all means," Eleanor said. "We are vegetable farmers by trade."

"First thing," Scruffy said as he pointed up the row, "If the weather holds, we can grow clover between these rows to eliminate those thirsty weeds."

"I like that," Robert said as he shot a look at his mother, who nodded her agreement.

"Second, prune the canopies." Scruffy slid a look at Eleanor to gauge her interest and added, "The owner of the orchard I worked for, Mr. Pinchwell, was a learned man when it came to growing fruit." He lifted his brow to Eleanor, who said with her eyes for Scruffy to continue. "Mr. Pinchwell emphasized the importance of pruning to allow sunlight penetration and at the same time to develop the structure of the tree to support the crop load."

"Makes sense," Robert said as he glanced at his mother.

"Indeed," Eleanor replied.

"When it gets a bit colder," Scruffy said, "we can prune this entire orchard. Also ..." He went on about the advantages of root grafting over seeding and other methods of raising an orchard.

"My goodness, Scruffy," Eleanor said with a pat on his shoulder, "for such a young man, you sure do know your apple growing."

"Funny thing," Scruffy said as he ran his fingers over the bark of a limb, "I never even thought about it until I heard myself talking. Guess I picked up a thing or two."

Eleanor eyed Scruffy as though an idea had come upon her. "Before you leave us, I have a favor to ask."

"Yes ma'am."

"I would like to paint you."

For the next couple of weeks, Scruffy tended to the apple orchard by weeding, planting clover between the rows, pruning trees, and explaining to Robert and Edward about budding—the grafting of the upper portion of a singular graft. "You want to do this when the buds are beginning to open."

Every evening after supper, Scruffy sat in a straight-back chair with his arms placed on the wooden armrests for an hour in the den while Eleanor stood behind an easel, painting her subject.

At the start of the first session, Eleanor had told Scruffy, "I want you to sit up straight and think about where you have been in your life and where you see yourself down the road."

Eleanor went on to say, "I strive for my art to represent not only the subject but also the heart and soul of the individual."

During portrait time, they exchanged life stories. Eleanor had grown up on a dairy farm in Superior, Wisconsin. "Up in the Northern Highlands, you might as well have been living on the North Pole as cold as it got in the winter," she said as she sat behind her easel, tilting her head to the side to study her subject.

Scruffy told his family history, including his losing his father the day he was born. "I have a stirring inside me." He looked at Eleanor as though to say, *Do you know what I mean?*

"Painting quiets my demons. I suspect seeing America is having a quieting effect on yours."

A still silence fell over them.

Eleanor dipped her brush into paint on a circular palette she held in one arm. "We have something else in common. I am also an only child and one quarter Chippewa, also from my mother's side."

She went on to say that in the frigid winter months, her mother had taken up art. "In the evening, when the endless chores were done for the day, she taught herself and me how to paint with a watercolor paint box given to us by a neighbor's wife who had developed severe arthritis and could no longer paint."

"Funny how one person's tragedy turns into another person's fortune," Scruffy said as he sat up straight, his back against the stiff rails of the chair.

"And," Eleanor added, "change the direction of one's life."

But during the silence, when Eleanor was absorbed in her task, as though trying to intuit what lay below the surface of her young poser, Scruffy let his mind wander back in time, reliving his life up to this point, and thinking, *What if ...*

What if his father, Logan Lomax, had lived? How different a person would Scruffy have been? He probably would not have been called "Scruffy," but rather "Junior" and eventually "Logan." He would probably have been living on a fertile stretch of land his parents owned, with no desire to leave.

His mother's memories of his father rose in Scruffy's mind. "It was his eyes," Nantes had said. "There was something trusting about his true-blue gaze that put me at ease." She looked off as though seeing her past and possibly what could have been her future. "Logan Lomax was a good, intelligent, caring man ... Yes he was."

Scruffy thought about how wonderful it would have been to have a father to work with, to talk with, and to provide perspective on the vagaries of life. He considered what it would have been like to have bonded with a man whose blood coursed through his veins: a man he would never meet in this life—a man he could only dream about.

How different it all would have been. He was so close to his mother, yet with a silent distance, as though she held something back—no doubt a byproduct of her upbringing and the crushing death of a husband. That silent distance would not have existed had Scruffy's father lived, in its place a three-way harmony between father, mother, and son.

One month to the day since Scruffy had arrived at the Logan farm, and the day before he was to depart, he and Robert were pruning in the apple orchard.

Robert grabbed a branch that was growing downward and said, "Need pruning, Scruffy?

"Yes," Scruffy replied, "and remember: gentle strokes backward only, a bit off the base to leave a collar."

Robert placed the teeth of his saw blade at the base of the limb and sawed back four times, dropping the branch.

"So, Robert," Scruffy said from across the row as he inspected a tree, its thin branches crisscrossing helter-skelter, "is this where you are going to settle with Attu and Robert Junior?"

"Part of me wishes I had never been to Alaska." Robert reached for another downward limb. "This one too?"

Scruffy nodded. "You were saying?"

"Course, if I had never been there, I would not have met Attu and had a son, but damn, Scruffy, that life gets in your blood."

Robert placed the saw blade on the limb an inch from the base and stroked backward. "Out panning for gold, roughing it outdoors in a tent, moving into town when the weather got too cold," he said in a remembering, wistful voice.

Robert grabbed another downturned limb and, without conferring with Scruffy, placed the saw blade an inch off the base and took a backward stroke. "The view, my god … the mountains, the wildflowers blooming in the spring, the deep blue sky … and it was as though it was just me and the good Lord at times. It was a powerful feeling."

Robert took a final stroke with his blade, dropping the limb. "And the cherry on top of the pie?" he said with a rise in his voice. "I lived— lived as free as the wind."

"Free, you say, huh," Scruffy said as he cut a wayward limb interfering with a branch growing toward the sky.

Edward appeared in the orchard and said, "Ever since your arrival, Scruffy, the weather has been good—sunny days with rainfall in the evenings." He looked up, the sky was dying in a plush of violet, before settling his gaze on his guest.

"If I did not know better, I would say you are a good luck charm." Edward's genial expression was replaced by that of a businessman farmer. "Scruffy, let's walk and talk," he said with a glance at Robert, who grinned as though to say, *Good luck, Dad.*

Scruffy figured where this was going.

Down the row a ways, Edward stopped. They were in a section that had already been pruned. "Fine job of pruning, Scruffy."

"Thank you, Edward."

"This was all Eleanor's idea," Edward said with of lift his hand toward the row of trees. "She was right about adding an orchard."

Edward cleared his throat to introduce a new subject. "I will get right to the point, Scruffy. We would very much—and I mean everyone in the family—like you to stay."

Scruffy started to speak, but Edward raised his hand. He looked down the row, eyeing Scruffy's freshly grown clover, which looked like a thick carpet of green. "I will put you in charge of expanding the orchard. Stay here as a member of the family." Edward looked at Scruffy, his eyes desperate for a yes. "Establish roots, Scruffy."

"Thank you, Edward, but I am set on riding the rails down to Florida and then up to New York City before heading cross-country and north to Big Bear."

"Big. Bear. Alaska." Edward's expression was that of one having met his match. "Well," he said with a lift in his voice as though the matter was settled, "I thought you would want to depart us, but I wanted to give it a try."

Edward put his hand on Scruffy's shoulder and said, "Eleanor and Attu are making a farewell dinner. Let's head on in and wash up."

The table was set with a checkered tablecloth topped by a platter of thick slices of juicy roast beef, a bowl of steaming mashed potatoes, a ceramic sauce boat thick with brown gravy, a platter of diced yams, and a basket of golden-brown biscuits. It looked and smelled delicious.

Edward sat at the head of the table, with Eleanor on his right, Scruffy on his left, Robert next to Scruffy, and Attu next to Eleanor.

From up the stairs, the whimpering cry of Robert Junior, whom Attu had just put down, caused Robert and Attu to exchange worried looks across the table.

"He will be fine," Eleanor said. "Let him settle down."

"Scruffy," Edward said, "would you lead us in grace?"

Hands were held around the table.

This was a family tradition that Scruffy had come to appreciate. He had attended church services from time to time with the Pinchwell children back in Yakima, but his mother wanted nothing to do with it.

But Scruffy liked the way a simple prayer, with hands held at the dinner table, could provide a sense of unity with those he sat with.

Scruffy decided against repeating the standard prayer he had heard given for the last month at this table and speak from the heart. "Thank you, Lord … for bringing the Logan family into my life." Scruffy felt

Edward give his hand a squeeze of approval. "Thank you for giving me the opportunity to work and live with such good and decent people— people I shall remember for the rest of my life—Amen."

"Thank you, Scruffy," Edward said. He gestured toward the food. "If you would do the honors."

As Scruffy dipped the ladle into the mashed potatoes, he glanced around the table. Robert had a look mixed with envy and sadness; Edward, a grudging understanding; Attu was hard to read, her expression placid, but her eyes had downward slants at their corners, like Nantes when something threw her off kilter; and Eleanor had a more pragmatic, though forlorn, look of understanding at the upcoming departure of her guest.

Scruffy passed the bowl of potatoes to Robert and said, "I also want to thank you good folks for taking me in and bringing me back to good health."

"Scruffy," Attu said in a voice so small and faraway that all eyes turned to her. "I … we …"—she lifted her hand to the table—"will be grateful to you for the rest of our lives." She dabbed a tear streaking her cheek, leaned back into her chair, and stared into her plate.

After the meal, Eleanor took Scruffy into the den. She removed a cover from the easel and said, "Come and see."

Scruffy took a close look, studying the portrait of himself from the waist up wearing his red flannel shirt. "That sure is grand, Eleanor. Mighty grand indeed."

"I am going to place it over the fireplace," Eleanor said with a lift of her hand to the back wall, "as a reminder of the man who saved my grandson's life."

It was a dead-on replica of Scruffy, with the high cheekbones and strong chin, and the gentle curve of his nose. She had captured not only the shape and color of his dark blue eyes but also, in his gaze, a look of adventure, as though he was ready to take on life for all it was worth.

"I knew you would not be settling here with us, Scruffy, much as the family wanted it to be." Eleanor looked at Scruffy reflectively. "I knew from our conversations while I painted you that the road was your mistress."

CHAPTER 12

THE FOLLOWING DAY, EDWARD DROVE Scruffy to the Kenosha train
depot. Before Scruffy got out of the car, Edward insisted that he
take fifty dollars as payment for time spent working the apple orchard.
"I do not want you riding the rails all the way to Florida without a
cent to your name." He stuffed the money in Scruffy's shirt pocket and
put his strong hand on Scruffy's shoulder. "If not for you, Lord knows
where my progeny would be. No arguments."

Inside the depot, Scruffy checked the schedule and discovered
the *Arrowhead Limited*, a passenger train, was arriving shortly. He did
not want to pay, and since there would be no boxcars, he decided to
try to ride in the baggage car, not sure if there was any room or even
whether the door would be unlocked. He sensed that the baggage car
was a long shot.

If so, he would hop on the platform at the front of the baggage car,
up in the front next to the tender, where there was no door. In essence,
he would be riding the blind. He heard Harvard's voice warning him
against such a foolish venture, but Scruffy decided that if he was going
to be a true hobo, he had to experience the blind at least once.

Down a hundred feet from the train station, Scruffy waited in a
weedy patch off the tracks. There was a chill in the air; it was going to
get cold tonight. But he dismissed the idea of quitting now.

After the unloading and loading of passengers, the steam engine
released a sharp whistle, followed by the banging of doors shutting
and the hissing of steam as the engine chugged forward, its monstrous
V-shaped cowcatcher mounted at the front, appearing capable of clearing
the tracks of any debris.

For a moment, Scruffy had second thoughts. He could wait for a freight train, where he would have the inside safety of a boxcar. But he shook off such a sensible suggestion and secured his bedroll over his shoulder, grabbed his bindle, and made a beeline for the baggage car. He reached for the door—locked!

The train was beginning to pick up speed. Jogging along ahead of the passenger cars, and not wanting to be spotted by a passenger or especially a conductor, Scruffy took a furtive glance up and down the rail line, saw no one, and hustled toward the front of the baggage car.

Running alongside the train, he placed his bindle on the steel platform and threw himself onto the hard metal, chest first. He carefully positioned himself with his back to the wall of the tender and brought his knees into his chest. Now all he needed do was make it to Chicago without falling off.

No more than ten minutes after the train had picked up a head of steam, it hurtled around a bend, catching Scruffy off guard. He started to slide off the platform before he grabbed hold of the ladder rail.

By the time the train entered the Chicago rail yard, Scruffy had sworn off riding the blind. Not only did his body feel like one big iceberg, but he could barely get himself off the platform, his chilled body seemingly unable to function as he walked, stiff-legged, over to the freight yard, where things were unreasonably quiet. There was not a soul around—nothing but tracks filled with boxcars.

"Psst. Hey, boy," said a raspy unseen voice.

Startled, Scruffy looked over his shoulder to a line of coupled boxcars, one of which had an open door.

"Get yourself out of the open," the voice said.

At the open boxcar, Scruffy said, "Friend or foe?"

"Depends." The voice came from a dark shadow in the rear corner.

"Name is Scruffy Lomax. Trying to get myself down to Florida."

The shadow moved, and the figure of a man emerged—an older-looking man wearing a stocking cap, a tattered red-and-blue-checkered mackinaw, and dungarees with holes in both knees. He looked like he would have fit right in with the group of 'bos in Brainerd.

"Get on in here," the man said with a wave as he moved back into the shadows.

Scruffy placed his gear inside the car and hopped up.

At the back of the car, Scruffy sat against the back wall, with a space between him and the man. "Am I in the right place to get down south?" Scruffy asked.

"No," the man said, "there will be a southbound freight coming later tonight."

"Awfully quiet," Scruffy said.

"Haaah," the 'bo spat out in his raspy croak. "These rail workers are all bohunks and micks." He leveled a knowing slant to his eyebrows and said, "Sundays they attend mackerel-snapper service and then supper with their horde before showing up for their shift, all of 'em with a bit of the Irish flu—even the bohunks."

"You taking the southbound freight?"

"Uh huh."

"Mind company?" Scruffy asked.

"Depends."

A silent beat passed before Scruffy said, "I am trustworthy."

The 'bo leaned forward and over into Scruffy space. A grimace skipped across his weathered, cross-hatched face as he squinted a once-over. "I believe you are." He extended his hand and said, "Joshua Decker here."

By dusk, the rail workers had arrived, and soon there were the creaks and groans of freight cars moving, and shouts and orders of men at work. Joshua and Scruffy were down a ways outside the yard, kneeling down behind a tool shed.

"That's our ride to Chattanooga." Joshua lifted his chin in the direction of a freight train across the yard from them being loaded at a warehouse.

In the dimming light, Joshua pulled a pair of binoculars from his knapsack and watched the train being loaded. "They didn't load the last two cars," he said. "We just might have us a roomy accommodation."

In the cover of nightfall, as the freight train began to move out, Joshua looked left and right. "Wait 'til it passes," he said.

Scruffy sensed he was in the company of an experienced hobo—a careful one at that.

When the train had exited the yard, they scurried across a series of tracks and then alongside the freight train slowly heading out. Joshua hopped on a ladder and tried one of the empty boxcar doors, but it was locked. He reached into his back pocket and pulled out a steel rod, fiddled with the handle and popped open the door, and swung himself around and into the car. "Scruffy," he said, "come on, boy."

Both men situated themselves against the back wall.

"Got us a long, straight shot," Joshua said.

They were peering out the open door, the rattling, clanging whir of the train rolling into the night. A crescent moon sat low in the sky, the stars beginning to reveal their twinkling light.

"And with a fine view to boot," Scruffy said. He reached into his burlap bag, removed a can of beans, and held it up. "Hungry?"

"Why, I got me some beef jerky that will go mighty fine with legumes."

And so it began—two men sitting in a boxcar, sharing their meager vittles, and talking.

Joshua said he had been a schoolteacher in the Upper Peninsula of Michigan. "Couldn't take one more day of dealing with obstinate, stubborn farmers and their obstinate, stubborn children." He said he had graduated from the University of Michigan with a degree in education and with aspirations to teach "rural folk."

He went on to say that he had been riding the rails doing odd jobs across the country for ten years. "How old you think I am, Scruffy?" Joshua said as he took a bite of his jerky and handed it to Scruffy, who passed the can of beans.

Scruffy thought him to be at least fifty, maybe fifty-five, but he didn't want to offend. "Forty?"

"You are being kind," Joshua said with a shrewd lift of his brow. "I am thirty-five, but I have aged exponentially ever since I hit the road less traveled by—if I may paraphrase Mr. Frost."

He laughed a deep, knowing chuckle. "Not that I regret it," he said. "Well, I do regret getting arrested down in Mississippi and having to work on a chain gang for six months before I and two others fellows escaped." He sunk a spoon into the can of beans and took a thoughtful chew. "One bit of advice," he said with an air of superior knowledge. "Stay the hell out of Mississippi."

"What made you decide on the hobo life," Scruffy said as he took a swig of water and handed the bottle to Joshua.

"Probably same thing that causes many a man to give up on a life and start anew—a woman."

Joshua said he had been engaged to a young and beautiful German woman who spoke limited English and came from a poor background. "She was swept off her feet by the son of a wealthy farmer who promised her a big house that she could run as she saw fit."

Joshua shrugged and exhaled through his teeth. "I had even been studying German," he said with a look of remembrance. "Ich bin fix und fertig!"

Scruffy looked at Joshua, a question in his eyes.

"It means I was completely knackered," Joshua replied in a soft voice. "I thought, 'What the hell? Why put up with the bad winters and dumb students for little pay?'"

Joshua went on to say that each year he promised it would his last of riding the rails and doing itinerant work from town to town. He lifted a cautionary finger and said, "But damn, the life on the rails gets in your blood."

Joshua took a swig of the water, handed it back to Scruffy, and said, "I will be getting off in Chattanooga, but if you like, I can tell you how to get to ... Where exactly is your destination?"

"Miami, I reckon."

"All right," Joshua said, "I can tell how to go about it and, if you are so inclined, a few lessons I have learned riding the rails."

By early morning, the train was slowing down. "Chattanooga depot up ahead," Joshua said as he went to the door and checked the front and rear of train. "Got me a woman in this here town that takes me in—no questions asked." Joshua looked over his shoulder, flashing a smile of pure lust at Scruffy.

He then hopped off the train with Scruffy right behind him. They both strode over to the side of a massive shed storing boxcars. Up ahead was an imposing brick-and-limestone depot featuring a large arched center section with smaller horizontal wings. In his travels, Scruffy had seen a variety of train depots—all of them fine-looking structures.

Joshua reviewed his instructions on where to catch the train to Atlanta, and from there to Tallahassee, and on to Miami. "Keep your eyes peeled when entering a yard, even if the train is only stopping for water," he told Scruffy. "I have learned that when you least expect it, trouble can come a-calling."

During the ride to Atlanta, Scruffy rode with a shifty sort who asked too many questions. Scruffy kept his answers short and never dozed off, even when Shifty nodded off.

At the Atlanta rail yard, Scruffy hid behind a storage shed, waiting for the freight train heading to Tallahassee. He spotted a beefy bull in a dark blue uniform who was armed with a holstered pistol and gripping a nightstick while inspecting boxcars. Scruffy remembered O'Hurley's warning about the mean bulls in Atlanta, and this man certainly looked the part.

When the train pulled out, the bull crossed the tracks and began inspecting another train, but Scruffy waited, remembering Joshua's words about trouble coming when one least expected it.

Most of the train had passed Scruffy, and it was picking up speed. As he was about to go for it, the bull returned, looking down the rails while pounding his nightstick in his palm. Finally he left. Still Scruffy waited, counting to thirty before heading straight for a boxcar ladder. He hopped up, jerked the handle open, and stepped inside his free ride.

The freight train Scruffy jumped in Tallahassee had two brothers on board: Joe and Tom Whitmore from Philadelphia, both down-to-earth trustworthy men who were heading to Miami to find work as carpenters.

Joe told Scruffy, "Having skilled hands finds us work anywhere, might as well be in a warm climate."

"Where did you lean carpentry?" Scruffy asked.

"Our dad worked at the rail yard, and he framed our house mostly from wood planks from out-of-commission freight cars," Joe said. "We learned from him."

"Yeah," Tom added, "the railroad supplied us with food on the table and roof over our head."

"And you thought it only appropriate they supply you with free transportation," Scruffy said with an admiring grin.

"Exactly," the brothers said in unison.

Four days after departing Chattanooga, Scruffy arrived in Miami, tired and sore from sitting and sleeping on unforgiving boxcar floors.

Miami was crowded and awfully hot. Never in his life had Scruffy been in such warm, humid weather—and in November, no less. He could not imagine what July would be like in this climate. He spent his first and only night in Miami sleeping on the beach, which was a comfortable change from the boxcars.

But Miami, a noisy, growing city of tall buildings and clanging trolley cars, did not suit Scruffy presently. Joshua had mentioned that "Key West is a different sort of place, with a nice sea breeze, provided by the trade winds, that tempers the heat, and without a lot of rules."

So, at the East Coast Railway Station in Miami, Scruffy waited for a freight train. But after three hours and only passenger trains, he decided to buy a ticket on the Overseas Railroad to Key West. It cost two dollars, but it turned out to be worth the price, for the views were amazing, as the train traveled over a series of overseas trestle bridges. The turquoise water was crystal clear, the rural beach towns preparing to burst out of their slumber as civilization made its way through this windswept archipelago plush with exotic plants and trees.

Scruffy got a botany lesson from his seatmate, who was a botanist for the State of Florida. "The Florida Keys are rich and plentiful in a variety of flora." The botanist lifted his open palm toward the window, which Scruffy was next to. "Right there you have gumbo limbo with its showy red bark, green buttonwood—which is an evergreen—palm tree, mahogany tree, almond, mango ... I could go on and on. And, of course, banana"—he pointed at clusters of greenish-yellow bananas attached to gnarly limbs—"which are not a tree but a plant, and the banana is technically a berry that grows toward the sun—negative geotropism."

The botanist clicked his tongue and said, "Wildlife oftentimes, like people, is not what you think it is."

Along the way through this oceanic paradise, the train passed buildings, roads, and houses under construction. It appeared work was plentiful.

In Key West, Scruffy got directions to the chamber of commerce, and with brochure and map in hand, he spent the remainder of the day walking about, getting a feel for the place.

It was much bigger and more developed than he had expected.

Duval Street, which ran north and south from the Gulf of Mexico to the Atlantic Ocean, seemed to be the main commercial area. Beyond Duval Street, on the Atlantic side, Scruffy watched workers grading out sand, dumped from trucks, along the shore.

From the brochure, he learned that a barrier reef protected the beaches from storms, but it also prevented sand from washing onto the shore, so in many spots sand was imported.

There were shops lining both sides of Duval Street, three- and four-story wood-sided buildings, painted white, with front plate-glass windows, some with deep balconies on the second and third stories. Telephone poles ran the length of one side of the street, which had concrete sidewalks on both sides. And clanging down the middle of the street came a streetcar.

At each end of Duvall Street were rows of Victorian mansions adorned with turrets and dormers and wrap-around porches; and beautiful Spanish-style bungalows with white exteriors, arched porches flanked by vines and potted plants, and red-tiled roofs.

There was a festive atmosphere in the air as people were bustling up and down the street, talking and laughing as though having a grand time for themselves. Also in the air was the faint smell of cigar smoke, which grew more pronounced as Scruffy approached a table of men outside a cigar shop who were puffing on fat cigars and speaking in Spanish.

During his first night, Scruffy slept under a palm tree on a Gulf of Mexico beach that was mostly dirt. The gentle crash of waves on the shore lulled him into a deep and restful sleep.

The next morning, Scruffy headed back to Duval Street and McGill's Restaurant, where the day before he had noticed a Help Wanted sign for a dishwasher. Mr. McGill hired him on the spot. "Our name is only temporary," McGill told Scruffy, with a glint of the devil in his eyes, "until Prohibition is repealed and we go back to our original name—McGill's Tavern."

Scruffy's pay was only ten cents an hour, but it included a room upstairs and all the food he could eat.

Scruffy had a grand old time for himself. He worked from noon to ten six days a week, with Sundays off.

It was here that Scruffy had his first drink, in a speakeasy in a back room of McGill's. The drink was a boilermaker—beer and a shot of whiskey. That led to his first hangover. There were characters galore in Key West, which was a booming town with lots of construction and real estate deals.

Oftentimes while sitting at the bar, Scruffy would hear stories about deals gone wrong and people losing everything, and also great success stories of tin-can tourists arriving with everything in their cars and striking real estate deals that paid them handsomely.

A young and pretty Cuban woman, Mariel, was a waitress at McGill's. She took a liking to Scruffy, and before he knew it, he was *hacer el amor* with Mariel. It was more than he had ever imagined. Mariel was a patient and giving lover.

But by March, with the weather heating up, Scruffy was ready to move on to New York, though not before Mr. McGill gave him a twenty-dollar bonus and threw a grand after-hours farewell party. Scruffy spent his last night with Mariel, who told him that she would miss him but added, "We have lived a lifetime in a short time. Now for our next chapter."

New York was a mistake. It was bigger and noisier than Chicago, and Scruffy stayed less than a week before he headed west, with an adventurous destination in mind—Big Bear Alaska or bust.

He stopped in Yakima and learned that his mother had moved to Mexico with one of the migrant workers. She had left a note with Mr. Pinchwell for Scruffy:

Dear Logan,

I hope your travels have suited you well. I have decided to go with Juan, a man I met during the harvest, back to his village, Yelapa. I want you to know that I will think about you every day for the remainder of my life, and for you to live a good and free life.

With love,

Your mother,
Nantes

Remorse flushed over Scruffy, as he had thought little of his mother since his departure. He assumed she must have had many a sleepless night wondering about her only child's well-being.

He had a sense that he would never see Nantes again. There was a tone of inevitably in her missive—an acceptance that their lives were on different paths, in different orbits. A "good and free life" was something Nantes had never experienced in Yakima. She had been born on the reservation in poverty, and when opportunity was on the horizon, her husband died and left her with a newborn. Scruffy hoped that his mother would find happiness in Mexico.

Upon arriving in Big Bear in the late spring of 1923, Scruffy had experienced enough of the life on the rails and had no further inclination, presently, to live that way. He got a job at the Long Branch Saloon washing dishes and cleaning up the bar in the morning, compliments of a letter of recommendation from Mr. McGill that ended "Finest worker I ever have employed."

Scruffy worked out with the owner of the Long Branch an arrangement for free room and board that was basic—a cold cut lunch and dinner that included yellow cheese and beans—plus fifteen cents an hour. His room was on the second floor. It was small, but he only slept there, and he had bath privileges three times a week. And just as Robert had told him, Prohibition had not touched this small town in the Alaskan Territory; no one had even mentioned it.

Scruffy planned to work at the Long Branch long enough to get a lay of the land—to listen to the trappers and prospectors who came into the bar and swapped stories about "heading up country" to pan for gold or trap beaver or muskrat. These men were characters of varying ages, all with gleams in their eyes and notes of anticipation in their voices.

Needle Nose Lagos was a few years older than Scruffy but seemed as though he had already lived a full life. He told Scruffy he had come all the way from Nova Scotia back in 1915 at the age of fifteen and had been trapping since he was "old enough to follow the trail of the traplines."

Needle Nose had an unforgettable face with a sharp, pointy nose, a constant five-o'clock shadow, alert eyes, and a head that was too big for his body. Atop that oversize head was a thrash of coarse and curly black hair that only added to the aura of the wilderness about him. And his yarns about roughing it told over drinks at the Long Branch Bar were captivating.

By that autumn, Scruffy had established a friendship with Needle Nose and asked if he could accompany him on his next trek out into the wilderness.

"Ever lived outside society?" Needle Nose said as he cradled a whiskey.

"Tramping the rails," Scruffy replied.

Needle Nose looked at Scruffy with a glint of appreciation. "Damn, boy, you must got some sand to you."

And so it was agreed that Scruffy would accompany Needle Nose "out yonder" to trap beaver.

Needle Nose warned Scruffy that it was a rugged and lonely existence that involved living for up to a couple of months "without so much as seeing another living soul."

"I am in," Scruffy said.

After six weeks out yonder, Scruffy had learned how to use various types of traps from drowning snares to leghold traps, but the misery suffered by the animals wore on him. Upon their return to Big Bear, Scruffy told Needle Nose that he was done with trapping but would like to join him panning for gold the next time he went out.

"I am a trapper by trade," Needle Nose told Scruffy, "but I will be glad to teach you the little I know about prospecting."

CHAPTER 13

Big Bear, Alaska, March 1925

IT HAD BEEN A LONG, frigid winter, but the old man of the north had begun to loosen his grip. There were still patches of snow on the ground, but the temperature had been steadily rising, and today had the feel of spring in the air—an Alaskan spring, where anything above freezing was considered favorable.

When back in town from prospecting, Scruffy did odd jobs: early-morning cleanup at the Long Branch, stocking shelves at the general store, and assisting a carpenter on a mill being built. He had continued to rent a room upstairs at the Long Branch but had grown tired of the lack of privacy—drunks had been constantly stumbling into his room by mistake. So a couple of months back, Scruffy had rented a room from the Widow Morlock, who was also the schoolmarm.

After three treks out in the wild panning for gold with Needle Nose, Scruffy had gained enough confidence to go out on his own the previous autumn. Though he never struck it rich with or without Needle Nose, Scruffy panned enough gold to keep him wanting to keep trying.

He enjoyed the independence that such a life afforded: heading out with a pack on his back, pitching a tent near a stream, collecting dried aspen for firewood, and eating a meal by a campfire.

The experience of riding the rails, the 'bos he had met whom life had kicked in the teeth, the murder in Brainerd that he almost witnessed, the murder that he and Harvard did witness, and getting beaten unconscious and robbed in Chicago and dumped in an alley had all left an indelible mark on Scruffy.

Not that roughing it was not dangerous, but it would not be one's fellow man that would be the culprit in this great frontier. Instead the danger would be presented by a lack of vigilance in properly storing one's food so that bears or wolves did not come a-calling, in carefully packing all the necessary supplies, and in avoiding injury with no help nearby.

But to return from roughing it and belly up to the bar at the Long Branch and say, "Barkeep, a round on the house—compliments yours truly, Scruffy Lomax," was the greatest feeling in the world.

A heartfelt roar would come from the patrons, mostly trappers and prospectors. They were a good group of men. Some of them were dreamers, and many had an inclination to tip one too many. But the core of the group was a hardworking, hard-drinking lot who enjoyed nothing more than swapping tales at the Long Branch. That was something that had yet to grow old.

And speaking of old, Scruffy had yet to turn twenty, but he had gained valuable lessons in the school of hard knocks. He had traveled across America, worked in a big city, and lived and worked in the Florida Keys, where he'd had a relationship with a fine-looking woman.

I am an old nineteen, he thought as he headed over to the Long Branch after a double check on his gear back in his room for his trek the following day out to the frontier in search of pay dirt.

The Long Branch was a converted storage barn with a winding staircase leading to the loft, which was lined with rooms for renters and staff. The bar was long and U-shaped with a plate glass mirror bearing a scroll design along the edges. There were a few tables about, and a piano that Scruffy had never heard played. The bar was the heart of the place.

Scruffy was greeted at the bar with back-slaps. "Well sir, pardner," Pete Prescott said as he slid a sly look from his seat in the corner, "you gonna hit pay dirt out thar."

"I am hopeful, but if nothing else," Scruffy said as he signaled for his usual to the barkeep, "it is a fine walk in the wilderness."

Scruffy reached for his mug and said in a raised voice meant to attract an audience, "And if fortune comes my way, you can expect a night of drinks on the house." Scruffy threw a bug-eyed look at Pete and grinned.

The bar broke up in a wave of hooting laughter and shouted lines including "Now you are a-talking!" and "We can always count on young Scruffy to treat us right!"

Scruffy had a couple more beers and called it an evening. He got well wishes and good luck from the men at the bar. "Pardner, come back with nuggets as big as my fist," Pete said with glass raised.

Back in his room at the Widow Morlock's place, Scruffy heard a whimpering whine from outside his window, which he kept open no matter how cold the weather. In the shadowy darkness, Scruffy made out the figure of what appeared to be a little dog of no more than twenty pounds, sitting there looking up at him.

Scruffy lifted the window, reached his arm down, and lifted the little creature into the room. He put the dog down to get a closer look. It was a male—some type of terrier with a wiry dark red coat, pointy ears, and a deep chest. Its skull was flat, and its muzzle long.

Its eyes … Scruffy looked closer. One eye moved as it looked about the space, but the other eye remained in place. To Scruffy's shock, he deduced that the still eye appeared to be made of glass. It nearly matched the dark brown eye but was not quite as deep a color.

How in the world could a little dog with a glass eye appear seemingly from out of nowhere? It must have gotten separated from its owner somehow. But it would not have been anyone in Big Bear who would own a dog with an artificial eye. By the looks of the mangy condition of its fur and its emaciated body—when Scruffy had picked it up, he'd felt it ribs right up against the skin—this little dog had been out in the elements for a while.

"Let's get you some food and water, little fella," Scruffy said as he reached into his knapsack and quickly set up water from his canteen in a tin cup, and bits of hardtack biscuit and beef jerky in a bowl. The dog lapped up the water and then sniffed the food before gobbling it down.

After eating, the dog hopped up on the foot of Scruffy's bed, walked in a circle three times, and curled up, his good eye on Scruffy with a look that said, *I am good.*

The next morning, Scruffy took the dog to the Wiley's General Store to see whether anyone had been looking for him.

"That would be an Irish terrier, Scruffy," Mr. Wiley said as he gestured for Scruffy to bring the dog up on the counter. "Good lord, a glass eye no less," Mr. Wiley said after a cursory inspection. "I will put out the word, but …"—he shrugged—"it is a wonder that dog made it here from wherever he came from."

Scruffy said thank you, and as he headed out the door, Mr. Wiley called, "What are you going to name him, Scruffy?"

Scruffy stopped and turned, cradling the dog in his arm. "Well, sir, how about Rusty the One-Eyed Wonder Dog."

Mr. Wiley nodded and pointed a finger at Scruffy. "Exactly."

Scruffy decided to stay a couple of days in town to allow the dog to fully recover. During that time, he discovered that Rusty was well-trained. He barked on command, lifted his paw, rolled over, and could stand on his two back legs and go around in a circle. Within a day, he responded to his new name, and by the third day he was running at a good clip.

During this time, Scruffy also learned that Rusty could repeat words. He praised the dog after he had gone around in a circle on his back legs. "Rus … tee," Scruffy had said with a pat on the neck.

Rusty groaned back in doggy speak, "Russs … teee."

Soon Scruffy had him saying "Scruf … feee," "Beeeg Beeeaar," and "par … neeer."

The words were not perfectly clear—garbled growls, really—but still, it was pretty amazing.

"Well, Rusty," Scruffy said before turning in, "You ready for a month of roughing it?"

Rusty looked over at Scruffy from his spot at the foot of the bed and winked his glass eye.

Scruffy's mouth gaped open. "Damn," he said, "you *are* a wonder dog."

CHAPTER 14

A N OLD-TIMER AT THE BAR had told Scruffy about a potential
prospecting spot in the Kosar Valley. It was a good two-day hike
away.

The first day, Rusty kept pace the whole way right alongside
Scruffy, stopping when he stopped and heading out when his master
did. That night, Rusty slept at the front of the tent, body sprawled out
with head resting on paws. A couple of times during the night, Scruffy
woke to find Rusty standing, ears perked, before settling back down.
Scruffy had himself a watch dog.

Late afternoon on the second day, Scruffy came upon a stream with
a hillside nearby. This looked like the spot the old-timer had told him
about. In the distance, the snow-tipped Kosar Mountains stood guard
over the valley, flush with an array of wildlife: mosses, lichens, cattails,
sedge grass, and a line of aspen and spruce trees at their base.

The beauty before Scruffy took hold, as though a part of him were
incorporated into the substance of the land. To hike out here in this
gorgeous wilderness by oneself, with a pack on one's back containing
all that one needed to survive, offered a sense of well-being the likes
of which Scruffy had never experienced before arriving in Alaska.
That being said, he kept his guard up at all times, for as beautiful as
it was, there was danger: wolves, bears, unpredictable weather, and
getting injured and dying alone. Scruffy had heard enough tales at
the Long Branch about men heading out to prospect or trap and never
returning—nary a trace.

Sinking the tip of his trenching shovel into the side of the hill,
Scruffy dug out loose rock, clay, dirt, and, so he hoped, hidden flakes
of gold. He placed the contents into his metal pan.

Rusty watched with head cocked off to the side as though trying to figure out what this was all about. At the edge of the stream, Scruffy filled his pan partially with water and began shaking and sweeping out the dirt and clay. He flicked out loose stones and examined his pan. "No luck," he said aloud.

He made three more attempts, and still nothing.

"This will be the one, Wonder Dog," Scruffy said as he dug into the hillside.

After sifting out the debris, Scruffy had one small speck of gold.

Rusty, who had been sitting on his haunches and watching, came over and sniffed Scruffy's find.

"Nothing much, my little red dog," Scruffy said. "But it is a start."

Rusty barked once, went over to the hillside, and sniffed around before pawing furiously into the bank.

"What you got there, Rusty?"

Rusty stepped back and barked.

Scruffy dug into the spot and deposited the contents into his pan.

At the edge of the stream, Scruffy started the painstaking process of sifting out the debris, while Rusty stood observing every move.

After winnowing out the unwanted elements and washing away the clay and dirt, there were no gold flakes. "Awg," Scruffy said as he put the pan down.

Rusty put his nose in the pan and honed in on a piece of quartz. Scruffy picked it up and inspected it.

"Holy smokes," he said. Needle Nose had told Scruffy that bits of gold could be found in stone, but this was the first he had ever come upon, or maybe he had missed it previously. He was relatively new at prospecting and still had a lot to learn.

"By golly," Scruffy said as he ruffled the fur on Rusty's neck, "you are one talented dog."

For the next two weeks, Rusty would sniff along the hillside, scurrying back and forth, stopping to get good sniffs, and moving on until he honed in on a location. Nearly every time, Rusty found gold— not a lot, but enough to make it a worthy endeavor. And the couple of times Scruffy came up empty, he wondered if he had lost the gold in the panning process.

Eventually Rusty had sniffed out the length of the hillside—at least the bottom section that he could reach—so Scruffy picked up his little dog and let him sniff at chest level. And lo and behold, Wonder Dog found more flakes of gold.

By the end of the third week, Scruffy figured he had pretty well tapped out this spot and decided to head back to Big Bear. He had collected three, maybe four, ounces of gold, worth up to eighty dollars, which could buy a lot of supplies and maybe even a few rounds at the Long Branch.

The trek back turned out to be a miserable time. It began raining right after Scruffy departed his campsite and did not let up until he had pitched his tent at dusk. Inside his tent, Scruffy changed into dry clothes and then toweled off Rusty, who was shivering something fierce.

A fire was impossible with everything so damp and wet, so after a meal of beans and a piece of jerky, both of which he shared with the dog, Scruffy nestled into his sleeping bag and brought Rusty in with him, holding the still-shivering animal close to his chest. "Rusty?" Scruffy said, waiting for his dog's attention.

Rusty looked at Scruffy, his good eye lined red with fatigue.

"I want you to rest easy tonight, and I will keep an eye out ... understood?"

Rusty's mouth opened just a bit, and he looked at Scruffy as though making sure he had heard correctly. He licked Scruffy on the chin and nestled up against his owner's chest, and within a minute gentle breaths of a deep sleep were coming from the little red dog.

CHAPTER 15

THE ASSAY OFFICE WAS LOCATED in a separate space in Wiley's General Store; the access for the public was a door around back. Scruffy left his gear outside the entrance, and he and Rusty entered the space, which had the look of a workshop with an L-shaped bench, on which were the tools of the trade: crucible, tongs, forceps, anvil, hammer, brush. Shelves on the wall over the bench were packed with beakers, scales, glass tubes, and the like. It was run by Merle Heidelman, who was sitting on a stool at the bench, unscrewing the top plate of a scale. He was a stocky man with close-cropped thinning hair and wire-rim glasses, behind which were impassive gray eyes.

Heidelman put down his screwdriver and looked up at Scruffy. "Ah," he said with an air of congeniality. "Young Master Lomax, and what have you for me today?" His voice had a singsongy, oom-pah-pah resonance.

"My little dog and I have been roughing it for the last three weeks and …"—Scruffy dug his hand into his pocket and removed a sample glass—"would like to cash in our pay dirt."

"Your partner in prospecting?" Merle said as he glanced at the dog sitting at Scruffy's side.

"And my good luck charm."

Merle shifted his attention to the sample glass filled with shiny gold flakes. "Five-ounce glass," Merle said with a concurring nod. "Let me see what you have." His tone had changed to that of assayer and businessman.

The assayer placed the glass on the table. "I need to rebalance my scale," he said as he removed his glasses and wiped his lenses with a thin cloth. "Come back at the end of the day and we can settle up."

Past a wrought-iron gate coated in black enamel, Scruffy came up the stone walk to Mrs. Morlock's house, which was situated on a half-acre lot at the edge of town. It was by far the finest-looking house in Big Bear, with a decoratively trimmed side porch, bay windows, and vertical board-and-batten siding.

The interior was one the likes of which Scruffy had never before seen. It contained high ceilings with ornamental molding around the walls, floor-to-ceiling draperies, walnut floors, wide birch-framed parlor armchairs, a satinwood settee adorned in intricate scrollwork, a glass-encased armoire teeming with old books, and a mahogany dining table with six high-back cane chairs.

As Scruffy came up the front steps, a shrill voice said, "Well, well, will you lookie here. I was about ready to demand a search party be sent out." Sitting in a wicker swing suspended by chains at the end of the side porch was the widow, with a hardback book in hand.

She was of an unknown age—in Scruffy's mind anywhere from fifty to seventy, as she possessed a dignity in her bearing, an assurance of life experiences. Mrs. Morlock had gray-white hair that she normally wore in a bun, but today her tresses were cascading down to her shoulders. She touched a brooch on her white blouse with a frilly collar and settled her hands on her lap, which was covered by a long gray skirt. Rocking ever-so gently, her black ankle boots lifted slightly off the ground as a puckish smile creased her thin lips.

"Oh," Scruffy said. "Mrs. Morlock, I did not see you there."

"And how did you and your little companion do out in that godforsaken wilderness?" Her watchful eyes honed in on her young boarder.

"Not bad," Scruffy said as he desperately eyed the front door, with its fancy scrollwork on the lintel and its imposing oak presence.

A bemused smirk creased the widow's lips. "I imagine you are looking forward to an evening with your fellow prospectors at the local watering hole?" She raised her brow, her inquisitive eyes seeking an answer.

"It has crossed my mind," Scruffy said as he reached for the door handle.

She drew back in her seat, her eyes still on Scruffy. "It being Saturday, may I expect you to join me for dinner beforehand?" she said. "Say six o'clock?"

Scruffy had forgotten what day it was. He had been looking forward to the Long Branch for the last week of prospecting, but after three weeks of beans and jerky, a hot meal was most appealing, and he did not want to upset his landlord. "Why thank you, ma'am."

Mrs. Morlock flicked her hand in a sweeping motion. "Off with you," she said. She lifted a warning finger. "And do not be late."

Scruffy's room was on the first floor, at the rear of the house, off the drawing room. The upstairs had three bedrooms, two of which were vacant. He was her only boarder. His rent was two dollars a week, which included dinner on Saturday and Sunday and bath privileges. When Scruffy had mentioned to Pete that he was tired of rooming at the Long Branch, Pete replied, "The Widow Morlock rents out a room from time to time, if you can pass her muster, but I must warn you she is a bit eccentric."

"How so?" Scruffy had asked.

Pete shrugged. "I don't know," he said. "Nothing real crazy, she's just a real quirky lady."

On Scruffy's first Saturday at his new place of residence, he had begged out of dinner with the widow, having agreed to meet Pete for drinks at the Long Branch, but he saw the disappointment in her eyes and the droop of her bottom lip, though she recovered. "Very well," she said too quickly. "I shall dine in the comfort of my own company."

After that, when in Big Bear he joined her for weekend dinners, though she always inquired in a tone of expectation of his presence at the dinner table.

Back in his room, Scruffy stripped down and put on a clean shirt and trousers from his dresser, unpacked his gear, piled all his dirty laundry in a wicker basket, and took it to the kitchen.

From a kitchen closet, he grabbed a scrub brush, a bar of lye soap, a pot, and a large copper tub. He left the tub on a flagstone patio in the backyard and continued to a hand-cranked well that had a stone base and shingled roof, in the middle of a small vegetable garden, and filled the pot with water. Back in the kitchen, he lit the stove and waited for the water to heat up.

After three trips of filling the tub with warm water, he pulled a metal-framed chair with a matching latticework back splat and seat from a round cast-iron table and sat, scrubbing his dirty clothes with lye soap.

When finished, he hung the wrung-out clothes on a clothes line that ran three rows deep, strung with corded rope attached to cross braces atop wooden posts twenty feet across from each other. Scruffy had built the clothesline for the widow when the old one was damaged beyond repair when a branch from a willow tree fell on it. Without fail, every time Scruffy saw the willow tree, he thought back to the attempted hanging of BoJack and his subsequent murder.

He then went back inside and boiled more water for a bath. The bathroom was on the first floor and had a claw-foot cast-iron tub. He heated up three pots of water and eased his naked body into the hot bath. *Oh yes, this is the closest thing to heaven*, he thought as the warmth seemed to seep into his bones. He scrubbed himself well with the lye soap and rinsed off with a washcloth.

After drying himself, he dressed in his clean clothes. What a grand feeling—clean inside and out.

In his room, Scruffy found Rusty sleeping at the foot of the bed, sprawled out, head on paws. Wonder Dog slid a look over at Scruffy—*About time*—before returning to sleep.

CHAPTER 16

BEFORE JOINING THE WIDOW FOR dinner, Scruffy picked up his money at the assay office—eighty-one dollars and thirty-one cents.

It is the most satisfying feeling to have earned good money without having taken an order from one damn person, Scruffy thought as he returned to his room, where he mixed beans and jerky in a bowl and placed it on the floor under the window.

From his spot on the bed, Rusty eyed the food and then squinted a questioning look at his master.

"I will bring a treat back for you after dinner with the widow," Scruffy said.

Rusty tilted his head to one side, the ridge above his good eye raised.

"Wonder Dog," Scruffy said, "I wish I could take you to dinner, but you know the widow would not approve." He ruffled the fur on his dog's neck and headed for the door.

As Scruffy entered the dining room, the door from the kitchen opened and Mrs. Morlock entered, wearing a white apron over her blouse and holding a tray bearing two white porcelain dinner plates and cutlery. She had pulled her hair back into a neat bun tied at the back by a barrette.

"You are early," Mrs. Morlock said as she set the tray down on the table and lifted a pitcher of water and filled two stem glasses.

Scruffy asked, "May I help?"

"I have the roast in the oven, and the side dishes are warming," she replied as she set the table. She looked down at her apron as though surprised she still had it on. She untied it from the back, folded it, and placed it inside a drawer in a credenza that had a glass-encased cabinet with fancy liquor glasses on one shelf and bottles of liquor and decanters on the other.

Scruffy stood at the end of the table, his hands on the top rail of a high-back chair, waiting for her next move.

"Would you care to join me in an aperitif?" The widow asked through a thin, inscrutable smile.

"Beg your pardon?" Scruffy said.

"Sherry," the widow said.

Scruffy had never drunk such a fancy drink. He liked beer and, on occasion, whiskey to go along. "Thank you, ma'am."

She offered her hand to the credenza. "Be a good gent and pour two," she said, tapping a decanter of amber-colored liquid, "and bring them into the drawing room."

When Scruffy entered the drawing room, Mrs. Morlock was seated on the settee and opened her hand to a winged chair. Scruffy placed the drinks on a ship's wheel table in front of the settee and sat. He studied the table momentarily.

"The table is incongruous to the room's motif," Mrs. Morlock said. "My late husband was a ship's captain." She smiled a secret smile mostly to herself. She then raised her glass and held it, her brow raised as though an idea had come to her. "Would the gentleman be so kind as to provide the toast?"

Scruffy stood and held his glass out in front of himself. "May the sun always shine on the lives of those we cherish, may the wind blow gently at their backs, and—" he paused as a moment of heavy recognition came upon him—"that they advance confidentially in the direction of their dreams and live a life unexpected in common hours."

Mrs. Morlock's expression was one of wonder.

Scruffy sat and took a sip of his sherry. It tasted like liquid cake. *Not bad,* he thought. *Not bad at all.* He said to the widow, "The last part of my toast I paraphrased from Henry David Thoreau."

Mrs. Morlock sat back and took a dainty sip of her drink. She lifted her gaze to Scruffy, her pale blue eyes showing a glint of newfound appreciation. "It was well said, young man."

During their aperitif, Mrs. Morlock inquired about Scruffy's background. In his time living with her, their conversations had always been brief and limited to the weather, her students, or her desire to have a library built in town.

The sherry had settled Scruffy into a comfortable state of relaxed fatigue. He gave a brief but succinct description of his childhood in Yakima, including his mother's heritage and the death of his father on the day he was born.

Mrs. Morlock stiffened her posture and leaned forward with an inquiring look. "And where, might I ask, did you learn of Thoreau?"

English class in high school. We covered American literature thoroughly, and even Shakespeare and some of the Greek classics."

"And after all that, somehow you ended up here—and with no one to cherish?"

Back up in his room, a ten-foot by twelve-foot space with room for his bed, dresser, small table, and stiff wooden chair, Scruffy noted that the dog bowl had not been touched by Rusty. He pulled from his pocket a handkerchief covering a surprise. "Wonder Dog, lookie what I brought home for you."

Rusty jumped down off the bed, eyeing the handkerchief.

Scruffy emptied into the dog bowl two chunks of juicy red meat from the roast.

Rusty dived in, eating the meat, beans, and jerky in ravenous gulps. When he finished, he licked his lips from left to right and then right to left.

"Well," Scruffy said, "now that you are no longer upset with me, what say we head over to the Long Branch and say hi to the fellas?"

Rusty stood on his hind legs and turned in a circle. He then jumped back on the bed and sat on his haunches with a bark of approval.

CHAPTER 17

THE MURMUR OF CONVERSATIONAL VOICES and the interjections of laughter could be heard a block away from the Long Branch. "Sounds like we are just in time, Wonder Dog," Scruffy said as he stopped and took in the sight before him. Big Bear, Alaska, was more like a town out of the Old West than the twentieth century—he had yet to see an automobile in Big Bear, a one-block town with one- and two-story board-and-batten buildings lining the no-name dirt road occupied by the general store, boarding house, land assayer office, livery, recently founded bank, blacksmith, doctor's office (which was used by a young doctor who traveled, depending on the weather, by horseback or dog sled from town to town), a furrier who did a bang-up business, and, of course, the Long Branch.

In the distance, the Kosar Mountains shimmered in the black sky as a full moon floated over the snow-tipped peaks. Scruffy thought of the Yakama Indian myth about the powerful effect a full moon could have on a person if he or she was attuned properly to comprehend the signs.

The only time Scruffy had thought of his Indian heritage was when his mother, Nantes, with her cinnamon-colored skin and straight black hair that she often wore in pigtails, took on an expression of someone trapped in two cultures. It was a far-off look that came over her from time to time—a flinching wince and a downward slope at the corners of her full lips that registered as an uncertain identity before she recovered to her normal implacable mien.

Scruffy had never identified with any group of people. He was himself, born Logan Lomax—a name he had abandoned in his youth. He was Scruffy Lomax—a name he had received when he whipped the class bully by grabbing the scruff of his neck and not letting go—a young man with a roguish moniker who desired to live this life he had been given to the fullest. And part of that fullness had been the newfound satisfaction of independence.

As he stepped up onto the boardwalk in front of the blacksmith's shop, an uproar of laughter quickened his pace toward the saloon's double-wide oak doors.

Men were standing and sitting shoulder-to-shoulder at the U-shaped bar, talking and laughing, and everyone was having a good old time. At the far corner of the bar, Scruffy spotted Pete saying so long to a couple of fellows he did not recognize.

"Scruffy!" Pete hollered with a wave. "Come on over."

Scruffy lifted up Rusty, set him on the bar, and pulled back a stool.

Pete said to Scruffy, "Just heard the most interesting tale."

"Yeah?" Scruffy said as he raised his hand to the barkeep.

Scruffy ordered a shot of whiskey and a draft, adding, "And a sarsaparilla for my little dog." He turned his attention back to Pete. "You were saying."

"Those two fellas I was just talking with claim they were attacked by a giant hairy ape-man."

Scruffy looked at Pete, a question in his eyes.

The barkeep brought his order, placing the sarsaparilla in front of Rusty, who sat up, cradled the shot glass in his paws, lifted it, and drank it down.

"Never get used to seeing that," Pete said through an appreciative smile.

A fellow across the bar said with wonder in his voice, "Did you see that? Did you see that little dog throw down a shot!"

The old-timer, who had told Scruffy about prospecting in the Kosar Valley, slapped the man on the back. "Ha, ha!" he barked as he nodded with a pronounced wink over at Scruffy. "Around these parts, you never know what you might see—right, Scruffy?"

A rumble of hooting laughter erupted at the far end of the bar from a group of trappers, diverting Scruffy's attention for a moment.

"Old-timer," Scruffy said in a raised voice. "That is why he is called Rusty the One-Eyed Wonder Dog." He slanted a crooked salute at the old-timer, threw down his whiskey, and followed it with a swig of beer.

"Yes sir," he said as general conversation, "that tastes mighty fine after three weeks roughing it."

Scruffy took another longer drink, finishing his mug, which he then raised to the barkeep. He then said to Pete, "There were stories similar back in Yakima about giant manlike ape creatures that the Indians called Sasquatch."

Pete petted Rusty on the back of his neck and said, "They said they were prospecting up north when this beast, standing on two legs, stood on a cliff and threw boulders at them while howling the most god-awful sound. They packed up right quick and skedaddled out of there."

"Anything is possible." Scruffy nodded a thank-you to the barkeep and cradled his mug of beer. "You know, Pete," Scruffy said as he shined a smile on Rusty, who was stretched out, head resting on paws, grinning his doggie grin as Pete scratched behind his ears, "I think it would be something magical if those creatures do exist."

Pete and Scruffy were joined by Needle Nose, who said he was going prospecting in a few days.

"Where you heading?" Pete asked.

"Working on that," Needle Nose said. "Any ideas?"

"Just might have one," Pete said as he raised a finger to the barkeep. "But it is a hike that I would not recommend going alone." He ordered a beer and then said to Scruffy, "You have any luck in Kosar Valley?"

"Not too bad," Scruffy said. He did not want to mention that Rusty had a knack for sniffing out gold. If word got out, someone desperate enough might try to steal him, though Scruffy had faith that Rusty would never consent to such traitorous action.

Scruffy asked whether Needle Nose was prospecting by himself.

"No," he replied as he took a short swig of beer. "Got a fella from Quebec I am partnered up with."

"French Canadian, huh," Pete said as he lifted his gaze to the front door. "Whoa, will you look at the size of him."

There stood the largest man Scruffy had ever seen in his life. He was six feet, six inches at least, with massive broad shoulders and a neck like the stump of an oak tree. There was a wild, untamed quality about this giant with a tangled thicket of dark hair and glowering black eyes that darted about the room until they homed in on Needle Nose.

"Yes sirree, he be French Canadian all right," Needle Nose said as a silence fell over the bar, all eyes on the approaching man mountain wearing a heavy flannel shirt and thick denim trousers held up by suspenders.

"Lagos," the big man said with a thick accent so that the name came out "Lay ... ghost."

"Pete Prescott, Scruffy Lomax," Needle Nose said with a lift of his hand to the big man. "Meet Frenchy Dupree."

Pete held out his hand, which was engulfed in a massive palm and closed over by broad fingers with fingernails as thick as turtle shells.

"Hellloo," Frenchy said.

After shaking hands with Scruffy, Frenchy clenched Scruffy's wrist, examining his hand. "That big hand for any size man. Oui."

Frenchy slid a look over at Rusty, who was sitting up, giving Frenchy the once-over.

"That be my dog," Scruffy said. "He answers to Rusty."

Frenchy leaned forward to get a closer look and bolted back. "He got only one good eye?"

"That is right," Scruffy said.

The giant was eyeing Rusty, not sure what to make of him, when Rusty winked at him with his glass eye.

Frenchy's bottom lip pouched out in a silent "Huh" as he put his hand on Scruffy's shoulder. "Mere dè dieu," he said in a low voice teeming with apprehension.

"Nothing to be worried about, Frenchy," Scruffy said as he gestured to the barkeep. "What are you drinking?"

Once Frenchy got a few drinks in him, he alternated between beer and whiskey. He settled down, though he kept an eye on Rusty.

Rounds were bought, and stories emerged. Needle Nose told about coming across Canada from Nova Scotia, not knowing where he was headed other than "away." He ended up in Alaska, where he had been "trapping mostly for nearly ten years now," he said as he ordered a round for his three companions. "But sooner rather than later, I am going to head down to the States and see what I see."

Pete Prescott, who was older—at least forty, maybe forty-five—said he was born in Yuma, Arizona, and got the moniker Pistol Pete from working as a deputy marshal, "Back when the West was still the West.

I carried a Colt forty-five on my hip ..." He stopped and took a swig of his beer and wiped his lips with the back of his hand. He made a face as though trying to remember what he had been talking about.

"You were a deputy in Yuma?" Scruffy said.

"Yeah, yeah," Pete said. "Once had a varmint try to draw on me, and I whipped my pistol out of the holster lickety-split and shot that gun right out of his hand." Pete shrugged. "Haven't carried a firearm since. When I departed Arizona, I left it all behind, including the handle Pistol Pete."

Scruffy looked over at Frenchy, who was sitting in the corner, his massive shoulders up against the wall, listening.

"Frenchy," Scruffy said. "I hear you are from Quebec."

Frenchy stared into his mug of beer and looked up, his dark eyes glinting a remembering look. "The backwoods of Quebec."

"Let me guess," Scruffy said. "You were a logger—and a good one at that."

Frenchy put his forearm on the bar and said, "Yes, logger. And yes, I was good."

The barkeep put the round on the bar, and Scruffy reached for a fresh mug of beer. "But I am a guessing that you also got the wanderlust."

"I see that," Frenchy said in a deep and rumbly voice, "Scruffy Lomax and his little dog, Rusty, see things."

As Scruffy headed back to his room, the moon was now high overhead, spilling light on the street almost like a street lamp in Chicago. It had been a grand night at the saloon. Frenchy Dupree was a most interesting man. Scruffy guessed he was somewhere in his early thirties, a larger-than-life backwoods figure in his flannel and Mackinaw.

And a deal had been agreed upon: in three days, all four men would prospect together at a location a three-day hike away that Pete had heard about. "There is safety in numbers when roughing it," he said.

Prospecting alone in the Kosar Valley with only Rusty had gotten a tad lonely for Scruffy, so joining up with three men sounded appealing, though Scruffy wondered whether after a while they might get on each other's nerves, and if so, whether they would learn to adjust to each other.

Time will tell, Scruffy thought as he opened the door to his room. He was not exactly inebriated, but had a pleasant sense of well-being—though a tired well-being. Three weeks of prospecting had caught up with him, and a good night's sleep in his bed was calling. He took off his shirt, trousers, and shoes and socks, and pulled back the covers. "Had us a fine old time tonight, Wonder Dog," he said through a big, arms-stretched-over-head yawn.

Rusty hopped up on the end of the bed, walked around in a circle, and lay across the bed, head resting on paws, sliding a look over at his master.

"Yeah, we are both pretty tuckered out," Scruffy said as he got into bed. He lay back with fingers laced behind neck as the day's events scrolled through his mind.

It had been a full day, from finishing the last leg of the walk in from prospecting to ending with drinks and an agreement at the Long Branch. But what rose in his mind was his toast during the aperitif with the widow that ended with "May the sun always shine on the lives of those we cherish." That had triggered the widow's comment, with a question implied: "And after all that, somehow you ended up here— and with no one to cherish?" Of course, Scruffy had planted that seed with his words.

Who did Scruffy cherish in this life other than himself, a mother he would most likely never see again, and a little dog sleeping at his feet? He did wonder whether someday he might want to marry, have a family, and maybe own a little spread of land and plant an orchard.

Maybe down the road, he thought as a heavy sleep came over him.

CHAPTER 18

A T DAWN ON APRIL 15, the four men met at the edge of town four days after they had come to an agreement at the Long Branch. Frenchy had a mule packed with gear, including Pete's sluice box, which none of the other three had ever used. On their backs, each man carried a large canvas knapsack supported by a metal exterior frame packed with essentials: clothes, tools, first aid kit, compass, and pans and vials for prospecting. And a sleeping bag was attached to the top of the knapsacks by a rawhide strap. The mule carried all the food, which lightened the burden, but still each pack weighed at least twenty-five pounds.

Needle Nose had told Scruffy that Pete was the only one of the three that had any real experience prospecting. Frenchy, like Needle Nose, had little experience. "Pay attention to how Pete goes about prospecting," Needle Nose had said. "We could learn a good bit about finding gold from him."

It was cold, but the sky clear, though there was always a chance of snow up until June. "Got us over twelve hours of daylight," Needle Nose said. "So let's get a move on."

They headed out, Scruffy and Rusty at one end and Frenchy and his mule at the other. A mile outside of town, they were on a prairie. The wild grass that had been dormant all winter showed signs of life, its color beginning to change from brown to a faint green. Interspersed with the grass were pussy willow, Canadian thistle, and hogweed, all of which Rusty plowed right through. In the distance, enormous cumulus clouds loomed over the dark outline of hills.

The men walked in a comfortable silence, as though they had been friends for years. They were four men with a wanderlust—four men who had taken a road less traveled.

Around noontime, Pete suggested they break to eat. They were at an outcrop of rocks in the middle of this vast stretch of grassland, with a smattering of trees nearby: firs and willows, and aspens with young buds on the verge of bursting out.

Before departure, they had agreed not only to share food but also to split the profit from any gold. Scruffy liked that; "One for all, all for one" was the motto of the Three Musketeers, the heroes of one of his favorite stories about a young man who leaves home and travels to Paris to join the three most formidable musketeers of the age.

"I have beans and jerky," Scruffy said.

"I start fire," Frenchy said as he reached into a saddlebag on his mule, pulled out a rawhide sack, and emptied on the ground five balls of what Scruffy figured to be mule dung.

"I will gather some twigs and such," Pete said as he eyed a copse of aspens that were anywhere from ten to thirty feet in height.

Needle Nose gathered some loose rocks from the outcrop while Scruffy dug out a fire pit with a trenching shovel.

Over a crackling fire, Frenchy hung the handle of a cast iron pot on a spit made of a thick stick suspended across two forked sticks driven into the ground. Inside the pot was a pool of water and lard, beans, jerky, potatoes, and carrots—he called it *gouloache française*. He dished out four plates and handed them out.

Scruffy saved a little jerky and beans for Rusty that he served him in a bowl.

"You feed dog people food?" Frenchy said with an inquisitive lift of his brow.

"That a problem?" Scruffy said as he met Frenchy's stare.

Frenchy took a spoonful of his goulash, swelling his cheek. "I feed Annie," he said with a tilt of his head to his mule, "some oats, and the rest she eat the wild grass."

"Good for Annie," Scruffy said. "I feed Rusty what I eat." He grinned a crooked grin at Frenchy. "We good with that, big man?"

"Yah, we good. We good."

By late afternoon, they had reached a small creek at the base of a line of foothills thick with jack pines. "What say we set up camp here?" Pete asked as he scanned the steep terrain before him. "We have us some climbing to do tomorrow."

"Yah," Frenchy said in a weary voice. "Good with me."

Scruffy thought it must be difficult for a man that size to walk for hours on end carrying a load on his back. *Frenchy must weigh close to three hundred pounds, and with little fat—an oversize ox of a man.*

Without another word, tents were pitched as unseen woodpeckers and smaller birds knocked and chirped from the pine trees.

Frenchy took his gear off of Annie and walked her over to the creek for a drink, with Rusty trailing after. Annie and Rusty stood at the edge of the creek, quenching their thirst.

Scruffy wished he could stop time and take this all in for a good long spell: bask in the clean, crisp air; view the sun sitting low, yet still strong in an azure sky; and savor the camaraderie of his companions and the powerful sense of well-being that living a life of freedom and independence offer to a man.

After they finished eating, there was still light, though dusk was around the corner, as the bright light had faded and in its place was the first hint of twilight. The men sat around the campfire in silence as though not yet ready to give up on the day, not wanting to give in to the fatigue of tramping in the wild, for there was time to savor the stillness of sitting and being—to let the day's events settle in their bones with the satisfaction of a full belly of grub and enjoy the company of like-minded men.

With Rusty's head nestled on the top of his thigh, Scruffy looked across the fire, which was smoldering with licks of yellow and gold. Frenchy was sitting Indian-style, his massive legs crossed one atop the other, his dark eyes staring into the fire as though entranced.

Pete poked at the fire with a stick, and red embers flared up overhead before they vanished into the cool air. "Figure we got another day and a half 'fore we get to Header's Creek."

"Header's Creek, huh?" Scruffy said. He knew little about where they were going. He had agreed to go the other night at the Long Branch, and in the intervening time before departure, he had not inquired. He had been glad to join up and to learn some of the finer points of prospecting from Pete.

Pete grinned at Scruffy. "Teach you how to sluice for gold."

"Me too," Needle Nose said.

"What makes you think we will find gold at this location?" Scruffy said to Pete.

"Nothing guaranteed in prospecting," Pete said as he tossed a stick into the fire. He went on to say that it was an abandoned mining site from the gold rush at the end of the old century and that a lode deposit may have eroded enough to have washed downstream and settled in a riverbed. "We are searching for black sand," Pete said.

"Black sand?" Scruffy said.

"You will see."

Before turning in, Frenchy said that bears could smell food from twenty miles away. "We must hang all food in trees," he said.

"I got an idea," Scruffy said.

"What is that?" Pete said.

"I get on Frenchy's shoulders and string it up high."

"Yah," Frenchy said. "You smart, Scruffy."

Frenchy got a roll of rope from his gear and pointed Scruffy over to a tall pine. Frenchy got down on his haunches as Scruffy took the rope and stepped on a boulderous shoulder, placed a hand against the tree, and stepped up with his other foot. Frenchy stood, with Scruffy rising so that his head was over twelve feet above the ground. He tied the end of the rope onto a thick branch.

Scruffy jumped down and secured their food in a burlap sack onto the middle section of the rope. They repeated the lifting process at a nearby tree and looped the other end of the rope on a branch. Scruffy pulled the rope taut, stringing the sacks of food high overhead, and tied the end of the rope tight to the branch.

"Now that is something," Needle Nose said. "Teamwork. Yes sir, men working together."

In the dead of night, Rusty began to whine.

Scruffy, still half asleep, sat up, as he thought he heard the cracking snap of wood breaking. Silence. *Probably my imagination*, he said to himself. But Rusty was at the front of tent, whining something fierce.

From outside came a low, growling howl. The growl grew in strength into a haunting hair-on-the-back-of-your-neck scream.

Everyone emptied out of the tents. Annie was whining and braying something fierce. Rusty ran over to the edge of the forest and began barking.

Frenchy calmed his mule, and Scruffy called Rusty over to his side.

Then it was completely silent. There was not a chirp of a cricket, hoot of owl—nothing. Dead silence.

"What in God's name was that?" Needle Nose said.

"Look," Scruffy said as he went over where the food had been hung. The line was down at one end, but the burlap sack containing the food was attached and intact.

"What in the world could reach up that high up ?" Needle Nose said as he examined the rope still tied to the branch that had been broken off the tree trunk.

"You know that story those two prospectors told me about the giant ape-man?" Pete said. Everyone looked at Pete standing there in his long johns, his face illuminated in a slant of moonlight. "Header's Creek is where it happened."

CHAPTER 19

THE CLIMB UP AND OVER the foothills was a challenge. Scrub trees and brush littered the ground, the land thick with pine trees. The trail had been grown over in parts. Wild grasses and sedges wet with morning dew caused Annie to slip and list to one side before Frenchy grabbed her by the flank, steadying her.

But besides the challenge of walking uphill, Scruffy had a sense that they were being watched. Last night after the bloodcurdling howl, and Pete's tidbit about the supposed Sasquatch attack at their destination, he went on to say that Header's Creek had a reputation of spooky things happening, and that it had been avoided for years. "Pack animals disappearing at night, rocks thrown at prospectors by someone or something unseen, strange noises, and god-awful smells."

Needle Nose said to Pete, "You didn't think to tell us that we were heading into a giant ape-man's neighborhood?"

"Would it have deterred you?"

Needle Nose looked up into the dark forest. "Cannot say it would." He then said, "Frenchy, Scruffy, you fellas okay with this?"

Scruffy was not discouraged by the idea of a hairy ape-man among them, though he would stay on high alert. "I am good," he said, looking up at Frenchy, who in the dark shadows of night could be mistaken for a giant ape-man.

"Safety in numbers," Frenchy said in a low voice. "I am good too."

◄◦►

By late morning, they came to the crest of the foothills; a valley below of prairie land was a welcome sight. "What say we break for chow," Pete said.

"Yes," Frenchy replied. He looked at Needle Nose and Scruffy for confirmation.

They nodded their agreement, and Frenchy opened his saddlebag and set up a feed bag with oats for Annie, while Scruffy dished out beans and jerky for Rusty, who gobbled it down.

The men sat on a log overlooking the valley, eating beans, hardtack biscuits, and jerky. "How far we got?" Scruffy asked Pete.

Pete took a thoughtful bite of his biscuits and lifted his hand to a string of low hills in the distance. "Beyond them hills is Header's Creek."

"You been there before?" Scruffy asked as he fed Rusty a nibble of biscuit.

"Years ago," Pete said as he bit into his jerky. "Had no luck." He shrugged and looked off. "But over time things change."

CHAPTER 20

DURING MIDAFTERNOON ON THE THIRD day, the four men crossed, single file, a rickety pedestrian bridge over a fast-running stream.

A couple of miles downstream, they came to an embankment cut through by timber steps that led to a clearing. At the rear of the clearing was a weathered wooden barrack, set back along the perimeter of thick foliage of bushes and trees. On one side of the barracks, a stone chimney ran along the exterior.

"That livable?" Scruffy said to Pete.

"Might have to run off some varmints," Pete said as he dug his hand into the embankment, pulled out a handful of earth, and ran it through his fingers, "but it beats sleeping out in the open." Pete went on to say that the structure had been built during the late nineteenth-century gold rush. He then motioned over his shoulder for the men to follow him.

The barrack sat three feet off the ground, raised by thick timber pilings. Steps led to the landing of an imposing timber-framed door that Pete opened. He peeked inside before entering the building, which looked capable of housing forty men or more.

Pete opened a window and stuck his head out. "Little dusty, and not smelling too grand, but we get rid of the critter poop and we should be just fine. Come on in," he said, his eyes twinkling with adventure.

The inside was empty, save for a row of wooden frames for bunk beds that ran along the back wall. A huge stone fireplace with a hearth was at the far end and appeared to be sound. The space had a dank, musky wild animal smell from the hardened scat that was scattered about here and there. Frenchy picked up the scat with an empty dung sack, careful not to touch it with his hands, and dumped it outside.

"Might help if we open the windows and get some air in here to clear out the stink," Pete said. He then went down the front and began opening windows. Only a few were completely intact, some with cracks or missing panes. There were six windows in front and six in the rear, two of which Frenchy had to use his strength to force open, splitting the bottom frame of one.

Back outside, Pete said, "What say we get a lay of the land."

Down at the creek, Pete looked up and down the stream. "I am hoping that some placer gold has found its way from there," he said, pointing upstream, "to here." He lifted his chin to a bend in the creek. He went on to explain that the leading and trailing edges of a bend were where gold could settle. "So we are going to want to work in these bends."

"I think for the remainder of the day we get things squared away," Needle Nose said.

Frenchy offered, "I will cut wood."

"I brought a fishing line and a lure," Needle Nose said. "How about I try to catch us dinner upstream."

"Damn," Scruffy said, "I like that." He turned to Frenchy. "You cut the wood, big man, and I will haul it inside."

"While you fellas are doing that," Pete said with his eyes on the water, "I will check out the bends."

Whacking and thwacking fallen branches with a razor-sharp axe, Frenchy began each cut by bringing the axe overhead. With a swift and powerful stroke, he would bring the blade down, splitting the branches in a single stroke, one after another, like a human wood-chopping machine.

Scruffy worked up a good sweat carrying armfuls of logs up the steps inside the barracks doorway, stacking the logs, and then heading back into the forest, where more wood had been cut. After six trips, they had plenty of wood inside, and Frenchy had a half-cord stacked where he had been working. "Frenchy Dupree," the big man said in a singsong kidding voice, "is a *bûcheron*."

Scruffy looked at Frenchy—*What?*

"Woodsman, Scruffy, I am a woodsman."

"You surely are, big man."

On the way back from the forest, Scruffy spotted a table and two benches made of red cedar at the back of the barrack. A patina of dirt and grime covered the surfaces, but after applying a wet rag with plenty of elbow grease, it would do just fine for meals.

After Scruffy and Frenchy cleaned the table in the front of the barracks, Needle Nose came up the embankment steps with a string of big silver-colored fish that were at least five pounds each.

"We are eating big tonight," Needle Nose said as he lifted his catch. "Silver salmon!"

"Mon dieu!" Frenchy said in a booming voice.

Scruffy stated, "Beans and jerky or what have you is gonna ruin the taste of that good-looking fish."

"Fish and biscuits has a good ring to it," Needle Nose said with brow lifted as though to ask, *What do you say?*

Dinner was a treat: fat, moist salmon—which Needle Nose cleaned on a flat rock at the creek and pan-fried over an open fire—and piping hot hardtack biscuits.

They ate all three fish, with Rusty cleaning up the entrails. Frenchy put away as much of the succulent salmon as the other three combined.

When they were done, everyone was food drunk. "Damn," Needle Nose said as he leaned back from the table, hands on belly, "I have not eaten that well or that much since—"

"Since never," Scruffy said, to laughter.

"Let's make sure," Pete said with finger raised, "that we clean up good."

"Oui." Frenchy lifted his gaze to the forest, which was forming into a solid shadow in the fading light. "Bears or ..." His voice trailed off, but the implication was understood.

Since breaking camp that morning, Scruffy had been on alert, looking and listening—though for what, he was not certain; the rustling of branches could have been overhead wind through the trees, and the faint knock of wood on wood off in the distance could have been a chipmunk clucking. The most disconcerting of all was the sense that they were being observed by unseen eyes.

"Big day tomorrow," Pete said as he stood and stretched his hands over head. "Let's get a fire going in the barrack and call it a night."

By sunrise, Frenchy and Needle Nose were digging into the embankment and panning their find for gold, while Scruffy was receiving his first lesson in sluicing.

"First thing, Scruffy, a sluice box is nothing more than a man-made channel." Pete ran his hand over the fixed ridges at the bottom of the box. "These riffles are set in the bottom to collect gold, the heaviest material." He put his hand on the flare and added, "The water enters here and washes right on down, sweeping away unwanted debris, while the gold settles down between the riffles."

Pete placed the box in a shallow channel along the edge of the creek. "We need to get this set at the right angle, which is dependent on the strength of the water flow."

"You set it in black sand," Scruffy said.

"That is where gold likes to hide," Pete replied. He then took a spade full of black sand, picked out the large stones, and placed the contents in the flare of the sluice as the current ran through it, washing out the dirt. Scruffy watched closely as Pete continued to run black sand through the sluice.

After a couple of runs, Pete emptied the contents into a pan and handed it to Scruffy. "Take it from here," he said.

After Scruffy had swished out unwanted dirt and small stones, bits of glittering gold emerged. "Look at that, Pete."

"Yes sir," Pete said with a lift in his voice, "we have us some placer gold."

That afternoon, Scruffy switched places with Needle Nose, working the embankment with Frenchy. Rusty, who had spent the morning watching Scruffy and Pete sluice where they had collected a couple of grams of gold, sniffed at the embankment before stepping back and barking.

"Rusteee," Frenchy said. "What is it?"

"He thinks there is gold in there," Scruffy said.

"Noooh?" Frenchy said with a look at the hillside and then the little dog.

"One way to find out," Scruffy said as he sunk his shovel into the hillside and emptied the contents into his and Frenchy's pans.

As Frenchy and Scruffy swished out unwanted dirt and debris at the edge of the creek, nearby, Pete and Needle Nose were leaning over the sluice box as though examining its contents.

"Eureka," Pete hollered. "Lordy, lordy, look what we sluiced out." He pulled from the bottom of the sluice box a shiny stone that looked like a large golden pebble.

"Bet that weighs a couple of grams, Pete," Scruffy said.

By the end of the day, they had roughly a quarter ounce of gold—not a bad day's work. Rusty had some success sniffing the hillside, though Scruffy was beginning to think it might be pretty well tapped out. The real opportunity, he thought, was in the black sand, as the others had even less luck than Rusty, who Frenchy now thought had a *cadeau spécial*—a special gift.

CHAPTER 21

A S THE DAYS WERE GROWING longer, there now being nearly thirteen
hours of daylight per day, Pete, who was now considered the leader
of the group, suggested they not overdo it. "In my old age, I need my
beauty sleep to concentrate on sluicing."

The men agreed to work no more than twelve hours a day, and
a routine was established in which Pete and, usually, Scruffy would
sluice for gold, while Frenchy and Needle Nose handled a variety of
tasks: Frenchy took care of cutting and stacking firewood, as well as
setting traps for rabbits, grouse, and squirrels, the latter of which Scruffy
thought tasted like chicken.

Needle Nose collected wild berries and continued to fish, but the
salmon must have migrated up stream, though he caught some halibut
and northern pike. Some days he came up empty-handed, and others
he had some luck.

The tedium of routine was tempered for Scruffy by the friendships
he was establishing with each of the men. Pete was a patient teacher
with a keen understanding of sluicing for gold; Scruffy was surprised
he had not struck it rich yet. There was little small talk when sluicing
with Pete, but Scruffy enjoyed the calm, deliberate manner in which
Pete went about his business.

Needle Nose was a likable, go-along-with-the-flow type of man
who had an agreeable disposition and a solid work ethic. He possessed
a seize-the-day look about him that was contagious. The man was a
pleasure to be in the company of and to work with.

Frenchy was, for the most part, a gentle giant, but there were times
when he became abrasive, such as when Needle Nose was assisting with
stacking wood and Frenchy bellowed, "No! I said we crisscross the logs

end to end!" Scruffy and Pete, who were sluicing in the creek, heard his voice, which might have been heard from miles away. There was also a time at dinner when Scruffy had Rusty on his lap and fed him a morsel of rabbit, and Frenchy looked across the table with a scowl of disapproval. Scruffy had been ready for just such a confrontation, and the previous day he had wandered out into the woods with Rusty and taught him a couple of apt words in doggie growl.

Scruffy turned Rusty's head to the side so that his glass eye was facing Frenchy. "Wonder Dog, what have you to say to Frenchy?"

The little dog grinned out of the side of his mouth, revealing a row of tiny but sharp teeth; it was an outrageously wicked grin, like that of a doggy version of Scruffy. He then growled in a whiny groan, "Fren … chee … wab … biitt goo … ood."

As Needle Nose and Pete exchanged disbelieving looks, Frenchy said, "Mon dieu!" in a low, rumbly voice as he leaned back on the bench with a look of suspicious discomfort.

Pete and Needle Nose burst out in an uproar of laughter.

"Frenchy," Needle Nose said, "Wonder Dog is not to be messed with—no sirree."

Everyone—even Frenchy, for the most part—was an admirer of the little dog, though the sentiment was not always reciprocated. A few days back, Needle Nose had no luck fishing, so he decided to try his hand at panning the embankment, but he had little luck. He asked Scruffy if he could borrow Rusty to sniff out gold.

"Sure," Scruffy said. "You can take Rusty to the mountain, but I cannot promise he will cross the mountain."

Pete took Rusty to the embankment, but Wonder Dog showed no interest in sniffing out gold unless Scruffy was with him.

Frenchy came around to making peace with Rusty, even feeding him a bite of freshly made pemmican, a new concoction that was game meat and berries pounded into meal and cooked in animal grease. When cooled and condensed, Frenchy packed it into bags from the hide of the game. This saved time, as the men could grab a hunk of pemmican with little pause in work. It was right tasty, and Rusty lapped it right up. Frenchy would cook a fresh batch every day and store inside the barrack. At an evening meal, he held up a patty. "Pemmican," he

CHAPTER 22

THREE DAYS BEFORE THE PLANNED departure date from Header's Creek, Pete told Scruffy, "I want to head downstream a good ways and see if we do not find a pot of gold."

They departed at sunrise, Scruffy wearing his knapsack crammed with pemmican, water, pans, and the disassembled sluice box.

They walked in silence, with Rusty sauntering along between them. By the time they passed the farthest spot they had previously sluiced, the current was barely a trickle. Scruffy was not sure how they could sluice in such a weak flow, but he trusted that Pete knew what he was doing.

Pete slanted a look at Scruffy, as if he registered what his comrade was thinking. "I am hoping that farther down the current picks up ... might find us a falls." They were walking in and out of the shade of the forest that loomed over both sides of the stream, which was thicker and denser than before with tall cedars, spruces, and the ever-present pines. Pete went on to say that where they were headed was considered uninhabitable.

"And now you tell me," Scruffy said.

Pete lifted his brow, his eyes grinning. "Thought you were due a surprise."

"Mighty generous of you," Scruffy said as he picked up Rusty to avoid a thicket of tall sedge grass.

Around a bend, they came to small clearing off to their left where trees forty and fifty feet or more in height were down, lying crossways one atop another. "Let's take a look," Pete said.

Each downed tree had a jagged break at the base; it appeared as though someone or something had snapped them down.

They stared dumbfounded at what lay before them.

"No man could have done this," Pete said. "Not even a man as big and strong as Frenchy—not even close."

"Sasquat—"

They both turned around to the splash of something heavy landing in the water. From across the creek behind the cover of bushes was a shadowy figure—massive, it was.

"What the Sam Hill," Pete said.

Rusty tore off splashing across the creek, barking up a storm.

"Rusty!" Scruffy yelled. "Come, right now!"

Rusty stopped halfway across, barked once more, and scooted back to Scruffy.

"It's at times like this I wished I carried a firearm," Pete said.

Scruffy said, "'Live and let live is my motto.'" He picked up Rusty. "Let's keep moving and find us some gold."

By late morning, they reached a pronounced bend in the creek with a small falls that flushed a strong run of water over its edge. "Lookie, black sand in that channel," Pete said as he pointed to a shallow area along the shore.

"All right," Scruffy said with a lift in his voice. But he could not help scanning up and down the shoreline, not sure what he was looking for. A sign of a great, hairy ape-man? That sense of being watched had returned since they'd left the site of the downed trees. Scruffy was not sure whether he was spooked and it was his imagination or whether his feeling of being observed was genuine. But the splashy *kerplunk* of something hitting the water was real—too damn real.

"Let's eat and then sluice," Pete said as he scanned their environment. Thick, massive trees bordered a six-foot hillside, below which flat-surfaced rocks followed the wide bend of the shoreline up to the falls. Overhead, the sky had turned gray as though a blanket had been spread. The once promising morning had turned, and a chill came into the air.

They sat on the rocks, feet dangling over the edge, nearly touching the surface of the water, and ate pemmican in silence.

Scruffy suggested that he pan the hillside and Pete sluice. "So we get the most out of the time we have," he said. He looked up at the threatening sky and then at Pete, who nodded his agreement.

After Pete assembled the sluice box, he fiddled with getting it at the right angle against the flow of the current. Scruffy went right to panning the hillside. By the first hour, he had found gold in all four pans, and Pete had sluiced some nice-size nuggets.

"We got us some gold, Scruffy!" Pete exclaimed as he extracted from between two riffles of his sluice box a star-shaped nugget the size of a silver dollar.

"Lordy," Scruffy said as he swished away debris in his pan to see five specks of shiny gold. "We hit us a mother lode, Pete."

Gold fever struck the two men as they worked furiously, picking out gold and storing the big nuggets in a moose-skinned satchel, and the smaller bits in Scruffy's sample glass. At first they did not notice the innocuous flakes of snow that swirled in the northerly breeze. Every time Scruffy swished or Pete angled the sluice box in the current, they came up with more gold.

Scruffy was in a zone he had never before entered—a feverous, focused state of unbridled greed. He reminded himself not to work too fast or to lose any gold as he swished and washed away unwanted debris, concentrating with every ounce of energy he could summon. He entered a rhythmic labor: ladle a shovel of soil from the hillside into the pan, swish and swish until more gold was found, store the gold, and start all over again. His mind went blank as he continued to pan. Each new find drove him into a deeper state; soon he saw only what was right before him as he toiled away.

A strong gust of wind swept down the creek, ruffling the current and swirling the heavy, wet snow. It was as though Mother Nature was angry at these two invaders for finding her secret treasure.

"We'd best pack up and skedaddle, Scruffy," Pete said as he removed the sluice box from the creek.

Scruffy looked around as if seeing things for the first time since his first pan. The ground was covered in snow, and poor Rusty was sitting on the outcrop, shivering, with a look that said, *Remember me?*

"Holy smokes," Scruffy said as he snapped out of the gold fever that had infiltrated his being. They had a long and difficult trek back to the campsite. Even with long days of sunlight, Scruffy knew that it would be a challenge to get back before darkness.

After packing up, Scruffy secured the knapsack, the weight sinking into his shoulders as a wave of fatigue came over him. He had expended a tremendous amount of energy getting here and had also experienced the mental exertion required by panning. Tired as he was, he scooped up Rusty and held him tight against his chest, the poor little guy shivering something fierce.

At the site of the downed trees, which appeared like an amorphous mass of white humps on the ground, Pete raised his hand for them to stop. The relentless snow was blowing sideways, making the visibility minimal. Rusty, a limp, wet little ball of fur, pressed tight against Scruffy, whose arm was numb from holding the dog, his shoulders screaming from the weight of the pack.

"We got us a whiteout," Pete said through the howling wind. "Need to find us some cover."

They entered the woods, where the wind subsided among the protection of the trees, but the temperature had dropped to below freezing. Rusty's body was no longer shivering, and Scruffy knew the life of his little dog was in danger.

As they treaded farther into the woods, the remaining sunlight was snuffed out, darkness ruling the day.

"We'd best turn around," Pete said in a weary voice that Scruffy had never heard from him before. It said they were in trouble—big trouble.

"We will figure something out, Pete," Scruffy said as they turned and walked back from whence they came.

CHAPTER 23

SCRUFFY WOKE WITH A START, his vision blurry. He caught a strong smell of something like a dead skunk, only worse. Blinking, Scruffy's vision cleared. He was inside a teepee-like shelter made of branches and sticks. Shafts of sunlight peeped through cracks in the high, conical structure.

He sat up. Across the space was the carcass of a small deer, with its head and legs intact, but the torso had been picked clean, exposing the ribcage. In another pile was a cluster of blackberries still on the vine.

Something moved at his side. "Rusty," Scruffy said as he ran his hand over the neck of his dog. "You okay, boy?"

Rusty was lying on his side. He tried to sit up, but Scruffy had to help him into a sitting position.

"How in the devil did we get in here?" Scruffy said.

The last thing he remembered was the snowstorm getting so bad that he, somehow, got separated from Pete.

"Pete," Scruffy had screamed. "Pete!" But it had been useless, as the furious wind drowned out every other sound.

He had pushed on into that bitter wind, the blinding snow swirling every which way, as he clung to Rusty. Scruffy made it as far as the downed trees. At that point, he could barely stand up, so great was his fatigue. The last thing he recalled was sitting against a tree, stroking Rusty's neck—not sure if his little dog was alive or dead—before he blacked out.

Scruffy tried to stand but had to sit back down, as he felt feverous and lightheaded, his forehead wet with perspiration. He looked around the hut for his knapsack, which held all the gold, but he did not see it.

His eyes flickered sleepily as though he were in a trance. *Sleep a bit*, he thought to himself, *and then get back to the barracks.*

Scruffy awoke, not sure how long he had slept. Though he was still listless, his fever had broken. He ran his fingers over a thin, cakey layer of dried perspiration on his forehead. A hunger for food rumbled in his stomach as inside his pockets he found two patties of pemmican.

He shared one patty with Rusty, who nibbled at it half-heartedly, and saved the other for the way back.

Emerging from the hut, Scruffy was not sure where he was. The snow had stopped, but the air had a chill to it. Spring was nowhere in sight, as a thick blanket of wet snow covered the forest floor. Scruffy checked the sky, seeing shafts of morning light splintering through the foliage. He headed in the direction of the rising sun and, he hoped, the creek.

After a couple of hours, Scruffy came to the downed trees. He had a pemmican pod left and, though hungry decided to save it, just in case.

It was a tough go, slogging through snow that came up to his ankles. Though weak from the ordeal, he continued on, carrying his little dog while trying to block the pain of each step from his mind.

By dusk, they made it to the previous farthest point Scruffy and Pete had prospected. It being too far to make it to the barracks, Scruffy found shelter in a recess in an outcrop of rocks along the creek. With nightfall, the air grew cold, and a chill ran through Scruffy.

Awaking at sunrise from a fitful, bone-chilling sleep, Scruffy found his body damn near numb, and Rusty was shivering something fierce. He broke off half the pod of pemmican and shared it with his dog, who nibbled before refusing to eat anymore.

"Need to get to the barracks," Scruffy said aloud as he stood and took on the day.

By noon, Scruffy had arrived at Header's Creek, but the place was empty. Inside the barrack, a rawhide sack of pemmican was on the mantel over the fireplace.

Scruffy thought about starting a fire and staying, but he had no matches. So they rested a bit, lying on the hard floor. Before departing, they ate. Rusty's appetite had picked up some, but the little dog was still listless.

The sun was out, but the air was brisk. How could it be spring one moment and then winter the next?

After two more days of trekking and sleeping one night in a small cave, the other in a copse of bushes, they finally made it at dusk to Big Bear, Scruffy barely able to hold his stiff-as-a-board dog in the crook of his arm.

CHAPTER 24

WITH THE LAST BIT OF strength he could muster, Scruffy pulled the heavy front door of the Long Branch open. The bar was packed, but the spirit of the place seemed off key, as though someone had died. Murmuring voices of unintelligible words floated around the room.

Stepping off to the side, Scruffy needed to gather himself to collect the wherewithal to make it to the bar without collapsing. He brought his hand to his numb face. His eyebrows were caked in ice, his hair also, and his body was sore from head to toe, every muscle exhausted.

His loyal dog was frozen stiff in his arms. The little dog, Rusty, had given his all.

The booming roar of Frenchy's voice broke Scruffy's concentration. Over in the far corner, Frenchy was speaking to Pete in an animated manner, appearing to lecture Pete. Needle Nose put a hand on Frenchy's arm that the big man jerked away.

Scruffy figured what the disagreement was about and began walking over, stiff-legged. When Scruffy was halfway there, the old-timer spotted him and hollered, "Lord have mercy. Look who has returned from the dead."

The room erupted in an uproarious cheer. Pete rushed over and took the frozen dog from Scruffy, while Frenchy and Needle Nose helped him to a stool. Pete placed the dog on the bar, his scraggly coat covered in knots of ice.

The entire bar came over, patting Scruffy on the back and welcoming his return.

"We thought you dead, Scrufeee," Frenchy said in a voice seized by sharp emotion.

"I thought I was a goner too. Unfortunately," Scruffy said with a tap on Rusty's neck, "my little dog did not make it." He lifted his finger to the barkeep, who was standing across the bar in his starched white shirt and black bow tie, and ordered a draft and a shot of whiskey. He then raised his finger and said, "And a sarsaparilla in memory of my one-eyed wonder dog." Scruffy's mind flashed back to when he had first found Rusty outside his window, the little dog with only one eye. He'd been such a good and loyal companion.

Scruffy stroked Rusty's side as the matted ice melted away from the dog's fur in little droplets on the bar and a thin vapor of steam rose off the body. *Wait a minute!* Rusty's shoulder twitched. Scruffy leaned close, the musky, wet doggy smell filling his nostrils. When the tail twitched, Scruffy barked with disbelieving laughter.

Frenchy crossed himself and said in a reverent tone, "Mon dieu."

"Looks like me little wonder dog has returned from the grave," Scruffy said as a surge of rejuvenation, like a life force, entered his being.

As the barkeep served the drinks, Rusty sat up on his haunches and looked around as though orienting himself to his surroundings. He stood on all fours, shedding the crackling icicles and exposing his dark red fur. The dog then sat, padded the sarsaparilla in his paws, lifted it, and drank it down.

Another cheer erupted from the patrons.

"Should have known it would take more than a little snow and ice to keep my wonder dog down," Scruffy said as he took a towel from the barkeep and patted Rusty dry. Scruffy then took a sip of whiskey followed by a long, thirsty drink of his beer. He wiped his mouth with the back of his hand and said, "That tastes mighty fine—mighty fine indeed."

After things settled down a bit and men returned to their seats, Pete said to Scruffy, "When we got separated in the storm, I looked for you, Scruffy, but the only thing I found was your knapsack. The gold was in there, and I have your share."

Pete went on to say that he'd found cover in a tree hollow and waited out the storm before making it back to the barracks. "The next morning, we looked and looked for you, but you were nowhere to be found—not a trace."

Needle Nose said, "I suspect you have a story to tell us."

"You've got that right," Scruffy said as droplets of melting ice dripped from his hair and eyebrows. The barkeep handed him a fresh towel. After wiping his head and face, Scruffy signaled for another beer.

"I woke up in a teepee hut made of branches and twigs." Scruffy threw his hands out in front of himself. "Have no idea how Rusty and I got there."

He paused momentarily and took a hearty swallow of his beer. "There was a deer carcass and a pile of berries in a corner."

"You think it was a Sasquatch hut?" Frenchy said.

"Don't know," Scruffy said. "But I wasn't going to wait around to find out."

"Yeah, Scruffy," Pete said with a concurring nod. "Skedaddle on out of there."

Scruffy looked around and discovered an audience of men two rows thick standing so very still to his rear. "I picked up Rusty and turned to leave."

Scruffy could feel the breath of the old-timer wheezing on the back of his neck. "Fellas," he said, turning, "if you could give me a little room."

In unison, the cluster of men took one step back.

Scruffy nodded a thank-you. "If I had run into a Sasquatch, you know what I would have done?" Scruffy looked around the bar and settled his gaze on Frenchy.

"The evil eye?" Frenchy said.

"Exactly, big man." Scruffy threw down the remainder of his beer and lifted his mug to the barkeep for a refill. "I would have put Rusty right in front of that hairy ape-man. But that was not the case, so Wonder Dog and I left and headed on back to Big Bear."

After telling of his return to Big Bear over a couple more rounds, Scruffy called it a night and headed over to the Widow Morlock's house. A pang of guilt came over him because he had gone directly to the Long Branch. At the front gate, he saw a light on in the parlor.

Scruffy looked down at Rusty, who had refused to be carried, walking over as if he was as good as new. "Well, boy, prepare yourself for a talking-to."

At the front door, Scruffy glanced at his mackinaw and trousers, which were splotched with dirt and grime. Imagining he looked a sight, he knocked, not wanting to frighten the widow. He heard the clattered pit-a-pat of her heels on the hardwood floor and then the creak of the door opening.

The widow rocked back, her hand covering her mouth, her eyes wide with disbelief. "You are alive," she said with a slant of the brow as though to certify it was really him.

"Yes, ma'am," Scruffy said in a sheepish little voice.

"Get in here this moment," she said, stepping back, with a sweep of her arm.

Mrs. Morlock gave her tenant the once-over. "You look like death warmed over," she said in her schoolmarm tone. "Nothing a hot bath and a good meal will not fix."

"I am some kind of tired, Mrs. Morlock," Scruffy said in as weary a voice as he could muster.

"Lord have mercy, young man, you appear as though you have not eaten in days." She raised a sharp finger. "You shall wait in the parlor while I draw a hot bath, and then I will prepare you a meal." She pulled her chin into the high, frilly collar of her blouse. "Not another word," she said, casting a look that demanded obedience.

The warm water relieved Scruffy's achy body, and the lye soap scrubbed away the dirt and grime. He then put clean clothes on clean skin. The flannel shirt felt so fresh and soft, the dry socks seemed to massage his feet, and the corduroy trousers provided warmth and comfort. It was good to be back under the widow's roof.

The meal was leftover stew that the widow called English stew. Scruffy knew it as Irish stew but kept that to himself. It tasted wonderful, with a savory flavor.

Scruffy insisted on helping with clearing the table and doing the dishes. Afterward, Mrs. Morlock said, "You must be exhausted, so off to bed." She raised her finger, indicating one more thing. "Tomorrow I would very much like to hear about your prospecting adventure."

Up in his room, Scruffy dug into his pocket and removed a chunk of pot roast covered in a napkin. "Here you go, boy," Scruffy said as he put it in Rusty's bowl. The dog took his time eating, taking small bites. After each swallow, Rusty licked his lips before the next bite.

After undressing, Scruffy pulled back his sheets, which were clean and crisp—the widow always cleaned his room whenever he roughed it.

Pulling the covers over himself, Scruffy felt a nervous fatigue, as though he were too tired to sleep. He needed to ponder what had transpired after his separation from Pete during the blizzard. He had nearly lost his life, but an intervention by someone or something seemed to have occurred. It was an unsolvable riddle, but he had learned a lesson: Beware of selfish desire that can lead to calamity.

"This above all: To thy own self be true," a line from *Hamlet*, had rung true to Scruffy when first he read it in high school, but now it took on a much deeper meaning. There were certain guidelines in life that one crossed at one's own peril. Yes indeed, one must keep careful watch for possible danger or difficulties, especially during a heightened state, such as gold fever.

At last Scruffy's eyes began to shutter. Tonight he would sleep a deep and healing sleep, and tomorrow he would continue living the life he had imagined.

PART 2

CHAPTER 25

Yelapa, Mexico, August 22, 1930

THE HORSE RIDE FROM PUERTO Vallarta along the rocky coast was a slow but scenic trek. The water was crystal clear, the hills lush green with foliage. All Scruffy had to do was follow José, a migrant worker he had met in Yakima, on his way down from Alaska. Rusty was as snug as a bug in a wicker basket secured behind the saddle.

After seven years in Big Bear, Scruffy had decided it was time for a change of scenery. Besides that, his three best friends had moved on: Frenchy had returned to the back woods of Quebec nearly three years ago now; Pete, two years ago, had departed for Nevada to try his luck prospecting; and Needle Nose had left a few months back for his village in Nova Scotia.

"I need to get back in touch with my roots," Needle Nose had told Scruffy on his last night in Big Bear at the Long Branch. "See how the family is doing." He leaned on the bar, looking at Scruffy but not seeing him, as his mind seemed to be elsewhere. "Want to make sure everyone is good."

After Needle Nose left Big Bear, it was not long before Scruffy had the strongest desire to get back in touch with his roots. He decided to stop in Yakima on his way to Mexico to see if anyone had heard from Nantes since she had departed with a migrant worker for Yelapa. But no one had heard from her.

The day before Scruffy's departure from Yakima, José came to him with bruises on his face and asked whether he could join Scruffy on his journey to Mexico.

"Men in hoods came to the migrant camp and beat us with clubs."

José twisted his face so that his eyes were two slits of incomprehension. "I do not understand, Scruffy. Why they do this to us?"

"Desperate people are capable of terrible acts," Scruffy said.

"You help me get to border, and I help you to Yelapa," José said.

"Deal," Scruffy said. "Let's shake on it."

Shaking José's hand, Scruffy remembered what the old colored man driving the rags cart had told him in Chicago after he was beaten and robbed: "There is good and bad in folks of all kinds of colors—do not go thinking we is all bad."

As they came around a bend in the coastline, a sandy cove with a gentle arc came into view, backdropped by a forest of big-leaved trees and mosses and ferns. *My first jungle*, Scruffy thought.

There were trawlers in the water—some with sails—and small skiffs. A sea eagle soared over the bay, swooping down and snatching a fish out of the water. This was not what Scruffy had expected.

On a stretch of land, rows of adobe huts with thatched roofs stood in stark contrast to the thicket of viny jungle looming over them. Off to the side of the huts was a corral with a handful of horses that Scruffy thought were mustangs. They were a bit undersized but sturdily built.

In one of those huts Scruffy hoped to find his mother. He remembered her words in her letter to him: "I want you to know that I will think about you every day for the remainder of my life, and for you to live a good and free life."

He had lived a good and free life since departing Yakima as a seventeen-year-old boy, and now he wanted to let his mother know that he was doing just fine. And he needed to check on her to make sure she was in a good place. He hoped that she had finally found a happy life.

Scruffy had learned some Spanish during the harvest seasons in Yakima from the migrant workers, but José said he would ask around for his mother before departing for his village.

They stopped in front of an open-air structure with a thatched roof supported by wooden poles, where two women were working. One of the women was placing large green leaves in a cast iron pot suspended from a rope on a tripod made of thick branches. She was middle age and heavyset, with a placid demeanor as though her life's course had been set and she was content with its outcome.

The other woman was young and beautiful, with a tranquility about her as she sat at a table, threading a leather string through a hole in two pieces of leather stitched together in the shape of a foot. Her thick, dark hair was in braids that draped down her shoulders, her cinnamon complexion radiant. Her lovely face had a flawless symmetry: the chin strong yet feminine, the nose in harmony with her full lips, which opened to a devastating smile as her gaze took hold of Scruffy, rendering him lost in her lush brown eyes.

As José and Scruffy dismounted, Rusty let out a sharp bark.

"You too, huh boy," Scruffy said as he let the dog out of the basket and placed him on the ground.

A scraggly dog of multiple breeds barked at Rusty.

"Perro," the young woman said to the dog.

The mutt let out one more yip before it approached Rusty, its tail cautiously wagging.

Rusty stood patiently as the dog sniffed his behind and then returned the favor.

"Ah, sandalias," José said to the young woman working the leather.

She squinted a smile at José, who then turned his attention to the older woman and said, "Conoces a Nantes?"

An aggrieved expression came over the woman's heavy face as her almond-shaped eyes stared at José. "Oh," the woman said. She looked at Scruffy as if she had figured something out, and she then spoke rapidly to José. When she stopped, she opened her hands, palms up.

"Amigo," José said in a slow, sorrowful tone. "I have bad news. Two months ago …"

Everything seemed to stop, Scruffy's heart catching in his throat. He looked at the beautiful girl, her smile having faded and in its place a look that said, *I am so sorry.*

The young woman escorted Scruffy up to the edge of the jungle forest, its lush canopy so hauntingly beautiful, so hauntingly sad. Nantes was buried in a clearing among other plots, each with a pile of stones at the head. There was nothing to indicate who this person was buried in the ground that Scruffy stood over, Rusty stood at his side, his ears perked as though on guard duty.

As Scruffy absorbed the loss of his mother, Rusty sniffed along the perimeter before returning to his master.

"Nantes era muy querido," the young woman said.

Of course she was, Scruffy thought. *How could she not be loved?*

José said that Nantes had gotten a mysterious illness called *fiebre de salva* (jungle fever). He went on to say that the village medicine woman, the older woman they had met, had made a healing potion but it had not worked. Nantes's hombre, the migrant she had departed Yakima with, had died in the deep waters of the bay when a storm capsized his boat six month prior. "After that," José said, "she was never the same."

Scruffy also learned that his mother had found happiness sharing a hut with her man, Juan. She had learned how to make netting for the fishermen and how to pick the right plants in the jungle for healing potions, and she had assimilated into the fabric of this tight-knit community.

The young woman slipped her hand into Scruffy's, her touch warm and inviting like a cozy fire after a day roughing it in the cold. She placed her hand over her heart and then offered it to the grave. "Nantes hablaba a menudo de su hijo" (Nantes spoke often of her son), she said. She reached over and put her free hand on Scruffy's heart, and with those compelling eyes swallowing him up, she said, "Logan Junior."

After seeing José off, Scruffy decided to stay in Yelapa for a while. He needed time to digest not only his mother's passing but also what was next in his life's journey.

At the open-air hut, the medicine woman tapped her chest and said, "Carmella." She then leaned her head toward the young woman. "Elia."

Scruffy placed his hand on his chest and said, "Logan."

Carmella spoke to Scruffy, but he could not understand what she was saying other than the word "*casa*."

"Qué?" After a back-and-forth exchange, Scruffy was still unclear.

Elia took him by the hand and led him to a hut set back near the jungle with a clear view of the bay. The interior was basic: a round wooden table with two rustic chairs in a corner, a three-drawer dresser with hand-carved handles at the rear of the space, and a crudely framed bed with timber posts.

Atop the bed was a patchwork quilt bedspread with each square a different geometric pattern. It was his mother's quilt that she had hand-stitched in Yakima when Scruffy was a young boy.

A staggered distance of memories flooded Scruffy. He recalled the simple task of his mother making her bed each morning, carefully folding over the top of the spread back evenly across the bed. He also recalled sneaking into bed with Nantes after a bad dream. She would bring him in close, tucking the quilt under his chin, his cheek resting on her shoulder. How safe and comforted he felt in that moment. It was such a vivid, yet faraway, memory in the mist of time.

Rusty scooted over and hopped up onto the rear of the bed. He went around in a circle and lay down, his head resting on his paws. He lifted his brow to Scruffy as though to say, *I am good right here.*

Scruffy would be sleeping in the bed his mother had slept in, and covered in her quilt, which he projected would have a soothing and, at the same time, disquieting effect. He had been negligent in waiting too long to find her—waiting too long to appreciate all that she had done for him.

Elia was standing by, watching patiently as Scruffy took in his new living quarters. In the top drawer of the dresser, Scruffy found a photograph of himself during a harvest. He was picking apples on a ladder, his big hand displaying a Grand Alexander. It was taken right before he departed. His expression was that of someone confident in his place in the world—confident in his abilities.

It had been a long eight years, and Scruffy had learned some things about the world and the people in it, including himself. He was a survivor; that was for sure. And Scruffy Lomax was considered by the good men in Big Bear to be a reliable comrade and good company for sharing a drink or two and telling a good tale about roughing it.

But now he was in a different place—not just in the physical difference between the tropical climate of Yelapa and the ice and cold of Big Bear, but also in how he saw himself.

Wait a minute, he thought as he removed a pocket calendar from his gear and realized that today, August 22, 1930—the day he discovered his mother was no longer of this world—Logan Lomax had turned twenty-five.

Elia led Scruffy back outside, where over the course of the day he was introduced to many of the villagers, all of whom were related. Carmella told him that the village was founded by four families who had come down from the mountains and settled there. "Somos independientes" (We are independent), she told Scruffy.

One older woman Scruffy met pointed at his heavy, worn boots and shook her head. She said to Elia, "Debes hacerle sandalias."

Elia nodded her agreement. "Sí."

Elia and Carmella introduced Scruffy as Logan. And while he was here, he would go by that handle as he recalibrated. But in his heart he would always be Scruffy Lomax.

CHAPTER 26

SCRUFFY FELL RIGHT INTO THE rhythm of life in Yelapa. Elia made him a pair of sandals his second day in the village that were light and comfortable on his feet.

On Scruffy's third day in Yelapa, Javier, Elia's older brother and only immediate family, took him out to the bay on his skiff and taught Scruffy the basics of netting for fish. Scruffy took right to it. Soon he was tossing the circular net, which had small weights distributed around its edge, in a circular motion into the water, while keeping one hand on the hand line.

"You are strong, Logan," Javier said as Scruffy hoisted a heavy net of fish out of the water and into the boat.

As instructed, Scruffy hoisted the net into a basin, releasing the retrieval clamp and dumping the fish into the basin.

"Good job, Logan," Javier said as they stood in the flat-bottomed boat. "You are a fisherman natural."

"You speak very good English."

"I spent a season in California picking lettuce, and I learn your language."

"What did you think of America?" Scruffy asked.

"I wanted to experience what it was like in America." Javier lifted an eyebrow as he gazed at Scruffy reflectively, a look of irony in his dark eyes. "And I saw all I needed to see." Javier paused, considering. "America provide great—"

"Opportunity," Scruffy said.

"Yes, that is the word." Javier lifted a cautionary finger and added, "If your skin is white. Not so much for people of color." Javier shrugged, his expression neutral, as though he understood the ways of the world.

"I am freer down here than up there," he said with of lift of his chin toward the north.

Javier fished no more than four hours in the morning before paddling in his haul of sierra mackerel, pargo, red snapper, and grouper. It was a colorful rainbow collection of seafood—none that Scruffy was familiar with. And they tasted great cooked in one of the communal adobe ovens.

While the men fished, the women of the village went into the jungle and collected pineapples, mangoes, and papayas, and set snares and traps for iguanas, which they skinned and roasted. It took a minute to accept the fact that he was about to eat a lizard, but Scruffy got over it, and it tasted pretty good, though a little tough.

It was a completely new diet for Scruffy, and a new lifestyle. Everything in Yelapa took place at a slow pace: catching enough fish to provide for the family and sell to the *intermediario* (middleman), who took them to Puerto Vallarta; taking siestas after lunch; and playing with the children before dinner. It was a change from roughing it in Alaska, where the frigid and unpredictable weather—which Scruffy was all too familiar with—could put one's life at risk in a matter of minutes; and nearly every waking moment, there was work involved.

"Involved" had taken on a new meaning to Scruffy in regard to his relationship with Elia. By the end of his second week in Yelapa, they spent time together each day collecting fruit in the jungle, walking along the beach, or making love in Scruffy's hut.

It had been a good long while since Scruffy had been with a woman. A dogsledder Scruffy had met a few years back at the Long Branch had a delivery route that included Fairbanks. Scruffy hitched a ride into the big city from time to time, and they visited Miss Eleanor's Lucky Strike. It was a slam-bam affair that took no more than ten minutes, with some rough-around-the-edges women, paid for by a hard-earned dollar, but it satisfied a need.

The only other woman Scruffy had been with whom he had not paid for was his first, Mariel, in Key West all those years back. As with Elia, Spanish was Mariel's native tongue. But unlike Mariel, Elia spoke no English, so each evening they taught each other their languages. After a few weeks, Elia had a rudimentary understanding of and limited ability to speak English, and Scruffy's Spanish had improved to the point that he could usually get the gist of what she was saying, and vice versa.

During the times they could not understand each other, Scruffy and Elia spoke a silent language. A lift of Scruffy's brow and a what-do-you-think expression meant "Let's get intimate." Elia would offer a shy smile and a tilt of her head, letting Scruffy know that she liked his suggestion.

Elia was a generous lover, her lean, supple body bending and arching in passionate sex. Scruffy had never been in love before, but he was sure that he was close, if not already there. Whenever he met her after coming in from the bay, there was a thump in his chest like a pit-a-pat of his heart preparing to launch from his chest cavity. Walking the beach holding hands, the horizon over the water glimmering in the red-streaked light, the outline of the boats bobbing in the shadowy water, brought a tranquil joy—a joy like nothing Scruffy had ever before experienced.

Making love was like the cherry on the pie—a perfect ending to a perfect day with a perfect woman. But with all that said, Scruffy remembered what the old-timer back at the Long Branch had once told him: "I do not trust happiness." It was during a quiet night, and the old-timer spoke with a look of reminiscence. "Been in love twice, and both of them broke my heart something fierce." He took a sip of his whiskey, gave his stubbly chin a thoughtful scratch, and said, "But I would not have changed any of it." He then nodded his knobby head and said through a thin, knowing smile, "To have lived a full life, you must have experienced regret and disappointment."

CHAPTER 27

"Como es la vida en America?" Elia asked Scruffy as they walked the beach barefoot at sunset.

They came to a halt, the cove still, the trawlers and skiffs like shadowy toys. "Life in America," Scruffy said, "is faster—*más rápido.*" He lifted his brow as though to say, *Comprende?*

Life in America had also gotten rough. In Yakima there had been a drought, and employment was lean, resulting in the migrants being looked upon with scorn.

Mr. Pinchwell had passed away a few years back, and his oldest son, John, ran the orchard. He was no longer the friendly boy Scruffy had grown up with, but a mean-spirited boss who worked the pickers with a ruthless zeal—especially the migrants.

Up in Alaska, there had been reports of things getting difficult in the States, but Scruffy was shocked at the changes not only in the weather, which had ravaged the orchards, but also in the mood of the citizens, who were looking for someone to blame.

Scruffy had now been in Yelapa for three months, and he had seen the faltering economy up north work its way to Yelapa. The intermediario, who bought the fish, was not coming down from Puerto Vallarta nearly as often, and when he did, he did not purchase as many fish.

But Javier showed no concern. "We can catch our own food, and the women can provide us with fruits and medicine from the jungle." He shrugged with an air of nonchalance. "We will not miss a little business, amigo."

One thing that Scruffy did miss was the camaraderie of the characters at the Long Branch. And he missed the adventure of heading out to prospect, not knowing what lay in store—the adventure of the unknown.

In Yelapa, each day was pretty much the same: fishing in the morning with Javier, maybe joining Elia for a bareback horse ride on the beach or in the jungle to pick colorful wild fruits, such as guava, pitahaya, guanabana, and cherimoya, the latter being Scruffy's favorite. Cherimoya looked like a beaten-up green apple, but its soft flesh was delicious.

"But do not eat the seeds," Elia had told him. "They are poisonous," she said with an air of superior knowledge. "There is danger lurking in the jungle."

Elia, on the other hand, was Scruffy's wild card. He no longer considered himself in love with her, but rather immersed in the company of a beautiful woman—a woman who was her own person, an independent person, who seemed to feel the same way about their relationship. She enjoyed the company of the *Americano*, comfortable in their relationship, but she had never given any hint of interest in marriage. Scruffy had a sense that she considered their relationship a temporary arrangement.

"You are a *vagabundo*, Logan," she told him after he told her of riding the rails across America. She had raised her eyebrow coyly. "El camino es tu amante" (The road is your mistress).

Scruffy remembered Eleanor, all those years back in Wisconsin, making a similar comment.

And of course Elia was right. The road *was* his mistress, Scruffy gave her hand a squeeze as they stood under the glittering night sky awash in low-hanging stars and a pale moon spilling silver light across the blue-black water. "Brilla brilla pequeña estrella," he said, letting the words roll off his tongue.

"When you return up north, what will you tell them about Yelapa?" Elia said as she raised Scruffy's hand, examining his palm.

He turned to her and smiled. "If I go up north, will you not miss me?"

She ran her middle and index fingers over a vertical line running from the base of Scruffy's palm up to the base of his middle finger. "Your fate line confirms that your destiny is vagabundo." Elia shrugged as though to indicate there was nothing that could be done to change one's destiny.

They stared into each other's eyes, the only sound the water lapping on the shore.

"Tomorrow, Logan, you must come to the jungle with me to pick fruit."

Elia had a knack for avoiding questions, it was like a verbal sleight of hand. But Scruffy, too, had been avoiding an internal yearning to search for new adventure, as a little voice kept asking when he would hit the road to go to parts of the States he had never seen: the Grand Canyon, Yellowstone and Yosemite National Parks—three must-see destinations he had promised himself to visit—the Southwest, which he had traveled through in transit across the Sonora Desert as a 'bo but barely seen other than a couple of cacti and some tumbleweed; and maybe on to New Orleans.

But another, stronger voice told him that heading back to the States seemed unwise presently. Javier had heard from the intermediario that migrants who had returned to Puerto Vallarta said not only that jobs were hard to come by but also that some people were starving. A massive dust storm had swept across Texas, killing people and livestock and resulting in failed crops.

So as long as Scruffy was still welcome in Yelapa, he would bide his time and let things come as they may.

CHAPTER 28

A H," Elia said, "look at that beautiful cherimoya out of reach."
Scruffy and Elia were standing in a cluster of trees in the jungle,
looking up at the top of the tree that appeared to be thirty feet high.
The lower-hanging fruit had been picked clean.

"Javier needs to purchase a ladder from the intermediario," Scruffy
said. "I will climb up."

"Do not damage the tree, Logan."

"You worry about the tree and not me, Elia," Scruffy teased.

Elia cocked an eyebrow and smiled her enigmatic smile.

The lower branches were similar in size to the apple trees back in
Yakima—not huge, but sturdy enough to hold Scruffy's weight. He
gripped a branch at eye level, put his sandals against the tree trunk, and
pulled himself up to where a branch grew out of the tree. The higher
branches were not as sturdy, but Scruffy thought them strong enough to
support him. He stretched his arms up, not quite able to reach a branch
four inches in diameter.

"Logan," Elia said in a cautionary tone. "It is not strong enough."

"Trust me," Scruffy said as he wrapped his arms and legs around the
trunk and shimmied himself up to a sitting position in the crook of the
branch. He reached out to a nearby cluster of the dimpled pale green
fruit and twisted the main stem. The fruit fell to the ground.

"Bueno, Logan," Elia said as she collected the fruit into a handwoven
basket made of palm leaves.

Scruffy continued stripping the branch of the fruit until he could
not reach any farther. He extended his body out onto the branch that
held him. After stripping the branch of its fruit, he climbed higher.

Scruffy extended himself out on a branch that sagged from his weight.

Elia gasped but said nothing.

There were two fat clusters of fruit dangling at the end of the branch, just out of reach. Scruffy did not want to leave this tree without taking down the fruit. As he shimmied on his belly out onto the branch, it passed in his mind that this was the first thing even close to a daring act he had performed in Yelapa.

"Looo … gaaan," Elia said drawing out his name in raised concern.

"Almost there," Scruffy said as he reached out and wrapped his fingers around the stem of a cluster. He tried to twist it free, but he had little leverage from his awkward position. He shimmied out farther and reached out with a firm grip on the cluster stem, and his weight forced the branch down.

Scruffy fell forward and off the tree, but he grabbed the branch with one hand and then the other, hanging on, nearly twenty feet off the ground. He was hanging between the two clusters of fruit. He wrapped the crook of his arm around the branch and, with his free hand, twisted off a cluster, dropping it to the ground.

"Loo … gaaan," Elia said, once again drawing out his name, but this time her tone said "Impressive."

Scruffy twisted the other cluster off the tree and received another impressed "Looo … gaaan" from Elia. He then gripped the branch with his strong hands and fingers and worked his way back to the trunk and shimmied his way down the tree.

"You are a jungle man," Elia said as she looked over Scruffy as though having discovered a new and interesting side to this man from north of the border.

Ever since Scruffy's display of fruit picking, Elia had subtly triggered some sort of shift between them. She was more attentive when he spoke, smiling and laughing as if on cue. She would look at him as though there was something intriguing about him, having some heightened sensitivity of understanding. She had recently begun to refer to him as "Mi hombre, Logan."

No longer did Elia mention Scruffy departing for the North. It was as though she had subconsciously recalibrated where he stood—where they stood. Now during sex her warm body, thrusting and grinding with abandon, was a physical pleasure the likes of which Scruffy had never imagined. It was as though their bodies were in sync in a rapturous cocoon, and afterward she would stroke his face while softly kissing his neck.

"Looo … gaaan," she would coo, "I could stay in this *momento* for *eternidad*."

Scruffy was enjoying his new status with Elia, but he was doing so with a dose of caution. He sensed that at some point she would mention a more permanent relationship. What would his response be? To live here with her for the rest of their lives, to take her to the States and settle down, or to leave Yelapa alone?

There was only one solution that made any sense, as hard as it would be.

CHAPTER 29

"YOU KNOW LOGAN," JAVIER SAID as he watched Scruffy pull in a net full of fish into the hull of the skiff, "you have become a *bueno pescador.*"

Scruffy emptied the net of fish into a bucket, a wayward red snapper slipping out, its pink tail slapping the floorboard. "I will get to you in a moment, *mi pez*," he said as he griped the hand line and tossed the net in a circular motion out into the water.

Javier nodded his approval of the casting and said, "I spoke with Juan's family, and they are willing to give you Juan's net and skiff. It would be a way to honor the memory of not only him but your mother."

Scruffy heard his mother's voice whisper in the back recesses of his mind, "It would be a good life for you, Logan—a good life with a good woman."

He picked the still-flapping fish off the floor, its slimy scales making it hard to get a firm grip. As Scruffy went to drop the fish in the bucket, it wiggled out of his hand, propelling itself out of the boat and plunking into the water.

"Ha, amigo," Javier said through a toothy grin, his pearl-white teeth in perfect contrast to his cinnamon-hued face. "Maybe I speak too soon."

"That one was determined to escape," Scruffy said as he looked at the basket teeming with an array of brightly colored fish.

"Sí, amigo," Javier said as his grin opened into a wide, brightening smile. He was a handsome, masculine version of his sister. "And you, my friend"—the smile faded—"are you preparing to leave us? Or … stay and make an honest woman of my sister?"

A warm, gentle breeze blew in from the bay, its horizon gathering light, above which a bank of billowy white clouds drifted across the pale morning sky. Other fishermen were scattered about the cove, their skiffs and small trawlers a reasonable distance apart, allowing each other room to operate.

Scruffy lifted his gaze to Javier, whose expression said, "Well?" Various thoughts flashed through Scruffy's mind: The intermediario had recently said that word from the States was that things had gotten even worse. Crops were damaged not only from a lack of rain but also from a boll weevil plague across the South. Things were bad in the big cities also, and the streets were getting crowded with homeless men and even some women. The thought of returning to Alaska was instantly nixed. *Been there, done that.* So what remained was the choice he had thought he would never agree to.

"I will talk with Elia," Scruffy said.

Javier's mouth lifted at the corners, his gorgeous smile flashing his agreement. "Bueno," he said with a bow of approval—a bow, it seemed, he had not expected to make.

By noon Javier had caught enough fish for the day, and Scruffy headed back to his hut, where Rusty was patiently waiting at the door, stretched out with head on paws, eyes at half-mast, appearing sad and bored. Javier would not allow him aboard his skiff. "Well, Wonder Dog," Scruffy said as he bent down and ruffled the fur on his dog's neck, "there has been a change in plans—*cambio de planes*, as they say here in the native tongue."

Rusty sat up, his ears perked.

Scruffy sensed that his dog was ready for a change of scenery. Being by himself not only when Scruffy was out on the cove in the morning but also during the time Scruffy spent with Elia, Rusty had lost the one-on-one time with his master.

Rusty seemed to miss the adventure of roughing it for weeks on end and returning to Big Bear and heading straight to the Long Branch, where, perched up on the bar, he was the center of attention. Here in Yelapa, he was just another dog—albeit, a one-eyed dog—El Tuerto—who had little interest in the village dogs.

Scruffy realized that he had been neglecting his dog, but soon he would take him out in Juan's skiff and they would be sidekicks again.

That evening Scruffy took Elia for a walk on the beach. As the sky was dying in a plush of violet, Scruffy got down on his knee and took Elia's hand.

"Elia, ¿quieres casarte conmigo?"

"Sí," she said softly, in a tone that led Scruffy to believe she knew beforehand of this proposal of marriage.

The following morning, Javier handed Scruffy a gold band that he said was his mother's wedding band. "For my sister," he said, as he lifted his index finger. "My only family. Also, with your blessing, the intermediario will bring a priest from Puerto Vallarta to perform the wedding." Javier nodded as though approving his own suggestion. "And after, of course, a *grande* fiesta." Javier nodded again, indicating the case was closed.

That was the moment that Scruffy realized the weight of his decision—that a lifetime commitment was expected of him, and that for the rest of his life, he and Elia would live in this small village along a secluded cove in Mexico.

Was this where his life journey of adventure ended? Married and with children? Scruffy told himself not to overthink it and leave his fate in destiny's hands.

CHAPTER 30

SCRUFFY HAD NEVER BEEN SO doggone nervous in his life. Today was the big day. After the wedding, which was being held on the beach, a village fiesta was to take place.

With Rusty curled at the bottom of the bed watching, Scruffy slipped into a white guayabera—a traditional cotton wedding shirt. It had four patch pockets on the front and a long, straight hem so it could remain untucked. Elia had made it, and Scruffy had to admit it fit very well and was light and smooth to the touch.

Javier had given Scruffy a large mirror to hang over his dresser to "Prepárate para la boda." The sharp features of his face had softened from the easy life in the warm clime of Yelapa, his skin highlighted by a radiant glimmer from the benevolent sunshine. His high cheekbones still had a ruddy hue, but now with a tint of gold that gave him—dare Scruffy think it—a handsome quality. "Not bad," he said to himself as he took one last look at the mirror before slipping into his cotton trousers that Elia had also made.

He thought it very thoughtful that she had taken the time to make his outfit, though that seemed to be the way of the people of this little village. Marcella and a couple of other women had made Elia's wedding dress, others had prepared dishes for the fiesta, and some of the men had hunted for deer and wild boar in the jungle that they salted and hung in the curing hut.

As Scruffy departed his hut, he thought about how easily he had been accepted into the village, with not a hint of resentment of the Americano. And he considered the good-spirited manner with which they had pitched in for the wedding, though he realized it was mostly for Elia; still, he appreciated the hard work.

The priest was late. The entire village—save Elia, whom Scruffy had not seen for two days—of over one hundred people was standing around a pulpit with a hand-carved cross on the front, which the village men had made years ago from jungle timber. The women were dressed in colorful blouses and skirts, some with intricate geometric triangle and angle patterns, the men in plain brown trousers and short-sleeve shirts that were brightly colored but monochromatic.

A murmur came from the villagers as all eyes turned to the trail along the coastline. Here came the intermediario approaching on horseback, and alongside him the priest, who was wearing a long beige clerical robe. Behind them were three riders wearing short jackets, white shirts with wide bow ties, fitted trousers with sparkling white buttons down the outside seam, and, atop their heads, sombreros. The last rider rode atop a huge roan pulling a cart covered by a tarp.

"Mariachi," the people murmured with the wonder of what they were seeing.

"My surprise for you and Elia," Javier said with a nudge of his elbow in Scruffy's ribs. They were standing before the pulpit as the priest approached.

The priest stood in front of the pulpit, facing Scruffy. "La novia?" he asked Scruffy.

Scruffy pointed a finger to a flash of white emerging from Marcella's hut. Elia was in her wedding dress, and never in his life had Scruffy seen such a vision of beauty, which was accentuated by the simplicity of the long white dress in perfect contrast to her cinnamon-colored skin.

Her hair, woven in interlaced strands, flowed down her shoulders. Atop her head she wore a wreath of Bougainvilleas, bright purple flowers that grew on thorny vines in the jungle, bringing to mind a rainbow casting its brief hypnotic light over a waterfall.

Elia's gentle eyes wrinkled in a shy smile as she stood next to Scruffy. He took her hand and laced his fingers through hers as a sense of calm came over him. This moment seemed so right, so appropriate.

Scruffy heard the priest's voice, the words slowly and carefully said. At the same time, he was thinking about how pleased his mother would have been to have witnessed this moment. How pleased she would have been that her Logan had, at long last, found his place in this world.

"El anillo?" the priest said.

Javier handed the gold band to Scruffy.

Elia offered her right hand, and Scruffy slid it onto her finger.

After a few more words and "hagos" from Scruffy and Elia, the priest said, "Yo os declare marido y mujer."

A huge cheer erupted from the villagers as Scruffy kissed Elia.

Javier wrapped an arm around Scruffy's shoulder. "Congratulations, my brother, Logan," he said as he leaned back, smiling and appraising his new brother-in-law. "So how does it feel to be a married man?"

"Good." Scruffy took a deep breath and said, "First wedding I have ever attended turns out to be my own." He lifted his shoulders, open palms out to the side. "Javier, what does a fella have to do to get a drink around here?"

Javier raised his index finger. "The mariachi band has brought tequila."

"Tequila?" Scruffy said. "Never had the pleasure."

The mariachi band played lively foot-stomping music from two guitars and rattles clutched in both hands by one member; all three sang along in loud, slightly off-key, voices.

The food was delicious: pork, marinated deer meat that was tender and succulent, roasted potatoes, mashed guanabana, guava, and mashed cherimoya, which was used as a sauce over everything.

The tequila had a sharp warm flavor and was accompanied by a lime and a salted rim. It was the first alcohol Scruffy had seen in the village. Javier had told him that a few years back, the village council, of which Javier was a member, had banned alcohol except for special occasions. "Some of the men," Javier said with an air of superior knowledge, "they"—he threw his hands in the air—"are no good with alcohol."

The priest, who had been so serious and formal during the ceremony, was having a grand time for himself. He sat on a bench, tequila in hand, laughing and talking to one and all as he waved his hand to the beat of the music. He was heavyset, this middle-aged man in the long robe with a tangle of steel-gray hair atop a large head anchored on a thick, fleshy neck.

Everyone was having a grand time. People were dancing and talking in rapid-fire Spanish that Scruffy had difficulty understanding, but he nodded and smiled as though he understood.

The fiesta went on deep into the night, with Scruffy feeling a tequila-induced bliss. He was in the moment during this time—his first hours of matrimony.

Elia, who had never had alcohol before, had two tequilas and was beautifully drunk, kissing Scruffy on the cheek as they danced to a slow song and hanging on him for balance before her head dropped on his shoulder. "I think, Logan," she said in a slow but happy voice, "I need to sleep."

After Scruffy put his wife to bed, he returned to what remained of the fiesta. The band and priest had retired for the evening as guests in people's huts. A few men remained, sitting on the sand down at the beach, talking softly. A full moon cast shafts of light down on the cove, illuminating the boats.

So this is where I am going to spend the rest of my life, Scruffy thought.

CHAPTER 31

IT TOOK NEARLY TWO YEARS, but with the help of an herbal potion that Marcella had prepared, Elia was with child. And it had a most unusual effect on Rusty, who now followed Elia everywhere she went, as though on guard duty.

Besides being the medicine woman, Marcella was the village midwife. She checked in on Elia every week in private. Scruffy was not sure what went on, and he never asked Elia for any details other than how she was progressing. "Bueno" was all he could get out of her.

The thought of being a father reinforced in Scruffy his willingness to continue his life in Yelapa. A few months after the bliss of the wedding had worn off, Scruffy began to feel the pull of the road, but it was tempered by the fact that the States were still in the midst of a terrible depression. The intermediario, Pedro, whom Scruffy had gotten friendly with since he took over Juan's skiff and sold his catch to him, had heard about great dust storms that had blown across the American heartland. "Muy mal en America hablado," Pedro had said the other day. The migrants said that the farmers in Oklahoma were losing their farms and packing up their humble belongings and departing the ravaged land and heading to California.

Still, Scruffy had mulled over departing this safe and married life in Yelapa when things got better up north. He envisioned himself riding out with Pedro to Puerto Vallarta and from there on to the States. He still had over two hundred dollars from his time in Big Bear. And he had also saved the equivalent of a hundred dollars in Mexican currency from fishing the cove. He knew it would be an act of cowardice to desert Elia, but Scruffy could not help how trapped he felt.

But when Elia told him she was expecting a child, a rush of paternal instincts kicked in. The urge to escape had been replaced with the dreamy aspects of fatherhood. If it was a boy, he would not only teach him the ways of fishing but also guide his maturation—something Scruffy never had as a boy from a father's perspective. And if it was a girl, Scruffy would leave the child-rearing to Elia but shower her with affection. He would teach the child English so he or she could feel connected to his or her American roots. The child would be half Mexican, one-eighth Yakama, and the remainder white.

Elia woke Scruffy in the middle of the night. "Logan, my water has broken," she said.

Scruffy rolled over, facing the shadowy figure of his wife. "I will get Marcella." He got out of bed and lit a match to ignite the oil lamp on the dresser.

The village was asleep, with nary a soul about. The sky and the cove appeared as a continuous black mass, as the moon was nowhere to be found. Scruffy weaved his way around the adobe huts until he came to Marcella's. He tapped lightly on the door—no answer. He knocked again. "Marcella," he said. He went to the window. Inside, a figure moved toward the door.

The door opened. Marcella was wearing a brightly colored serape. Upon recognizing Scruffy, the sleep vanished from her eyes. "Uno momento," she said with a lift of her finger. Within a minute, she reemerged dressed in a sack dress and holding a stack of sheets and towels that she handed to Scruffy. She then went back inside and came out with a black case that was similar to what a doctor would use. "Ven," she said as they headed back toward Scruffy and Elia's hut.

They found Elia tucking in fresh sheets on the bed.

"Elia," Marcella said in a gentle but authoritarian tone. She placed her case down and stepped in and finished the chore. She then turned to Scruffy, still holding the sheets and towels that were crisp and clean. She told him to put the linens on the chair and to wait outside.

Part of Scruffy wanted to stay and do—what? He was not sure. He squinted a questioning look at Marcella and then Elia.

"Logan," Elia said with a lift of her brow, her eyes asking him not to argue.

"All right," he said. "If you need me, I will be right outside the door."

CHAPTER 32

THE FIRST GLIMMER OF LIGHT came from over the hills as the village stirred awake. The men were heading down to the water and their boats; women were gathering the village children for school in a large hut that the board had ordered built last year.

It had been a couple of hours since Scruffy had begun waiting outside, and he had not heard a word. He peeked inside the door and saw Marcella tending to Elia in bed. There was a look of anguish in his wife's eyes—a look he had never seen from her before.

Scruffy had witnessed the birth of livestock in Yakima during his childhood and knew that it was a painful experience, but still it tore his heart to see Elia suffering so. He wanted to rush to her, but he knew it would not help the situation.

"Logan! Es Hora?"

Javier approached, a huge smile across his bronze face.

"Si," Scruffy said.

"It will be fine, amigo," Javier said.

"Waiting is not my forte."

"I will join you," Javier said. "Together we will wait the birth of your child."

Scruffy was about to tell Javier that it was not necessary, but he held up. "Gracias," he said.

Javier went and got two chairs so they could sit while they waited. And wait they did.

In the late morning, Marcella came out of the hut. Scruffy and Javier stood. Scruffy was hoping to hear that he was a father.

Marcella said that there was a problem; the baby was upside down in the uterus. "Recamara de nacimiento."

"That is how I was born," Scruffy said. "My mother said it was very difficult."

Javier asked Marcella if he should ride to Puerto Vallarta for a doctor.

"Si, pronto," Marcella said.

As Javier departed, a vague sensation of nausea rose in Scruffy's stomach. *Is a breech birth an inherited trait? Passed on from father to child?* "Can I see Elia?"

"For a minute," Marcella said.

Elia was sitting up in bed, wearing only a nightshirt, her legs spread, her vagina exposed. Her forehead was wet with perspiration, her lovely face contorted in agony.

As Marcella applied a damp cloth to Elia's forehead, Scruffy reached for her hand, which was very warm.

"Awwgg!" Elia screamed as she writhed in pain, her eyes wild like those of a trapped animal. She looked at Scruffy but seemed not to recognize him.

"Logan," Marcella said. "You must leave."

At the door, Scruffy took one last look as Marcella leaned over Elia, instructing her to breathe slowly. Elia took a breath and then gasped and moaned something fierce before Scruffy closed the door.

Scruffy sat but then decided against it. He was too damn nervous to sit. Out in the cove, the fishing boats were coming in for the day. On the beach, a fisherman was unloading buckets of fish from his dinghy. Even from a distance, Scruffy could see that he was pleased by the way he moved about with an easy, free-as-the-wind air. He knew that feeling from his many successful days fishing. It had been so different from prospecting in the cold of Alaska. Everything about Yelapa was different, from the language to the small brown people, and of course the warm weather.

But now it all seemed to be turning on him. His wife was in trouble. How much trouble Scruffy did not know, but he knew that if Marcella wanted a doctor, it must be serious.

He told himself to calm down, but it did not work. Nothing would work until his wife was safe and the child was born.

In the late afternoon, Javier arrived with a middle-aged man riding a bay that was saddled. He had thinning gray-brown hair and was of medium size, with eyes that were large and with the look of someone who had seen many things in this life. It appeared this would not be his first difficult birth.

After a brief introduction, Scruffy started to speak, but he stopped. He searched the doctor's face for some indication that it would be all right—that his wife and newborn would come out of it alive and well.

The doctor patted Scruffy's shoulder, those old-soul eyes engulfing him, before he silently entered the hut, closing the door behind him.

By dusk, Scruffy was barely able to think straight. His mind was a blur as he and Javier sat silently waiting. Since the arrival of the doctor, Scruffy and Javier had not heard a sound other than a couple of high-pitched moans.

When the door finally opened, the looks on the doctor's and Marcella's faces were ones of devastation. "Tengo una mala noticia," the doctor said. He was wearing a white shirt blotched with blood.

Scruffy's mind was not working well enough to understand. "Qué?"

"Tu esposa y tu hijo estan muertos," the doctor said in a heart-wrenching voice.

"Dead ..." Scruffy looked at Javier, who nodded confirmation. "My wife ... my son?" Scruffy fell to his knees, burying his face into his hands as he began to shake.

Javier spoke to the doctor, but Scruffy did not hear. He was in a lonely, desolate place far, far away.

CHAPTER 33

New Orleans, May 1934

S CRUFFFEEE," HENRI SAID FROM THE kitchen door. "I need steak au Poivre, tout de suite."

"Comin' right up," Scruffy said as he forked a strip steak, simmering in a pool of cognac-based cream sauce, from a cast-iron skillet onto a plate and poured the sauce onto the steak. He then pulled asparagus from a steaming pot with a pair of prongs and nestled it next to the meat, after which he lifted a sizzling frying pan of golden-brown fingerling potatoes from the oven and situated them on the other side of the filet.

He placed the plate on the raised counter and nodded *okay* at Henri, who loaded it on his tray and whisked his way out to the dining area.

Working as a line cook in a French brasserie in the French Quarter was a long way from Yelapa not just in miles but also in state of mind. Two days after the death of his wife and son, Scruffy had left Yelapa with the intermediario, Pedro, in his horse-drawn wagon.

From Puerto Vallarta, Scruffy had made his way via bus, which broke down twice, to El Paso—two hot grueling days with Rusty sitting on his lap. From Texas he hopped a freight train to New Orleans, his mind reeling from the events in Yelapa.

After the doctor had given Scruffy the heart-crushing news, he had burst into the hut, and what he saw there would be stamped in his memory bank for the remainder of his life. Two bodies were wrapped in sheets atop the bed, like mummies—one so very small. At that moment, Scruffy felt as though an axe had been wedged in his chest as he gasped to breathe. The baby had choked to death on the umbilical cord, and Elia had died soon after from a severe hemorrhage.

"El parto de nalgas es impredeible," the doctor said, his expression blank, while his eyes revealed the devastation.

Scruffy heard the doctor's words, but his mind did not comprehend. He looked at Javier, his eyes saying, "What?"

"He says," Javier said in a raspy whisper, "breech birth is unpredictable."

The burial was the next day; two wooden caskets were buried next to Scruffy's mother. Nantes now had the company of her daughter-in-law and grandson.

It had been three months or so since the death of his wife and son, and every morning upon awakening and every night before closing his eyes, the worst day of Scruffy's life rose in his mind.

During the course of the day, he kept himself occupied with work and frequenting the local watering holes, but the weight of that fateful day was always near. The old-timer in Big Bear had told Scruffy that time heals all wounds, but so far that had not been the case.

At midnight, Scruffy headed out the back door of the kitchen, where Rusty was lying on a sheet of cardboard that Scruffy had cushioned with a small blanket. Rusty lifted his eyes with a look Scruffy had come to know—one that seemed to say, *When are we getting out of this place?*

"What say we head over to Poor Boys Bistro and have us a drink, Wonder Dog?" Rusty stretched his front paws out and yawned. As best as Scruffy could figure, his dog was somewhere around twelve years old. But one would not know it, for he showed none of the traits of an older dog. He was still nimble on his feet and guard-dog alert.

"Come on, Rusty, let's make the best of things as they are right now." Scruffy motioned for his dog to follow, and they exited the alley.

One of the regulars at Poor Boys Bistro had told Scruffy that it was formerly a speakeasy, but since the repeal of Prohibition at the end of 1933, it had opened its doors to the public.

The joint was a few blocks away from the brasserie and was situated at the rear of an alley, behind a heavy wood plank door that still had a peephole. The place had a long bar at the back, heavy-duty wooden tables in the dining area, and booths along the walls. Poor Boys had a dusky feel to it, with sparse lighting from overhead lamps hanging in iron cages from the tin ceiling. Behind the bar was a full-length mirror with stacks of liquors on shelves. It was a nice place to sip on a beer and mull things over.

"Beer for Mr. Lomax and sarsaparilla for the Wonder Dog?" the bartender said in the tone of one who already knew the answer to his question. He was of middle age, a medium-built fellow with a handlebar mustache and dark hair that he slicked back.

Scruffy placed Rusty atop the bar and took a seat. "That will work, Royce."

Royce placed the drinks on the bar. "How is kitchen life?" he asked as he slid a look over at Rusty cradling his shot glass in his paws, lifting it, and swallowing it down. "That dog is something else," he said with a shake of the head and a smirky smile. Royce turned his attention back to Scruffy, who took a long, thirsty swallow of his draft.

"Kitchen life is not bad for a fella who had no experience in such an endeavor."

"A little bullshit can go a long way in these hard times," Royce said with a wink.

Scruffy had told the proprietor of Marigny Brasserie that he had worked in kitchens from Alaska down to Mexico.

Pierre Dufief was an elegant-looking Frenchman dressed in a silk pinstriped suit with a rose in the lapel. He looked Scruffy over, eyeing him from head to toe. "I do not need any help," he said. "Besides, I believe you have never worked in a restaurant in your life, monsieur." He lifted his brow—*Touché.*

"If I do not cut it, fire me without pay," Scruffy said with a lift of his shoulders. "What have you got to lose?"

Mr. Dufief stared at Scruffy. He pursed his lips and said, "You look like an interesting sort of man. Okay, I give you one day in kitchen, washing dishes."

Scruffy smiled at the memory. "Bullshit indeed, Royce," he hooted. "Worked my way up to line cook."

After two beers, Scruffy departed for his living quarters—a small room in a boardinghouse at the edge of the French Quarter owned by a Mrs. Julianna LeCroux. She was a widow but was younger than Mrs. Morlock, and she possessed a certain sauntering way about her that drew a man's eye. And her Victorian-style home with a magnolia tree in the front yard protected by an iron picket fence and gate seemed a perfect match for the house and its owner.

Scruffy's room was on the second floor, in an octagonal turret that brought to mind a castle tower. The space was small but cozy, containing a glass-door bookshelf along one wall, crammed with old dusty books; a single bed across the space; a window with a view of the street below; and a small desk and chair. There was something safe and secure in this nook, tucked away with Rusty.

A street lamp gave off enough light that Scruffy need not light the lamp on the nightstand. He got under his covers, and Rusty hopped up on the bed and rested his head across Scruffy's ankles. The dog let out a little sigh.

"I know, Wonder Dog," Scruffy said. This was the hour when Scruffy was most vulnerable and alone. And truth be told, it was also the time when he reflected how damn disappointed he was in himself. Before Elia's pregnancy, he had almost departed Yelapa so many times he had lost count. Such an act of cowardice it would have been.

And then, when he found out she was pregnant, that urge to run had disappeared like a puff of smoke evaporating into thin air. It was as though he were being punished for his lack of integrity regarding the urge to hit the road as free as the wind, not knowing where he would end up or how long he would stay.

And if mother and child had both come through the ordeal, would he, Logan Lomax, have gotten another itch to abandon his family? What was it about a lifelong commitment that scared him so? What was it about living a life of adventure that drew him so? Big Bear was calling.

Spending weeks roughing it and then coming into town and heading for the Long Branch and throwing down drinks and swapping tales—oh, that was a time. As was the first time he lit out of Yakima twelve years ago. Along the way, he had learned some skills: masonry aspects of the construction trade, net fishing, restaurant and bar work, plus what he had learned in the Yakima orchards.

Scruffy laced his fingers behind his neck and stared at the shadowy ceiling of the branches of the magnolia tree against the street lamps. As he had done every night since coming to New Orleans, he replayed in his mind the death of his family and his decision to depart for the States—hard times and all. Living in Yelapa was no longer an option.

Once in El Paso, he had decided that New Orleans was as good a place as any. But now came an urge—one he was familiar with: it was time to move on.

CHAPTER 34

$\mathbf{B}$ IG BEAR HAD CHANGED. NEW buildings had been erected in town for new businesses, and on the outskirts, homes and a church had been built.

The Widow Morlock's home had been purchased and converted into a new general store by Mr. Wiley. The widow had moved to Arizona to live with her sister. Merle Heidelman, the assayer, had bought the old store from Wiley and had taken on two employees. And besides the physical changes, the transient prospectors and trappers were down in numbers, and all new and younger. Even the old-timer was no longer about.

Scruffy negotiated with Merle Heidelman to rent the room in the back of his building that had previously been the assay office. The space still had a cast-iron wood-burning cook stove that Scruffy used for food and heat. He purchased a bed, dresser, table, and two chairs from Mr. Wiley.

After living in Big Bear almost a week, Scruffy realized that whatever he had been hoping to find was not there. Going to bed each night and waking up was still difficult. He had dreamt the other night that he was with his son, whom he and Elia had named Roberto, out in the cove, fishing. The boy was ten years old and was all that Scruffy could have ever hoped for in a child. He was a beautiful boy who spoke fluent English and adored his father. They were inseparable, other than when Roberto was at school.

In his dream there blossomed a joy, a revelation, and upon awakening, it was crushed by the reality of the moment. His son would never be. Elia had been but would no longer be. He thought of a line from *Hamlet*:

"To be, or not to be: that is the question." Those words had a new and powerful meaning to the adult Logan Lomax.

"We need us a prospecting expedition, Wonder Dog," Scruffy said as he headed back to his room after a night at the Long Branch.

Rusty let out a concurring bark and scooted ahead as though ready to pack up and go.

At the back entrance to his room, there sat Rusty, waiting, his head cocked to the side, his good eye with a look of expectation—a look his little dog had not had for a good long while.

The next morning, Scruffy headed over to Wiley's General Store to purchase gear for his prospecting trek. Behind the counter, which was situated at the rear of the first floor, where the Widow's living room used to be, was a young woman. The curves of her gave shape to the shapeless sack dress she wore. The face above the dress was so quick and aware it almost hurt to look at it.

The girl smiled at Scruffy as he approached. It was a smile of reassurance and other things that Scruffy sensed but did not know.

"Good morning," she said. "May I be of help?"

I believe you might, Scruffy thought. "I need dry goods to last a couple of weeks out yonder," Scruffy said with a lift of his hand over his shoulder.

"Prospector?" The girl said, her eyes opening wide with curiosity.

"For now, I reckon."

"I see you're back at it, Scruffy." Down the counter, Mr. Wiley was stacking canned goods on a shelf.

"Rusty insisted." Scruffy looked down at his dog, who was sitting at his feet.

"I have a new order of sluice boxes," Mr. Wiley said.

"No," Scruffy said. "I am going to keep it simple."

He turned his attention back to the girl. "Also need a lightweight pan ... net"—he pointed to a fishing net on a hoop hanging on the back wall—"and a sturdy knapsack."

After all his goods had been brought to the counter, including a tent, Scruffy said to the girl, "When I return, may I call on you?"

She leaned back, her eyes appraising. "You don't even know my name." A smile creased the corners of her mouth. "And I have just learned your ... nickname ... Scruffy?"

"Scruffy Lomax is what I go by." He put his hands on the counter, leaned forward, and whispered, "Christian name is Logan." He made a face—*Okay?*

"Marne Mayer is my name." She flashed a look down at Mr. Wiley, who was talking to a customer. "But I am afraid I am not so colorful as to have any sort of nickname." Marne smiled in a way that reflected her awareness that a flirtation was under way.

"How unfortunate," Scruffy said. "Some folks have no luck whatsoever." He cleared his throat, indicating new order of business. "So ... Marne ... Mayer"—he let the name roll off his tongue—"may I call on you upon my return?"

"Yes you may ... Scrufffeee Looomax."

CHAPTER 35

AT FIRST LIGHT, SCRUFFY AND Rusty departed Big Bear, heading for Header's Creek, the place where he almost lost his life, for the first time since he had been struck by gold fever.

It seemed strange to be back at prospecting—in Big Bear, no less. When he had last departed Alaska, four years prior, Scruffy thought that he would never return—that his life would be a continuous journey of seeing different parts of America and possibly the world. But life has a way of changing things.

And then there was a Miss Marne Mayer, whom Scruffy could not get out of his mind. After leaving the general store, Scruffy had gone to the assay office to buy glass vials for storing specks of gold. Merle Heidelman mentioned that Marne was Mrs. Wiley's niece from the panhandle of Idaho. "Not sure what would bring a fine-looking young woman like that to Big Bear," Merle said.

When he had turned in the previous night, Marne's beguiling face rose front and center in Scruffy's mind. How pretty she was, how intriguing, and oh, how he ached to *be* with her; to hold her in his arms; to kiss her lips, which he imagined were soft and warm; and to nuzzle her lush, thick hair. Scruffy fell asleep thinking about her.

In the morning he awoke at the end of a dream, with Elia waving farewell. "Have a good life, Logan," the ghostly figure said before fading away.

By noon, Scruffy had reached an outcrop of rocks in the middle of a vast stretch of grassland. He took in the beautiful vista of this untamed land. It was the same location where he had stopped with Frenchy, Pete, and Needle Nose on their prospecting trek. It had been a grand and dangerous adventure with three good men. Now he was going it alone. But going it alone had its advantages, such as having time by oneself to think matters over—not to determine any sort of plan but to wonder what might possibly be in store next and to walk this open land, with snow-capped mountains in the distance, the smell of sedge grass and wildflowers in the air. It was June, and the weather was perfect: fifty-five to sixty degrees, partly sunny, and a gentle breeze at Scruffy's back.

Rusty had a swagger—or, more accurately, an extra giddy-up—to his step as he scooted right along.

"You are enjoying this, are you not, Wonder Dog?" Scruffy said as they came to a small creek at the base of a row of foothills lined with jack pine trees.

Rusty flicked his tail and let out a whimpering whine of appreciation as he ran to the same creek where he had quenched his thirst with Frenchy's mule, Annie. The dog stood on the edge of the water, lapping up his fill before licking his mouth and scooting back over to Scruffy, who had begun to set up camp.

"Well, Wonder Dog," Scruffy said as he hammered a tent pin into the ground with the butt end of his hatchet. He eyed the foothills on the other side of the creek, "Looks like we got us some climbing to do tomorrow."

The following morning, the climb up and down the foothill was difficult, but it was nothing Scruffy could not handle as he weaved his way through the jack pines. He had packed lighter than in the past. Most of the food he had packed was patties of pemmican that he had bought at Wiley's General Store. He did not bring a frying pan or any clothes other than what he wore. He planned to live off the land, collecting wild berries and fishing.

At the crest of the foothills, Scruffy came to a valley of prairie land. "Remember this, Rusty?" he asked, taking in the vista of wild grass and wildflowers bobbing as a breeze swept down across the prairie. In the distance, an azure-blue sky met the sepia-hued land speckled with an array of colors. "If that is not medicine for a man's soul, I do not know what is."

Rusty barked his agreement.

"And dogs too," Scruffy said with a laugh.

By dusk, Scruffy and Rusty had dined on pemmican. After eating, he pitched his tent at the base of an outcrop, beyond which was a hillside of woodlands.

"Another half day, Wonder Dog, and we will arrive at Header's Creek." Scruffy was sitting on a flat rock, Rusty at his feet, stretched out, head on paws.

Scruffy scratched his dog behind the ears and ruffled the fur on his neck. "Didn't tire you out, did I?"

Rusty lifted his brow to his master and yawned a big, wide one. He then got up and went to the tent opening and turned back, eyeing Scruffy.

"I believe you have the right idea, my wise little dog," Scruffy said as he stood and stretched his arms overhead.

Tucked into his sleeping bag, fingers laced behind head, with Rusty stretched out across his ankles asleep, Scruffy had a sense of well-being that he hadn't experienced in a good while. He knew that in his future travels, when things got him down, a trip to Big Bear may well be needed. *See this great world while you are in it, but do not live by any set rules. Take it day by day and live each one to the fullest.*

CHAPTER 36

THE PEDESTRIAN BRIDGE AT HEADER'S Creek was down, but Scruffy found a shallow crossing and stepped over stones as Rusty splashed his way across. Down along the creek a ways, Scruffy came to the embankment in front of the barracks, which looked the same as before, if a bit more weathered, having faded to a pale gray.

Scruffy went up the timber steps of the embankment and over to the barracks, which looked like an inanimate ruler sitting up on its thick pilings. The inside appeared as though no one had been there in the last four years. The skeleton frames of the bunk beds were still along the back wall; a pile of ashes in the stone fireplace was all that remained from last time.

After unloading his gear, Scruffy said to Rusty, "You get some rest, Wonder Dog, I won't be long."

With trenching shovel in one hand and hatchet in the other, he headed out into the woods behind the barracks and dug up some worms he'd stored in a rawhide pouch and then cut downed branches and limbs for firewood. As he headed back, cradling a pile of wood, Scruffy stopped and turned around. He had a sense that he was being watched. He wished he had brought along Rusty, who could have smelled out anything hiding out there.

Scruffy peered into the thick woods bulging with massive trees and underbrush. It would be easy to find cover in such an environment, even for a creature as big as a Sasquatch, if they really did exist.

He thought about the strange occurrences that had taken place the last time he was in this neck of the woods. He recalled the huge downed trees that appeared to have been pushed over, the *kerplunk* of something heavy splashing in the creek, and the shadowy figure he had seen under the cover of the woods. And then he thought of the hut of tree limbs and leaves he had awoken in after losing Pete. How had he gotten there, and who or what put the pile of berries and deer carcass in there? This was something he had barely pondered on. Why that was, he did not know; but at the very least, there was something unexplained going in this part of the territory.

Back in the barracks, Scruffy grabbed his fishing net, braided string line, and a hook. "Come on, Rusty," he said. Let's find a good-size fishing stick and catch us some dinner."

Down the creek a ways, Scruffy broke off a tree limb about the diameter of his thumb. He snapped the branch in half with his boot, cut away the shoots with his hatchet, and tied the braided line to the end of the stick.

"Got us a fishing pole, Rusty," Scruffy said as he secured a worm on the hook. "Now we need us some fish to bite."

After a couple of hours with no luck, Scruffy decided to head back and try his luck panning. As he began the walk back, Rusty began running back and forth along the creek, barking and looking across the water. Scruffy did not see anything.

"Come on, Rusty," he ordered. "Let's skedaddle."

Back at camp, Scruffy began digging a hole at the base of the embankment with his trenching shovel. A young fellow he had met at the Long Branch, who had been prospecting for the last year, had said, "Dig a deep hole—or Mr. Pocket, as I like to say—where gold has been found before, and when you hit black sand, start panning."

Scruffy had asked if he'd had any luck.

"Not yet," the young man replied, "but if it was easy, everyone would be digging for gold."

The soil was loose and easy to dig, and Scruffy got into a rhythm. At a depth of five feet, Scruffy had found no black sand. He climbed out and began a second hole.

By late afternoon, he had dug three holes and had come up empty in all three—no black sand. "What you got there, Wonder Dog," Scruffy said as he watched Rusty sniff around the perimeter of one of the holes.

A splashing sound came from the creek. At the edge of the water, a good-sized fish, at least two feet in length, was swimming along the shore in a slow, listless manner. Scruffy ran up to the barracks, got the fishing net, and tore back to the creek.

Up and down the shoreline he searched, but to no avail. As Scruffy was ready to quit, Rusty entered the water, taking one slow step after another. Standing with his legs submerged, his body above water, the dog plunged his head into the creek and came up with the fish, holding it by the tail. Rusty rushed out of the water and over to Scruffy, presenting his master with his catch.

Scruffy placed his net under Rusty's mouth, and the dog deposited the olive-green fish splotched yellow and white along the belly. "I believe you caught us a northern pike, Wonder Dog," Scruffy said in an exuberant voice.

Scruffy left the fish in the net on the red cedar bench in front of the barracks and went inside to get his knife to clean the fish.

"Arf! Arf! Woof! Woof!"

What now? Scruffy thought as he pulled his knife from his knapsack and headed back outside. At the table, the net was still there, but the fish was gone—as was Rusty. A faint musky smell was in the air.

"Rusty!" Scruffy hollered as he strode into the woods. "Rusty!" He heard barking from deeper in the woods.

"Wonder Dog, come. Right now!"

A rustling sound came from the forest before Rusty emerged, trotting out wearing his guard dog look: his mouth closed in a thin, stark line; his eyes two slits of concentration; and his ears pointed up.

There had been recent sightings of coyotes in Big Bear. *Maybe it's a coyote, or possibly a bear, but that's a stretch. A hawk or some other bird of prey swooping down and flying off? All possible, but ... Nah.* Scruffy would not believe in a Sasquatch until he saw one.

Before turning in for the night, Scruffy moved a bunk bed frame against the front door. He then started a fire and slipped into his sleeping bag on the floor next to the hearth. The crackling fire settled down and provided comforting warmth.

Scruffy had packed light, but one thing he was glad he had brought was a flashlight that was nearby, as was Rusty, who lay at Scruffy's feet, facing the door.

The space was dark other than a flickering glimmer of light from the fireplace.

Scruffy drifted off into a deep sleep.

A low growl from Rusty stirred Scruffy to a sleepy consciousness. "What is it, boy?" Scruffy said, sitting up. He put his hand on Rusty's neck, which felt tight, as though a string had been pulled through the dog's body.

Rusty rose to all fours, eyeing the window next to the front door.

My god, Scruffy thought. Appearing in the window was a great, dark outline of what looked like a conical head—or was it a shadow from a tree?

Rusty bolted over to the window, lifted his paws to the windowsill, and turned his head, his glass eye aimed at the shadow.

Scruffy started for the window, but by the time he got there, the shadow was gone.

"Not sure what that was, Wonder Dog," Scruffy said as he lifted his dog off the sill, "but I suspect if it was real and you just gave it the evil eye, we will no longer have a problem with stolen fish."

CHAPTER 37

A FTER A FRUITLESS WEEK OF digging holes in search of Mr. Pocket, plus losing two days to rain that Scruffy spent in the barracks bored out of his mind, he decided to head back to Big Bear. There were holes all along the banks of the creek. It looked like the handy work of a swarm of giant groundhogs. He had found barely a speck of gold, and besides, he wanted to begin the courting of Miss Marne Mayer.

The two-and-a-half-day walk back was uneventful. Scruffy had no sense of being watched, and the weather held.

Midafternoon, Scruffy arrived in Big Bear and went directly to his room. With wooden bucket in hand, he went out back to a well pump.

After three trips to his room, he had half-filled a circular metal basin with water. He stripped off his dirty, smelly clothes and stood naked in the basin of cold water, scrubbing himself from head to toe with lye soap and a washcloth. It was a chilly cleansing, but he did not want to spend the additional time warming water on the stove. When he finished, the once clear water in the basin was a murky brown, but he was fresh and clean, though a bit chilled from the cold water. He put on clean underwear, socks, trousers, and a red flannel shirt.

As he combed his hair at a mirror over his dresser, Scruffy noted that he was beginning to show signs of aging, or, to use a description more to his liking, maturing. Fine lines, like fissures, crinkled in the corners of his eyes when he squinted. His ruddy face was speckled with a light growth of chin whiskers—or, more precisely, fuzz. He would probably never grow a beard—a trait inherited from his Yakama roots. His once smooth cheeks were now rough to the touch. But he liked what he saw. Age was inevitable, but before him was a fit and healthy man—a man who had never suffered any sort of major illness and who had overcome difficult times by moving on to the next phase of his life's journey.

"All right, now," Scruffy said as he turned from the mirror and headed for the door.

Mr. Willey was behind the counter, going over an inventory list. He looked up over his wire-rimmed glasses as Scruffy approached. "How did the prospecting go out yonder, Scruffy?"

"Not much luck," Scruffy said as he looked toward the door to the storage room behind the storekeeper.

As if on cue, the door opened and Marne emerged with a crate of canned goods. "Where shall I put these, Uncle Ernest?"

Wiley told her to leave them on the counter. He gave Scruffy a knowing lift of the brow and turned his attention back to his niece. "Marne, would you assist Mr. Lomax here?" With that, he straightened his papers and went into the storage room.

"May I help you with something, Mr. Lomax?"

Scruffy leaned back from the counter, looking into her honey-brown eyes that shone with some unknown knowledge, her olive skin radiant, her lips full and promising, her chestnut hair tied off to the side by a red ribbon. "Not here for business," he said.

"I see," she replied.

"I would like to call on you this evening after supper."

"That would be fine. Shall we say seven?"

Mr. and Mrs. Willey lived in the row of new houses at the edge of town. It was referred to at the Long Branch as Proprietor's Row. Some of the homeowners were the feed and lumber yard owner and his wife, with grown sons who worked in the family business; the president of the new bank and his wife and six children; a newly constructed timber-framed house that was the property of the family of a big mining enterprise that was going on a few miles outside of town; and the new reverend and his family, who lived in a parsonage built by his congregation next door to the church that was erected a few years back.

The Wiley house had a white picket fence with a latch gate and a stone path leading to a front porch where Marne sat in a glider chair.

"Good evening, Mr. Lomax," Marne said as she rocked ever so slowly.

Scruffy stood at the bottom of the steps, Rusty at his side. "Hello there."

"I see you brought a companion."

This here is Rusty," Scruffy said as he came up the steps. "He volunteered to chaperone."

"Well now, might you ask him to join us," Marne said as she slid over to the end of the glider.

Scruffy looked over his shoulder at his dog, who was lying on the walk, head on paws. "It appears he is going to provide us with a bit of space," he said as he came up the porch steps.

"May I?" Scruffy said as he offered a hand toward the glider.

"By all means."

After a period of silence, Scruffy said, "So how do you like living in Alaska—or should I say Big Bear."

"Good a place as any," she said in a matter-of-fact tone.

"This time of year almost makes up for the brutal winters."

As though a switch had been triggered, Marne's beautiful features assumed an expression of wounded bitterness. "Brutal? I could tell you about brutal," she said with a cool detachment in her voice.

They rocked on the slider as Marne seemed to go off inside herself.

"I am a good listener," Scruffy said.

Marne gave Scruffy a hard, probing look. "Can you keep a secret?"

Scruffy started to say *depends* but instead replied, "I have never been accused of being a blabbermouth."

Marne screwed up her eyes as though trying to decide. "I do not know you, Scruffy Lomax." She thought for a moment and pursed her lips as though a decision had been made. "I must talk with someone, and you appear my only option."

Scruffy took Marne's hand and said, "I have had some difficult times in my life and have learned a few lessons." He squeezed her hand gently and smiled. "I am a good listener."

"My folks," Marne said, "put my illegitimate child up for adoption— my daughter." She kept her beguiling eyes on Scruffy. "I spent one day with her, and then she was taken."

Marne gripped Scruffy's hand with surprising strength. She slid closer so that her thigh was against his, her lovely smell overwhelming him with desire. "I was banished not only from the home I grew up in but also from the town of Athol, Idaho—a tight-knit community where everybody knows everybody's business." Her tone was that of an indifferent observer, as though she were a witness and not the recipient of a shunning.

Marne went on to say that the father of the child was a married man with three children, and a prominent citizen. "I kept the books for his sawmill, and he wooed me something fierce whenever we were alone in his office, and next thing I know, I am with child."

She said it was her first time with a man and news of her situation devastated the young man she was on the verge of getting engaged to. "I never said who the father was," Marne said as she dabbed a tear streaking her cheek. "But my young suitor knew it was not he—as did his family, who made it impossible to stay."

She looked away, her mouth turned downward in the corners, before casting her gaze on Scruffy, her face glimmering with a faint hint of irony

Marne seemed to possess a repertoire of looks, like an actress playing a scene—a skilled and a beautiful one at that.

"If my aunt had not rescued me …" She let the words drift off, her thought incomplete.

Scruffy slid his arm over her shoulder and brought her in close. "Folks around here do not pass judgment so quick."

Scruffy was seeing Marne three times a week and even having supper with her aunt and uncle. Marne told it like it was. He found that refreshing but at the same time a bit concerning, coupled with the unemotional way she had revealed her past. He wondered whether the loss of a baby had not robbed her of sensitivity, or whether she was in a deep-seated internal pain that her outer self had crammed deep into her psyche. If that were the case, at some point it would all come home to roost. He also wondered how much of her story he should believe. She sounded convincing, but did it really matter? For besides the physical attraction—he thought her the most beautiful of girls—Scruffy was also drawn to her manner, that unknowable aura about her that attracted him to her like nothing he had ever experienced. Whether there was more to her past indiscretion or not was presently unimportant.

As far as intimacy, they had done nothing more than a bit of sparking on the porch. The first time Scruffy kissed her, she pulled away to inform him, "I will not make the same mistake again." Scruffy thought that it might take marriage for him to have his way with Marne. He was not close to asking for her hand; nor did he know whether she was even interested in him in that way. He decided to give it time and see. It almost seemed like a curse, the desire to be with a woman and have a family despite his urges to uproot and travel about free as the wind.

But right now he had no plans to hit the road, and not wanting to get himself bored lollygagging around town with too much time on his hands, Scruffy got a job at the lumber yard. He drove a flatbed truck, delivering orders of lumber as far out as ten miles to a network of cabins and shelters for crews building park roads. This was a change from when Scruffy first arrived. Progress was making its way into Big Bear and the surrounding area, and Scruffy was not sure how he felt about that. Part of him liked the isolation, and another part recognized the need for growth.

Things were different now. The Long Branch had not changed one bit, but its clientele had. Men working on the roads frequented the place, as did the some of the employees of the lumber yard. They were a decent enough group of fellas, but they did not have the spark of adventure that the old-time prospectors and trappers had back in the day.

But Scruffy enjoyed the freedom of loading up his order of supplies every morning and heading out—with Rusty riding shotgun, head out the window—on the newly paved macadam road.

Today he was en route to the Kennabutte Copper Mine, a big operation at the base of a foothill five miles outside of town. By the time Scruffy arrived, the operation was in full swing. Shuttle cars pushed by miners into and out of the mine on a dual track, running from inside the mine entrance to a crusher site. Large grinding machines, which reminded Scruffy of primordial iron monsters, were fed the ore by conveyor belts leading into the belly of the beast, and the by-product would exit on another belt. The grinded ore was loaded on to dump trucks by cranes to be taken to a nearby processing area.

Ned Gillespie, the foreman, came out of a cabin with a man who had the confident look of a boss. He was tall with broad shoulders that tapered down to a narrow waist. He also had the look of a former athlete, not only in his physical stature but also in the easy manner with which he moved, as though each body part was in perfect rhythm. They stopped walking as the man lifted his hand forward and explained something to Ned, who listened intently. The man then tapped Ned on the shoulder and walked back into the cabin.

Ned paused as though digesting his instructions. He spotted Scruffy and motioned over his shoulder for Scruffy to follow him to an area away from the mining operation.

"How you be, Scruffy Lomax?" Ned said as he came up to the driver's window.

"That the boss man you were talking to?" Scruffy asked.

"That would be Frank Kennabutte, the owner's son."

Scruffy asked whether he was living in the big timber-framed house outside Big Bear.

Ned nodded his affirmation and said, "Living in that big house all by himself."

Ned went on to say that Frank Kennabutte had graduated from the University of Pennsylvania with a geological engineering degree. "He has all kinds of ideas about *expediting* the mining industry."

"It is quite an operation, Ned," Scruffy said as he scanned the activity around them: miners, wearing blue hard hats, shuttling the cast-iron cars in and out of the mine; the whine and clang of the heavy machinery; the dust from the extraction process; and the big trucks coming and going.

"It is something," Ned said as he peered into the cab at Rusty, who was sitting upright at Scruffy's side. "Mining, grinding, concentrating, roasting, smelting conversion, and refining," he said with a finger jab. "We do it all."

"Well sir," Scruffy said, "let me get this unloaded."

Ned and Scruffy stacked the sixteen-foot two-by-eights and two-by-sixes next to other stacks of lumber. When they finished, Scruffy handed Ned an invoice sheet. "John Hancock it, and I will be on my way."

Ned pulled a pen from a leather pocket holder in his shirt pocket and signed it on a board. "I could use a good man as a jack-of-all-trades around here."

Silence.

"Driving one of them big trucks," Ned said with a wave of his hand at a green sixteen-ton dump truck getting loaded with crushed ore by a crane. "Hauling material here and there in a flatbed, office work when needed."

Ned looked off and then returned his gaze to Scruffy. "We are going to build a plant to process the ore, and I will be stretched out. I need a smart, quick-on-his-feet fella who sees things that others might miss."

The offer surprised Scruffy, as he had met Ned Gillespie only twice before.

"I can judge a man first time I meet him," Ned said with a knowing lift of his brow. "I knew you were the real deal within half a minute."

Ned mentioned Scruffy's salary, which would double what he was making delivering lumber.

There was something about this site and the job offer that had a stifling effect on Scruffy, as though it would squash his independence. "Thank you, Ned, but I am going to decline."

A knowing smile hovered about Ned's lips. "I figured you would." He smiled again, this time with a shadow of irony. "The good ones are the hardest to figure out, since they are not sure why they are that way, but just that they are."

CHAPTER 38

O N A LAZY SUNDAY AFTERNOON, Scruffy took Marne on a walk. It was late August, and the weather was temperate but held the ever-present hint of cold just around the corner.

"Scruffy Lomax," Marne said with an air of gaiety, "are you planning on settling in Big Bear?"

Scruffy slid a look over at Marne, whose gaze met his, her eyes inquiring.

This was the first time Marne had shown any sort of interest in his plans. She knew nothing much about his life other than that he was from Yakima and had traveled around the States and Mexico.

When he had mentioned riding the rails, she had only said, "That must have been an experience," before changing the subject and talking about her day at the store.

Marne did not know that Scruffy had been married or that he had lost a wife and son during childbirth—nobody in Big Bear did. Nor did they know that he had almost been hanged during his first week on the road or that he had witnessed the murder of a man. He was not sure whether Marne was not a curious person or whether she had no interest in his life.

When he had asked about growing up in Idaho, Marne had only said, "My past is dead to me."

They mostly talked about their days, Marne recounting what took place at the store—the inventory, rude customers, a fellow from the lumber yard coming by the store and stealing glances—but so far too shy to speak to her.

Scruffy did not know what to make of her talking about other men interested in her. The more time he spent with her, it seemed, the less about her he understood. And though she said she did not want to talk about her past, she had told him about giving birth out of wedlock the first time he spent time with her. "Incongruous" was a word Scruffy had looked up in a dictionary left in his living quarters; it meant *lacking harmony of parts.*

But now there seemed to be a shift in the air.

They were in a meadow of wildflowers on the outskirts of town, holding hands. Her warm touch sent a surge through Scruffy as they came to a gurgling creek.

"Let's sit," Scruffy said as he offered a hand to help her onto a large flat stone.

"You did not answer my question," she said, leaning her face toward his, her warm breath and sweet scent all over him.

Scruffy put his hand on her waist, bringing her in close, and kissed her on the lips.

Marne pulled back, both hands on Scruffy's chest. "Let me know when you have an answer."

After dropping Marne off at the Wiley house, Scruffy headed toward his room, pondering Marne's question. It seemed that if he wanted any sort of advancement in the romance department, a commitment was required.

His physical desire for Marne was tempered by her incongruous manner. Was that what it was, or was there something deeper going on with her? She was hard to figure out. And even if he did figure her out, did he want to spend the rest of his life with her?

But oh, how he ached to have his way with her. This was not just because of her physical attributes; it was as though he wanted to conquer her—to lie naked with her as she gave herself to him.

Back in the room, Rusty lay on the foot of the bed, giving Scruffy his why-did-you-leave-me look.

"Wonder Dog, what say we head over to the Long Branch for a libation."

Rusty shot off the bed and trotted over to the door.

There was a smattering of men at the bar, and a few tables were occupied. Ned Gillespie was situated at the corner spot of the bar, where Scruffy had held court on many an occasion back in the twenties. But this was a different time, and it seemed like a different place. Ned was talking with the boss man, Frank Kennabutte, who was leaning with his back to the wall, beer mug in hand.

Frank lifted his gaze to Scruffy as he approached their space, studied him for a moment, and said to Ned, "Malachite can contain up to fifty-eight percent copper."

Scruffy placed Rusty on the bar and took a seat one empty stool over from Ned.

Frank shined a smile on Rusty and said, "I believe this establishment has gone to the dogs."

Ned turned and said, "Hey now, if it is not Scruffy Lomax and his little dog Rusty. He twirled his finger in a circle to the bartender for another round and said, "What is your pleasure, Mr. Lomax?"

"Beer for me," he said, his eyes on Kennabutte, "and a sarsaparilla for Rusty."

"Frank," Ned said with a hand on Scruffy's shoulder, "this is the capable man I was telling you about."

"A jack of all trades, if I remember correctly," Kennabutte said as he took in the measure of Scruffy.

The bartender placed the drinks on the bar, and Rusty pawed his, lifted it, and swallowed it down.

"Now *that* is impressive," Kennabutte said in a changed voice. He held out his hand to Scruffy. "Frank Kennabutte here."

Scruffy shook his hand, the grip firm. "Scruffy Lomax here. Good to make your acquaintance."

Frank held Scruffy's large, rough-hewn hand, examining it before taking a swig of his beer. He looked at Scruffy, his grayish blue eyes meeting Scruffy's with a look of decisive appraisal. "What is it going to take to get you hired?"

Frank went on to sell Scruffy of the big plans he had for the copper mine. "We're going to build a processing plant not far from the mine, and there is a need for good men to join in this venture."

Scruffy was not sold on Frank Kennabutte, who appeared to be around thirty. It was as though he were putting on the act of a salesman selling his wares. His true self lay camouflaged below the surface. He figured there was a cold-blooded businessman at the core of this young entrepreneur.

Scruffy declined the sales pitch.

Frank lifted a hand, an expression of serious, yet false, modesty on his handsome face. "Think about it."

On the way back to his place, Scruffy remembered the old days at the Long Branch and how different it was: the laughter, the characters—he being one of them—and the stories told and repeated many times over.

He sensed he was coming to another crossroads. The two biggest so far had been his departure from Yakima at age seventeen to ride the rails and his leaving Yelapa after the death of Elia and their son during childbirth. Scruffy had been ready to live out his life in Yelapa with a wife and son, and maybe even a passel of children. At least that is what he told himself. But deep down, he was not certain that he would not have bolted. It pained him to think of himself as such a scoundrel, but it was a situation that he never had to face.

And now Marne had cast a spell over Scruffy. The beguiling, indifferent manner in which she had rejected his advance had ratcheted up his desire not only to have his way with her but also to *be* with her. She had gotten inside him like no woman before.

At the door to his living quarters, Scruffy looked up into the clear night sky, the crescent moon spilling shimmering moonlight across the land. He was not sure whether it was a waxing or waning moon.

CHAPTER 39

"WHAT DO YOU SAY, WONDER Dog?" Scruffy said as he shifted the flatbed truck into third gear. "More days, more dollars."

Rusty, paws on the open window, turned halfway as an acknowledgment and then returned to his favorite pastime—hanging his head out the window.

It was September, and the weather was beginning to turn. Mornings were brisk, with the first hint of snow in the air. But Rusty seemed not to mind the cold air blowing in his face. If the window was shut, he would whine until Scruffy opened it.

"Come wintertime, my faithful friend," Scruffy said, mostly to himself, "that window is going to remained closed. Understood?"

There was another half head-turn from Rusty, accompanied by a squint of disapproval, and then he was back to lapping in the wind.

Up ahead, a cloud of dust rose into the morning sky. Straight ahead was the construction site of the Kennabutte Mining Company's future processing plant.

Scruffy pulled in next to a tent that was the temporary office. Inside he found Ned Gillespie looking over construction specs.

"Ned," Scruffy said with a rise in his voice, "how you be?"

"Hey, Scruffy," Ned said as he lifted his gaze from a set of blueprints on a high round table in the middle of the space. "Where you been? Mason Junior brought the last three deliveries."

"Got in late last night. Spent the last ten days running errands in Fairbanks for Mr. Mason," Scruffy said.

"Ha!" Ned said as he packed his cheek with a chaw of tobacco. "Careful or he will have you marrying one of his plain Jane daughters."

Ned lifted his brow, his eyes grinning. "Run for the hills if he calls you *son*."

Scruffy grudged Ned a smile and said, "I miss anything around town?"

"Nah," Ned replied as he motioned Scruffy outside.

"It is something. Is it not?" Ned said with a wave of his hand.

They were looking at a full-scale big-time operation. There was a temporary concrete plant on the premises with a cement bin, mixer, batch hopper, and belt conveyor. It looked like a row of small silos on stilts. Men were pouring the concrete floor of the plant via a hose connected to the mixer. There were at least a dozen workers; two were pulling up the reinforcement wire as the concrete oozed out of the hose, while others spread the concrete with come-alongs, followed by a team of two workers screeding with ten-foot two-by-fours.

Ned pointed to a crew of carpenters building the temporary living quarters, which reminded Scruffy of the barracks at Header's Creek. "I will meet you at the far end over there."

Scruffy drove over and parked. At the rear of the bed, he loosened the security ropes from the lumber as Ned came up. They began pulling a load of sixteen-foot two-by-eights off the truck bed and stacking them on a line of wooden pallets.

Before his time spent in Fairbanks, Scruffy had been making deliveries out there a couple of times a week. He had previously told Ned that he did not have to help him unload, but Ned insisted. "I like to get my hands dirty every now and then," he had told Scruffy. "Plus I like your company, Mr. Lomax."

And Scruffy liked Ned's. He was one fellow who would have fit right in back in the day around these parts. Too many of the new breed around Big Bear were a hungry, almost desperate lot. Of course, most had come up from the States, where things were downright terrible. The tough times had left a mark on these men.

"Where's the boss man?" Scruffy said as placed the front end of a board on the pallet that Ned pushed forward. "Haven't seen him since he offered me a job at the Long Branch."

"Been away on business, and then when he came back last week ..."

Ned looked over at some carpenters hammering studs into toe plates. "Rumor has it Frank has met himself a young lady. He is a smitten."

"Around these parts?" Scruffy said as a sudden tightness swarmed in his throat.

"One of the carpenters was fishing and saw him taking a buggy ride with a pretty young thing out on the prairie."

As far as Scruffy knew, there was only one pretty young thing around these parts—Marne.

After unloading the lumber at the processing plant, Scruffy waved so long to Ned and headed back to town. He could not get out of his mind the image of Marne and Frank Kennabutte as a couple. And a fine-looking couple they surely would be: the tall, handsome Ivy Leaguer with the intriguing golden girl who had a vibration of energy that came off her as though her body hummed. And that hum drew Scruffy like nothing he had ever experienced.

At twenty nine years old, Scruffy had lived a life some men might have called full, including marriage, the heartbreaking loss of a wife and child, and time spent riding the rails all over the North American continent in some pretty sticky situations—and each time he had come out in search of another adventure. But Marne had stymied Scruffy's desire to roam. He wanted in the worst way to have his way with her.

What was it about her that drew him so? Beautiful she was, but it was more. It was her nature—that unknowable something yet to be reached that he wanted to pull from her and bask in.

If Marne was seeing Kennabutte, she must realize that he would find out. Was this some sort of game she was playing, or had she found a bigger catch in Frank? With his family wealth and status, she could live a life she had never dreamed of. Scruffy bet that she had not told Frank so freely about her child born out of wedlock. As far as he could tell, the only folks that knew were Mr. and Mrs. Wiley and himself. There had not been a mention of it at the Long Branch or by any of the men at the lumber yard, most of whom frequented Wiley's General Store.

He had told no one about seeing her, and he wondered whether she had not done the same.

Gonna meet it head on, Scruffy thought as he pulled into the lumber yard.

CHAPTER 40

APPROACHING THE GENERAL STORE, SCRUFFY came upon Mr. Wiley locking up for the evening. "Looks like I'm too late," he said.

Mr. Wiley pulled the key out of the lock and turned. "Scruffy," he said with a squinty look of someone assessing a possible problem.

"I was hoping to find Marne."

"Left early," Mr. Wiley said. He looked down the street as though hoping to make a quick getaway.

"Might I find her at your home?" Scruffy said.

Mr. Wiley winced, his gaze low. He sighed and said, "Scruffy, I am afraid she has met a fellow."

"Would you tell her I would like to talk with her?" Scruffy raised his hand. "I will not cause a scene. I just want to hear it from her." He shrugged as though to say, *What do you think?*

"She and I will be doing inventory early tomorrow morning. Come by before work."

Scruffy was up before dawn, having slept little during the night. He tossed and turned so much that Rusty hopped down and curled up on a throw rug at the side of the bed.

He had run through his mind so many different scenarios as to what to say to Marne. In the end, he decided to play it by ear to see what sort of frame of mind she was in and go from there.

The half-blue light of dawn glinted over the rooftop of Wiley's General Store. As Scruffy approached, the front door opened.

Marne was wearing a full-length gray skirt and white blouse

buttoned at the top so that her collar was neatly lying flat against the cotton fabric. Her hair was in a tidy bun secured at the back of her head.

"Come in," she said in an even, dispassionate voice.

Scruffy entered the dead-quiet store. He immediately sensed that they were alone.

Let's have a seat at the stove," Marne said, gesturing to a potbellied stove situated in a corner nook. It was a spot where men hung out and chitchatted about life in Big Bear.

They sat in high-arched wicker chairs at a round table across from each other.

"My uncle said you wanted to talk to me." Marne's voice was so utterly dull and droning, as though she were fulfilling a necessary obligation. And matching her tone was an expression of disinterest—her lips pursed, her eyes looking right through Scruffy.

"Are you seeing Frank Kennabutte?"

Marne sat perfectly still, her hands folded on her lap. She lifted her gaze out the window and away from Scruffy. "He has asked for my hand in marriage."

Marne was a gold digger—plain and simple. What a fool Scruffy had been, being strung along until a better prize was dangled before her. "That be mighty interesting," he said just as casually as he could muster. "Do he and his family know about your previous life?"

Marne turned to Scruffy. Her indifference vanished, her lips drawn tight and her eyes stretched wide as though she was shocked by Scruffy's words.

"I told that to you in confidence." She cocked her head appraisingly at Scruffy, her eyes saying, *Well?*

An idea was formulating in Scruffy's mind—a terrible yet satisfying idea. "I will be leaving Big Bear for good," he said.

"Oh," Marne said with a breath of relief.

"But there is a price for my confidence." An ache like a yearning was growing in his loins. Part of him hated himself for going down this road, but it was like riding the blinds, consequences be damned. He wanted her.

"You will need protection."

Scruffy got off work early. After straightening things up at his place, he found a packet of condoms in a drawer from his time in New Orleans. The agreement was that Marne would come by after work and would entertain one session of "No more than ten minutes. And afterward, neither I nor anyone else will ever see Mr. Lomax again around these parts."

At six there was a light tap on the door. It was Marne, still dressed in the white blouse and gray skirt. She went right to Scruffy's bed and began to undress. "Hurry please," she said. "I do not want to be missed."

As Scruffy tore off his clothes, Rusty curled up in a corner and faced the wall, as though not wanting to witness what was about to take place.

Marne lay on the bed, as naked as a jay bird. Her breasts were full and firm, her legs shaped as though on a lathe, and her pubic hairs a bunched thicket, behind which was her secret treasure.

As she spread her legs apart, her eyes were two slits, like those of a hardened poker player or, dare Scruffy think it, one of the prostitutes in New Orleans he had been with.

Scruffy secured a condom on and positioned himself atop Marne, her breath warm and inviting. He kissed her on the lips and received nothing in return. He put a hand on her breast and gently rubbed his thumb on her nipple—nothing. She may as well have been a corpse.

He slid his middle finger between her legs and inside her, gently stroking while entering her deeper. She began breathing in deep breaths as he probed with his long finger.

Her body grew warm.

He slid down and maneuvered his member inside her.

Marne's body erupted in a huge twitch as he began stroking back and forth. She began to moan with pleasure as they moved in rhythm, thrusting and grinding.

Scruffy came with an exalting groan of pure sexual relief.

Marne scooted out from under him and stood.

Lickety-split, she pulled on her underwear, bra, blouse, skirt, and shoes. She rearranged her bun, which had been loosened during their encounter. She then went to the door, stopped, and turned. "Remember our deal," she said.

Scruffy sat naked on the edge of the bed, feeling like a piece of white trash—a pitiful man who had coerced a young woman into sex not only to satisfy a sexual need but also to gain a sense of conquest over someone who had been dealt a tough hand early in life. Yes, she was a conniver, an out-for-herself woman, but was it any worse than him having the urge to run out on Elia after marriage?

But, he told himself, *I did not leave Elia.* Thinking it was one thing; going through with it was another.

PART 3

CHAPTER 41

A S THE TRAIN SLOWED COMING around a bend, Scruffy jumped off the freight car, trotted along the side of the train, and grabbed Rusty.

Up ahead was the Salem, Oregon, train depot. It was a stately structure made of cream-colored brick with tall Ionic columns framing arched windows. He hid behind a freight shed; nearby was a handcar on the side track.

As the freight train pulled out of the depot, Scruffy decided he'd had enough of freight cars. The ride from Fairbanks had been a long, miserable journey with numerous stops along the way. Scruffy had mostly ridden by himself, a few 'bos here and there, but it had been an uncomfortable ride involving sleeping on hard floors and eating pemmican day after day. It had taken ten days to get this far, and another ride in a desolate boxcar was not in Scruffy's plans.

He had a general idea of ending up somewhere in Southern California. The warm weather and the fact that he had never spent any time there was a good enough reason.

It was early morning, and there seemed to be no one around. There was not a soul on the depot platform or a yardman about.

"Let's have ourselves an adventure, Wonder Dog," Scruffy said as he headed over to the handcar.

He tossed his knapsack and sleeping bag on the floor, put Rusty in the front, and got behind the pump lever. Scruffy had never ridden a handcar, though as a boy he had seen railroad workers in Yakima riding by on one. He pushed down on the seesaw-like hand pump, and the car moved forward. He put his foot on the wooden brake shoe to stop it and then pulled up on the hand pump, moving it in reverse.

Scruffy looked around, saw no one, and pushed down on the lever. The car moved off the side track and onto the main line, heading south.

A mile clear of the station, Scruffy had the hang of it. *Use a little effort, but let the momentum of the handcar do most of the work.* Rusty was sitting proudly up front like a doggy hood ornament. "Better than riding with your head out the window, Wonder Dog," Scruffy said.

Rusty looked back and threw Scruffy a toothy Wonder Dog grin.

A couple of hours into the journey, the faint sound of a train whistle followed by a plume of smoke in the distance drew Scruffy's attention. He hit the foot brake. At the rear of the handcar, he lifted the two back wheels off the tracks and then did the same for the front end. He pushed the handcar off to the side and into the cover of scrub trees.

A few minutes later, a passenger train came clickety-clacking down the tracks, whizzing by like a blast of wind. Scruffy was sitting on a stump, Rusty at his side.

Scruffy dug into his knapsack and pulled out his last pemmican patty. He tore off a piece and offered it to Rusty, who sniffed, gave Scruffy a look that said, *Again?* and turned away.

Rusty had all sorts of looks he gave to Scruffy. It was as if he spoke a silent language. He had revealed a new one after Scruffy had done the deed with Marne. As soon as Scruffy got off the bed and began to put his clothes back on, Rusty hopped up onto the foot of the bed, sniffing the tangled rat's nest of sheets. He then looked at his master, mouth closed, his good eye with a questioning look that could only be described as disappointment.

Scruffy was not proud of the manner in which he had forced Marne into sex, but the guilt no longer gripped him as it had immediately afterward, and he was not going to lose any sleep over it. He had decided that she was a manipulator of men—a wily, cagey young woman who had her own self-interest front and center. It was not that he blamed her, but he was damned if he was going to feel any more shame about it. Besides, the completion of the deed had freed Scruffy from whatever hold she had on him, as though a valve had been released that had put a halt to his pining for her so. And by golly, once they got into it, she had enjoyed the encounter as much as he had; though the moment it was over, she reverted to being the calculating femme fatale.

Scruffy ate half the pemmican and offered it back to his dog. "Come on, Rusty, you need to eat," he said.

Rusty took a nibble and then another.

"I will find us some new vittles, old dog, don't worry," Scruffy said as he stood and began rolling the handcar back toward the tracks.

Rolling down the rails on a handcar provided a sense of freedom that Scruffy found exhilarating. And so did Rusty, who sat proudly erect up front, watching the world go by. They passed a cemetery, the tombstones lined straight and true, the grass perfectly mowed and so very green. Down a ways lay a field of stubble, followed by a vineyard, the vines wrapped around the rows of posts, which made Scruffy think of his years in the orchards in Yakima.

They were rolling right along, probably going a good ten miles per hour, when they came to a gradient that took work to get up. But Scruffy liked the challenge of it, liked the physical exertion, and when they reached the crest and then had a gentle slope downward, they picked up speed, hitting close to fifteen miles per hour. This was fun. This was an adventure.

In the late morning, Scruffy spied a large sign on the side of the tracks that read, "Southern Pacific Railroad, Eugene-Springfield, Oregon, Depot." Up ahead was a low horizontal red brick building with eave overhangs, tall double-hung windows, and dormers. It was not as grandiose as the depot in Salem, but it was a fine-looking utilitarian structure.

Scruffy pushed the handcar off the tracks. There were no obvious hiding spots, the land clear of any sizable foliage. But he did spot a small brick shed with a gravel road leading to the depot. There were empty crates stacked on the side of the shed. He hid the handcar and his sleeping bag behind the crates and headed toward the depot.

The depot was quiet. A few folks waiting on benches with suitcases were nearby. Since Scruffy had departed Big Bear, he'd had limited contact with people other than inside a boxcar. The depot seemed a bit strange to him, as did the looks he received from people that he passed by.

He lifted his arm and took a whiff of his armpit. *Good Lord!* He stunk to high heaven. He took a train schedule at the ticket counter and headed outside. He was going to ask for directions to town but decided against it, smelling as foul as he did. Scruffy had a change of clothes and a bar of lye soap in his knapsack. All he needed was to find water.

Past a small parking area, Scruffy headed out on to a two-lane road that led into a quiet tree-lined neighborhood. Two blocks into the walk, he came to a stone church with a steeple, and next to the church was red brick parsonage with a gambrel roof. Along the side of the church was a picket-fenced yard with picnic tables, benches, and a gathering of people having a picnic of some sort. The men were dressed in clothing ranging from suits and ties to what looked like hand-me-downs. The women were in dresses or skirts, but some had the look of poverty about them—the shoulders a tad stooped, the eyes with a what-in-the-world-happened look. But they all seemed like decent, God-fearing folk. One of the men, dressed in a cardigan sweater and trousers with a crease down the middle, waved hello to Scruffy as he approached.

Scruffy, with knapsack strapped over his shoulders, waved back and said, "Good day to you."

"New to town?" the man inquired.

"Yes sir," Scruffy said as he stopped. "By any chance is there a YMCA nearby?"

The man, standing at a gate to the fence, said, "It is a good long ways across town from here." The man was in his late forties. He was a big, sturdy fellow with a thick neck and big shoulders, steel-gray hair that was parted on one side, and a confident air about him.

"How about you and your little friend there"—the man slanted a look at Rusty—"come join us for potluck supper." He opened the gate and offered his hand to the picnic.

Scruffy hesitated.

"What do you say?" the man said.

"Truth is, I have been traveling for days and haven't had a chance to clean myself up."

The man waved off any notion of such a thought. "Ha. The meal is for those less fortunate during these difficult times. Some folks in attendance have not bathed for days."

"Well then," Scruffy said with a lift in his voice, "I accept." He stepped over to the open gate and held out his hand, which the man shook. "Scruffy Lomax here."

"Hello, Scruffy," the man replied. "Tom Wilson—or Reverend Wilson, as most folks call me."

The food was spread on two tables, and the reverend told Scruffy to head on over. There were baked beans and franks, hamburgers, potato salad, and pies and cupcakes galore. Scruffy filled his plate and sat at one of the picnic tables with a young family with three boys from around three to six in ages. There was a desperate edge to the parents, who sat silently eating.

Scruffy waited to get the eye of the young man who looked no more than twenty-five—but a hard, been-through-the-wringer twenty-five—with dark circles under his eyes and a general weariness that gripped his expression.

"Good day to you," Scruffy said.

The man grimaced a hello.

The three boys, who sat alongside Scruffy, began quibbling over one boy sticking his fork in the other boy's food. Their father told them to hold their tongues and eat. His voice had a defeated tone to it.

The man had the build of someone familiar with hard work. His physique was lean, and even in a flannel shirt that was two sizes too big, Scruffy sensed that under the clothes there was a restless muscular energy in need of physical labor.

Scruffy dug into his food, which tasted delicious: the beans hot and spicy, the frankfurter savory and oh, so good. Scruffy held Rusty in his lap and fed him a bit of burger, which drew the attention of the oldest boy next to Scruffy.

"Your dog eats people food?" the boy asked.

"Boy," his mother said in a voice that told him to be quiet.

"Like me, when we can," Scruffy said as he nodded hello to the mother.

She sort of smiled, crinkling the corners of her lips. She was thin like her husband, with light brown hair that hung over her shoulders and slate-blue eyes that at one time may have been filled with wonder and joy but now had a look of one going through the motion of living.

Scruffy said to the boy, "His name is Rusty, the One-Eyed Wonder Dog."

The boy shot a furtive glance at his mother and then a big-eyed stare at Scruffy. "One eye?"

The boy shot another look at his mother, who was looking at Rusty as though trying to figure something out.

"Yes, the other is glass," Scruffy said. "He was like that when I found him."

"Where was that?"

"Big Bear, Alaska, son," Scruffy said with a look at the father, who, like his wife, now had a look of interest.

Scruffy extended his hand to the man and introduced himself.

The man shook it with a strong, firm grip. "Brian Driscoll," he said, with a glimmer of interest. "Alaska, you say."

"Some good job opportunities in construction." Scruffy went on to tell about Kennabutte Mining needing carpenters "and anyone who is familiar with manual labor."

Brian introduced his wife, Agnes, and the three boys. He had been a logger, "And a good one at that," but he had not had any work in months. "There is a Resettlement Administration work camp being set up." Brian went on to say he hoped to find work there. "Alaska sounds interesting," he said evenly, "but not practical for a family with little."

Later on, when most of the people had left—but not before everyone pitched in and helped with the cleanup—the reverend came up to Scruffy, who was getting ready to head out.

"How about a hot shower before you depart," the reverend said.

"Yes sir, I would like that."

The reverend lifted his hand to the parsonage. "Outdoor shower on the far side."

The hot shower was a most wonderful treat, and the reverend even provided a complete change of clothes: a denim shirt, a rugged pair of tan dungarees, socks, and an undershirt. And to Scruffy's surprise, the clothes fit. It turned out the clothes had belonged to the reverend's son, who was attending seminary school back east.

The reverend also told him of a country store not too far away where Scruffy could buy supplies. "If you have the funds," the reverend added.

Scruffy was fortunate to have a good bit of money saved from his years working and living on the skimp. Here he was as free as a bird, with money saved, while folks like Brian Driscoll and his family and so many others had no idea where their next meal would come from.

It was midafternoon by the time Scruffy got back to the handcar stashed at the brick shed. He looked up and down the tracks—all clear—and lifted the handcar back onto the tracks, placed his sleeping bag and knapsack full of dry goods and canned goods on the platform, and off he and Wonder Dog went.

CHAPTER 42

B Y THE TIME SCRUFFY CAME to a sign that read "Klamath Falls, five miles," he had been pumping the handcar for three days. It had been a memorable journey so far, and with more to come. He had ridden through the heart of the Willamette Valley—a gorgeous land of fir and pine trees, fertile farmland, and breathtaking views along the Pacific Coast—before veering inland. He was not sure he was taking the most direct route to California, but there was no hurry.

Oregon was a neighbor of his home state, but in this short time, Scruffy had seen more of Oregon than Washington.

He had spent his first night of his handcar journey sleeping along the banks of a lake the name of which he did not know. But after working the pump lever all day, sleep came fast and was sound as he nestled in his sleeping bag.

The second morning, it rained, and after an hour of pumping in a downpour, Scruffy stopped and found shelter in maintenance shed that stored railroad ties, fasteners, and various tools—all to repair a railroad track. After a couple of hours and a change of clothes, the rain let up.

Back on the rails, Scruffy rode into a pine forest with a pristine lake, its water a rich, dark blue. Then he rode past a farm with a freshly painted bright red barn and a white farmhouse. A farmer on a tractor waved to Scruffy, who waved back. "Good day to you!" Scruffy shouted.

His second night, he had slept in a barn less than a quarter mile from the railroad. The barn was on an abandoned farm. The house had burned down, and all that remained were scorched timbers and ashes. It was like sleeping in a ghost town, but hay in the loft provided a soft bed and another sound sleep.

On day three, Scruffy fell into a comfortable rhythm of pumping and taking in the scenery: the green timberland, a farm every now and then, and the occasional flatbed truck with migrant workers in the back sputtering along a dirt road running parallel to the tracks.

The blast of a train whistle startled Scruffy. Less than a couple hundred yards straight ahead, barreling down the tracks, was a freight train.

Scruffy hit the brakes, lifted the back end and then the front end, and pushed the handcar off the tracks. No less than ten seconds later, the coal-black locomotive rumbled by, shaking the ground on which Scruffy stood.

The engineer stuck his head out the window of the locomotive and gave Scruffy a long, disapproving look.

Scruffy decided that when he got to Klamath Falls, it was time to get off the rails and find another way to get to Southern California.

CHAPTER 43

Klamath Falls, Oregon was a fine-looking town situated on Upper Klamath Lake, though it was a bit rural, with dirt streets leading into and out of town, and a church service being held in a large open-air tent. Giving it a cozy feel were the nearby volcanic mountains. Scruffy had learned this from a visitor's guide he picked up at the chamber of commerce.

Riding on the handcar for three days had made Scruffy want to get out and about, walking here and there around Klamath Falls, stretching his legs and resting his arms, which were tuckered out from pumping.

At one end of town, Scruffy came upon a group of men unloading a stake truck with "Civilian Conservation Corp" written in green letters on the side panel of the cab. They were a rough-looking lot that reminded Scruffy of the miners working for Kennabutte Mining back in Big Bear. The men, dressed in raggedy clothes, had going-through-the-motions expressions planted on their grizzled faces as they headed toward a row of small cabins in an alleyway.

Back in town, Scruffy walked up Main Street, which was lined with masonry buildings two and three stories high, some with columns, arches, and lintels; others were utilitarian horizontal boxes. On the corner of Main and Second Streets, Scruffy spotted across the street what he had been looking for. "There we go, Wonder Dog," Scruffy said as he stepped off the boardwalk. His eyes honed in on the words "Houlihan's Tavern" scrolled over the front door of a one-story brick structure that was nestled between the Pennywise Five and Dime and the Hotel Earley.

Scruffy picked up Rusty and pulled open the heavy wood-planked door with "Jack Houlihan, Proprietor" engraved on a steel plate over a porthole window. A long bar was situated in the back, and tables and booths in the front area. Heavy wood beams ran across the ceiling, from which hung hanging lantern lamps. The place was dimly lit, but like the town, it had a cozy feel. There were groups of men at the bar. Scruffy placed Rusty atop the bar, pulled up a stool, and sat.

The bartender came over and said, "No pets, friend." His voice had an edge to it.

"That so," Scruffy said as easy as you please.

The barman, a tall and big-boned fellow with a high forehead and a strong jaw, had a scar running down his left cheek that was partially covered by muttonchops. He put both hands on the bar and leaned forward. "You will get no service while that mangy mutt is on the premises."

"What if I told you this is no ordinary dog?" Scruffy asked.

A man sitting on a stool one seat over said, "Let me guess, I bet that there is a talking dog."

Scruffy slid a look over at a man dressed in a flannel shirt and bib overalls. "That and then some," he said.

"Look," the bartender said, "I don't care if he can recite Lincoln's Gettysburg Address, you are not—"

"I know," Scruffy said with a lift of his hand. "But have you ever had a talking dog who could raise a shot glass of sarsaparilla and down it in one fell swoop?" Scruffy stood and looked around the bar for encouragement.

"Do not make me come out from—"

"Hold on there, Lawrence," said a burly man sitting at the end of the bar, dressed in a dark suit with a bolo tie. He spoke with a heavy Irish brogue.

Scruffy figured this was Mr. Houlihan.

The Irishman came over to Scruffy. "Jack Houlihan, here, lad," he said with hand extended.

Scruffy shook and said, "Scruffy Lomax is what I go by." He gestured to his dog, who was still sitting on the bar, looking straight at Houlihan with his good eye. "This here is Rusty, the One-Eyed Wonder Dog."

"You a betting man, Mr. Lomax?" Houlihan said through a sly smile, his light blue eyes dancing with mischief.

"What do you propose?"

"If your wonder dog can throw down a shot and then say 'Houlihan's Tavern'—not some barking nonsense that is not understood—drinks on the house for the next hour."

The bar erupted in a mug-clattering cheer from the patrons, who were coming over to witness.

Houlihan raised his hand, his devilish eyes looking around as though he were savoring the moment. "But if he ... it is a he?" he said. Scruffy nodded. "If he does not, you pay me five bucks, and you and your little companion leave my fine establishment."

Scruffy pointed at the barkeep. "Lawrence, a shot of sarsaparilla and tall draft, if you please."

Lawrence looked at Houlihan, who nodded.

Lawrence put the drinks on the bar, and Scruffy grabbed his draft and took a long, thirsty swallow, downing the contents. "Ah," he said. "That is what I am talking about."

"I believe Mr. Lomax must have some Hibernian blood coursing his veins," Houlihan said with a nod of approval.

Scruffy threw a wink at Houlihan. "Just might be," he said through a mischievous grin. He then turned his attention to Rusty, whispering in his ear. He leaned back from his dog and said, "Understood, Wonder Dog?"

Rusty gave his master a pronounced wink and sat on his haunches, cradling the shot glass in his paws. He lifted it deftly to his mouth and downed it in a quick throwback.

The patrons, standing behind Scruffy three rows deep, let out a beer-thirsty roar of approval.

"Very fine," Houlihan said, "but now comes the difficult task of a dog speaking English." He crossed his arms across his barrel chest, his eyes on Rusty.

Rusty wheeled around, still on his haunches, which brought a gasp from the crowd, and faced Houlihan. Rusty whimpered as though clearing his throat and then let out, in a garbled, whiny, growly voice, "Hool ... la ... hens Ta ... vern."

The bar exploded in an uproar not only because of the free drinks but also at having witnessed a real, live talking dog.

Houlihan raised his arms for silence. After the bar had died down, he said in a ringing voice, "Lawrence … Cold pints all around … and then another … and another …"

Houlihan went around the bar, talking to one and all about what they had witnessed. "Saints be with me," he said to one group, "If I live to be one hundred years, I will never witness the likes of what took place this evening." He raised a hand toward his barkeep. "Lawrence, another round, if you please."

It was a merry old time, with Houlihan telling stories about his upbringing in Ireland. "Drank me first pint at ten and me first whiskey at twelve. Poor as we were, me and my lads ran the streets and alleys in dear old Dublin as though we owned them."

In the midst of this clamorous occasion, Jack Houlihan placed his hand on Scruffy's shoulder, his eyes shining on Rusty. "Mr. Lomax, as you and your Wonder Dog here"—he petted Rusty on the neck—"are me honored guests for this evening, might I entertain you with a song from the old sod?"

"By all means," Scruffy said.

"Lawrence McDonald," Houlihan said with a grand sweep of his hand, as though introducing an act, "grab ye Scottish fiddle, laddie buck."

The barkeep went to a door in the back and reemerged with a bow and a shiny dark-grained instrument that appeared out of place in this rough-hewn tavern of rough-hewn clientele.

Lawrence, his expression no longer that of a tough barman and bouncer, appeared busy in thought as though composing a musical score in his head as he went back behind the bar. He set his instrument on the bar, filled three pitchers with beer, and placed one at each end of the bar and one in front of Scruffy.

The barkeeper lifted his fiddle, his left hand on the neck, his right holding the bow, and tucked the body of the instrument into his shoulder as he rested his chin on the lower side of the body. He looked at his boss, his eyes saying, "Ready."

Houlihan raised his hand. "Lads," he said in a strong yet tender voice, "if I might have a modicum of silence."

The voices died down, and all eyes turned to the Irishman.

> I am a rambling Irishman
> In Ulster I was born and
> Many is the pleasant day I spent
> 'Round the shores of sweet Loch Erne
> But to be poor I could not endure
> Like others of my station
> To Amerikay I sailed away
> And left this Irish nation

Every man in the tavern turned in upon himself as they listened with rapt attention. There was something liltingly musical in Jack Houlihan's voice, but it also held a deep melodious quality with trilling peaks and valleys. He raised and lowered his register with effortless grace.

> Rantin-de-na, tan-tin-de-na
> Right antin-de-na in denandy
> Rantin-de-na, tan-tin-de-na
> Right antin-de-na in denandy ...

It was joyful and heart-wrenching as Scruffy absorbed not only the music but also the words, which seemed so appropriate for his life.

> The night before he went away
> I spent it with my darling
> Three o'clock in the afternoon
> 'Til the break of day next morning
> But when that we were going to part
> We lay in each other's arms
> And you may be sure and very sure
> It wounded both our charms

A respectful silence greeted the end of the song before Scruffy began to clap and the rest followed. Every man's hand struck the other, with nary a word said.

After the free pints had ended, most of the bar cleared, save some late arrivers Scruffy had seen unload from the Civilian Conservation Corp stake truck. They had cleaned themselves up, freshly scrubbed, though still there remained an edge of hostility about this group of men. They had arrived in two separate groups of four, and each group sat at the far end of the bar from the other.

Lawrence served each group. In one, each man ordered a shot of whiskey and beer, the other group just beer. And with the departure of the men who had basked in the free beer and music and the arrival of these others, the spirited mood inside the tavern died.

Houlihan pulled up a stool next to Scruffy and sat. He tilted his head toward one end of the bar and then the other. "We are in the midst of the unhappys," he said to Scruffy.

Scruffy mentioned he had seen them earlier.

"We have unhappys from Ohio," Houlihan said with a look left, "and unhappys from Kentucky, who prefer a shot of whiskey with their mug," he said with a glance to his right.

Jack went on to say that times had gotten tough for the farmers around these parts. "A plague of army worms and grasshoppers come through a couple of years back and wiped out a swath of crops."

"I have seen tough times all over this country," Scruffy said.

"Yeah, lad," Jack said. "But the locals do not appreciate the government shipping a labor force across the country to take jobs that they could use." He waved his hand as if to say, *Enough.* "Tell me about yourself, Scruffy Lomax."

Scruffy told of his life since leaving Yakima, without getting into the personal matters. He presented himself as a vagabond wanderer.

"Ah," Jack said. "You sound like an Irish traveler." He gestured to Lawrence for another round. "I was a roamer in the old country, wandering hill and dale. Never settling, always moving on."

"How did you end up in America?" Scruffy asked as he cradled his freshly poured mug.

"Let's say ..." Jack said with a remembering look, "that I got into a bit of mess that only the separation of an ocean could satisfy."

The two men stayed after hours, with Lawrence joining them. Jack sang a few more songs, accompanied by Lawrence on the fiddle.

Over the course of the evening, Scruffy mentioned he had worked as line cook in New Orleans, and Jack offered him a job. "I only serve cold sandwiches and hard-boiled eggs that I make meself, but if you are willing, I have room for a galley kitchen in the back." He leaned over on his stool, pressing his shoulder into Scruffy's. "I think we might make a fine team together, Scruffy Lomax."

But Scruffy declined. "Thank you, no, Jack." He looked at Rusty lying atop the bar, head on paws. "Me and old Rusty have us some more places to go, places to see."

"Cannot blame you any, lad," Jack said through a rueful grin. "There is an old Irish blessing that seems appropriate for Scruffy Lomax and his Wonder Dog: 'May the road rise to meet you, and the wind always be at your back.'" He lifted his finger with a twirl of dramatic flair. "'And may the sun shine warm on your face.'"

CHAPTER 44

AFTER SPENDING THE NIGHT ON a cot in a storage room at Houlihan's, Scruffy woke early a tad hungover but looking forward to meandering his way down to Southern California.

On the outskirts of town, he came to a paved road with a sign indicating that the California border was twenty-five miles away. He went to the side of the road and waited. "We're gonna hitchhike, Rusty," Scruffy said with a glance down at his dog, who had a squinty, unsure look in regard to this new mode of transportation.

Ten minutes later, a Mack truck approached carrying an open trailer of timber logs. Scruffy stuck out his thumb. The truck passed but came to a screeching halt. Scruffy picked up Rusty and ran up to the driver's side of the cab. "Heading south, are you?" Scruffy said, looking up at the driver.

"Scruffy Lomax," the driver said through a big grin, "and his Wonder Dog."

"Yes," Scruffy said, "you were at Houlihan's last night."

The driver directed Scruffy around to the passenger side. He stowed his gear in a spacious area behind the seats, put Rusty on the front seat, and climbed up.

"That was some performance last night," the driver said, shining a smile down on Rusty as he accelerated back onto the road.

"An all-around fine evening," Scruffy said.

After introducing himself, the driver told Scruffy that last night, "was a welcome relief from all the hard times." He went on to say that he was delivering his load of lumber to "Crescent City, Cal-i-for-i-aye." He threw a look at Scruffy. "Does that suit you?"

Scruffy was not sure where Crescent City was, but he said, "Yes sir, much appreciate the ride."

It was a scenic trip through small towns and open farmland by way of a new mode of transportation, a safer and more comfortable means of travel, and with a wide-open view of mountains in the distance, farmland dotting the landscape, forests, rivers, and lakes. It was beautiful country.

They stopped once for fuel and sandwiches at a country store, somewhere across the California border. If the place had a name, there was nothing to indicate such. This land was nearly as rural as Alaska.

When they arrived at a lumber yard a few miles north of Crescent City, the driver asked Scruffy where he was heading.

"Southern California," he replied.

The driver gave him directions to a spot less than a mile away where Scruffy would have the best chance to hitch a ride down the coast. "Not only the best route," the driver said, "but the prettiest ride you will ever experience."

The trucker had been right about the breathtaking views. Scruffy had hitched his way through a Redwood forest, the awesome size of the trees bigger than he could have imagined. He spent a night on a beach in Big Sur, a rugged, untamed area that combined rocky cliffs overlooking the Pacific Ocean and hills teeming with trees.

But prior to the breathtaking views, Scruffy had seen the underbelly of the Great Depression. Outside Oakland, he passed by people living in concrete sewer pipes stored above ground. It was like a small village of concrete tubular homes, the people all bearing defeated, desperate looks, the stunned children in rags, some of them barefoot.

Somewhere inland, while riding in the back of a flatbed truck, he passed a ramshackle encampment of tents where people were sitting and standing in clusters as though waiting for something, anything, to happen.

Scruffy realized his good fortune at traveling through these terrible times yet not personally experiencing them. Or perhaps it was that he was more adaptable to living outdoors, sleeping in the woods or on a beach, and thinking nothing of it. He had been hungry in this life, but it had never gotten him down. He had an inner belief in his ability to see any challenge through.

On the afternoon of his third day hitchhiking, Scruffy was dropped off in San Jose by a man driving a Buick convertible who said he acted in silent movies. "But my voice is not suited for talkies," he stated. Scruffy found this plausible, since the man had the glamorous look of a screen star: broad shoulders, cleft chin, and handsomely chiseled face. But his voice belied the face: squeaky and with a trace of a foreign accent, possibly German.

San José was a fine-looking town with a Spanish flair full of colorful abode buildings with scalloped roofs, but Scruffy had an urge to go farther south. Why this was he was not sure, but he did not question it.

On the side of US Route 101, Scruffy waited over an hour before he finally caught a ride from a trucker hauling material to build a set for Warner Brothers Studios in Burbank, California. While in New Orleans, Scruffy had attended a Marx Brothers movie, and he thought it not only entertaining but also bigger than life. Burbank, California, had a good ring to it.

When they entered the city limits of Burbank, Scruffy asked whether he could help unload the truck, and his offer was gladly accepted. They rode through the entrance of Warner Brothers Studio, where a uniformed guard stationed at a guardhouse waved them through.

The studio lot had hangar-like buildings dotting the vast space. People in various costumes were walking about: a cowboy leading a saddled horse, an Indian chief in a headdress, a beautiful blonde in a low-cut cocktail dress, her breasts nearly spilling out.

There were also workmen pushing carts of braced plywood painted with background scenery of a mesa with flat-topped buttes, and others with a lake surrounded by woodlands. It was like a small city of activity. The people were animated, which was so different from the defeated demeanors he had seen and encountered on his journey there.

The trucker backed up to a loading dock, with Scruffy guiding him right up, where a man holding a clipboard was waiting.

"You were supposed to be here two hours ago," the clipboard holder shouted in an aggravated voice to Scruffy.

"I got help, Nate," the trucker said as he unlatched the rear door of the trailer and opened it. "We'll get it unloaded right quick."

The inside was packed with crates that looked heavy and difficult to move. "We need a hand truck," Scruffy said, looking directly at Nate. "Two if possible."

The trucker and Scruffy began unloading the contents, whizzing in and out of the trailer and pushing the heavy crates where Nate directed.

When they finished, the driver had Nate sign an invoice and then said to Scruffy, "Thank you for your help."

Nate heard this and said to Scruffy, "I could use a quick-thinking, hardworking grip." He lifted his brow as though to gauge Scruffy's interest.

Scruffy was not sure what a grip was, but he figured it involved manual labor. "I accept," he said with a lift of finger. He went to the cab and grabbed Rusty. "As long as my dog, Rusty, can come with me each day."

"Ha! That is not a problem," Nate said. "This is the studio that made Rin Tin Tin a household name."

CHAPTER 45

T WO MONTHS INTO HIS JOB as a grip—which, as suspected, involved manual labor on the set—life at the studio was going just fine for Scruffy, as well as for Rusty. They showed up each morning at the guardhouse, and Scruffy flashed an ID card at the guard, walked over to the back lot, and met his team of grips. Nate, who was the construction coordinator, would give them their duties for the day. They worked long hours, and Scruffy only had Sundays off so far—not that he was complaining; the money was good.

He was renting a room at a boarding house two blocks from Warner Brothers, and near his living quarters was Dino's Bar and Grill, a seedy, run-down joint that had cheap drinks and decent food.

Scruffy's team was finishing up the background set for *Captain Blood*, a costume period pirate adventure. They had already assembled a huge water tank to represent the ocean, a West Indies beach complete with sand and artificial palm trees, and the exterior and interior sections of a three-mast Spanish man-o'-war. The crew consisted of seven men of various ages and backgrounds. All were glad to have the work, and all seemed to enjoy working in the land of make-believe.

Scruffy had heard that rehearsals had already begun, and there was a rumor floating around the lot that Warner Brothers had invested over a million dollars, and the two leads were a pair of relative unknowns: Errol Flynn and Olivia de Havilland.

Scruffy had yet to see any of the actors for this movie, but once they had completed all the sets, Nate said to him, "The director wants a competent grip during filming, and I have assigned you, Scruffy." Nate shrugged and splayed his hands out to his sides. "Not sure about Wonder Dog on the set, but this is an opportunity you do not want to pass up."

Rusty had fit right into the daily routine around the studio. He would sit nearby, watching, and he would follow when they went about the lot collecting or unloading materials needed. One of the guards even presented Scruffy with a dog collar that had on it a Warner Brothers ID tag. It was like being part of a family—a big go-with-the-flow family.

On the first day of filming, Scruffy reported to Sound Stage A at six in the morning to find a small crane, the top of the mast nearly touching the cavernous ceiling. He was early, but Scruffy wanted to get a feel for the environment he would be working in. The stage was set in the motif of a Jamaican town square with grass huts and shanties.

Scruffy had asked around the studio about the two stars, Errol Flynn and Olivia de Havilland, and had learned that they were both big dog lovers. The director was Michael Curtiz, who was Hungarian and was considered an innovative master of unusual camera angles and positions. Scruffy could find nothing out about the director's like or dislike of dogs, but word around the studio was that he was a decent enough fellow, though very passionate about his work.

Soon the set was alive with technicians, cameramen, production staff, and a man in a beige suit with a silk scarf around his neck that swept off his shoulder. There was something foreign in his appearance: the face above the scarf was quick and aware, as though busy with newfound ideas; the striking planes of his ruddy cheeks, long and smooth, brought to mind European aristocracy; and his concentrated look took in his surroundings as one in charge would be expected to do. *This must be Michael Curtiz, the director.*

"Vincent," the director said in a precise and somewhat musical tone, "Do we have an operator for the crane? And where are the three-strip cameras I was promised? He was speaking to a cluster of staff huddled in a corner.

A man emerged holding a clipboard and walked over. "Yes, Mr. Curtiz," he said.

As Scruffy was wondering what he was supposed to do, the director lifted his hand in an impatient manner and said, "I need coffee. Now."

Scruffy made a beeline to the coffee table. He poured a cup, put it on a saucer, and placed the drink on a tray, accompanied by a container of cream and sugar.

He walked directly over to the director and said, "Sir, your coffee."

The director, deep in conversation with Vincent, focused in on Scruffy. "Ah," he said, as he looked over the tray. He took the cup off the saucer and took a sip. He nodded his approval at Scruffy. "You are?"

"Scruffy Lomax, Mr. Curtiz. Nate assigned me as your personal grip."

Curtiz nodded again, this time indicating *that is all*. He then returned to his conversation.

Scruffy's old grip team showed up and began moving props under the direction of one of the production staff, which consisted of men with titles such as "production assistant," or "PA"; "production manager"; "assistant production manager"; "unit manager"; and many more. It was a wonder they all kept their duties straight. Nate had told Scruffy that his job was to stand by for specific orders from the director or "Uppity-ups." "You are not to get lost in the scrum of grip work."

And so he stood by, off to the side, with Rusty sitting at his side, no one yet having commented on Wonder Dog.

After the grips had set up a raised platform with steps in the middle of the realistic-looking Jamaican huts and shanties, a young man and very young woman walked over to Mr. Curtiz. They were both stunningly attractive. The woman wore a costume period long dress with lace and ruffled sleeves; and the man, buckled boots and high stockings, and a long jacket with a satchel across his shoulder. His hair was nearly down to his shoulders, and Scruffy wondered whether it was not a wig.

This handsome man had a certain look about him—a derring-do look of one who had already led a life filled with romantic adventure.

Vincent came over to Scruffy and said, "Mr. Flynn would like a coffee with a splash of cream, and Miss de Havilland, cream and sugar."

Scruffy filled a tray with the order and went over to the two stars sitting in high-back canvas chairs with their names scrolled across the backs.

Flynn flashed a smile at Scruffy that was the most charming of smiles, his teeth deepwater gems gleaming under a pencil mustache which he ran his finger over as he said, "Which is cream and sugar?"

The one on my left," Scruffy said as he held the tray.

Flynn handed the cup to Miss de Havilland and took the other. He then looked down at Scruffy's side and shined a smile on Rusty. "Who is this adorable little creature?"

His voice held a hint of what Scruffy took to be a British accent. It sounded so very sophisticated and at the same time hail-fellow.

"That is Rusty, the One-Eyed Wonder Dog."

Flynn flashed another brilliant smile on Scruffy. "I believe we have a good luck charm in your Wonder Dog, Mr. ...?"

"Scruffy Lomax, here."

"Of course you are," Flynn said.

Scruffy's job turned out to be errand boy. If Errol Flynn needed something from his dressing room or if the director needed more copies of the script, Scruffy hustled over to the editing department across the lot. But much of the time, he stood by and watched, since it took time to set up the lighting to Mr. Curtiz's specifications.

The director was extremely particular about how the light shone on his leading actors. "First shot of Errol, I want figure lighting with key light away from the camera ... fill light opposite the key light ... backlight from overhead. Understood?"

People would scurry about the set, adjusting tripod floor lamps and adjusting levers connected to the overhead lights.

By late afternoon, they were finishing up filming a scene in which Errol Flynn's character, Peter Blood, was auctioned off as a slave and purchased by Olivia de Havilland's character, Arabella Bishop.

Both, in Scruffy's opinion, were going to be stars—especially Errol Flynn. He had a certain insouciant charm that was infectious.

Olivia had more of a confident low-key poise that combined with her wholesome beauty. She was the girl next door, but next door in a very expensive neighborhood.

During the many halts in filming, as lights were constantly rearranged or Mr. Curtiz wanted a change in the dialogue, there seemed to be a silent attraction between the leading man and woman: a shy smile of admiration at Errol from Olivia, a glint of acceptance from him with a noble lift of the brow.

When finally the last "Cut" for the day had been announced, Scruffy decided to head over to Dino's Bar and Grill for a couple of cold brews and a hamburger.

Past the entrance gate to the studio, Scruffy turned right and headed west, the sun sinking below the golden hills lining the horizon in the distance. It was late October, and the temperature was mild, just as it had been every day he had been living here. The weather was predictably perfect, with little rain. One of his fellow grips had told Scruffy that living in Southern California was a dream life, if your idea of a dream was every day being the same.

Scruffy had decided that as long as he was employed at Warner Brothers or anywhere else in these parts, he would ride out the Great Depression right here. He had seen enough of the hardship and poverty many of his fellow Americans were enduring. There was a sense of family in this make-believe world of film teeming with artistic people, including actors, movie staff, and designers of costumes and sets. Warner Brothers Studio had a creative energy that was infectious and stimulating.

Scruffy also needed a rest. Ever since he had departed Yakima as a seventeen-year-old boy, he had been living a hard physical and mental existence. It was as though his thirty-year-old body and mind were telling him to hold up for a while and take it easy.

It had been some journey to this point: riding the rails across the USA, meeting people—good and bad—and visiting places like Big Bear, Chicago, Florida, New Orleans, and Yelapa. He tried not to think much about his time south of the border—about the woman he had married and loved, the son he almost had, the life he had almost lived. No, it was something he stored in the back recesses of his mind as he pushed forward in this life that he was cutting out for himself—this life in which he never knew who or what was around the corner.

CHAPTER 46

THREE WEEKS INTO FILMING *CAPTAIN Blood*, Scruffy had developed an appreciation for the craft of filmmaking and the unique characteristics of the Hollywood folk he worked with. It was so different from any other line of work. Making a movie was a slow process compounded by Mr. Curtiz's Hungarian accent. He once stated, "Wery nice, but I want poodle in this scene."

The prop master had looked at Rusty, but the director shouted, "No, I said poodle." A few minutes later, Curtiz was called out to see a standard poodle. "Vat do I vant with this goddamn dog?" he screamed.

"You said you wanted a poodle, Mr. Curtiz," the prop master replied.

"No," Curtiz said, "I vant a poodle of water!"

The entire set broke up in an uproar of laughter, including a chagrined Mr. Michael Curtiz, a man who wore his heart on his sleeve and whose bark was much worse than his bite.

Also eating up precious time, since each day of production was expensive, were meetings between the director and his staff, and discussions between the director and individual actors as to how he wanted a given scene played.

And when they did film, there were many takes and retakes before a final "Cut, print" as Mr. Curtiz explained, "Show your displeasure in your eyes, Errol, your eyes," or "Olivia, my dear, I vant you to freeze in terror—freeeeze."

At last, after over two months, Scruffy came to work for the final day of filming *Captain Blood*. It took three hours to get all the props exactly how Mr. Curtiz wanted them. After many takes of Errol sitting at a desk, covering his face in his hands, he looked up and said, "Good morning, Uncle."

Mr. Curtiz got up from his chair and looked around the set, a sly grin forming at the corners of his mouth. "Cut ... final print—It is a wrap." He then smiled a big beamer, and the set let out a great cheer.

Errol pulled his wig from his head and said, "Now we are about to have the best wrap party any of you have ever attended." He shot a glance at Mr. Curtiz. "Am I not correct, Michael?"

"Yes," Mr. Curtiz said with a shake of his fist. "The wery vest—at the Brown Derby, six tonight."

Scruffy had not been outside of Burbank since his arrival. He had been working nearly every day, and when he had a day off, he lazily spent it at Dino's. Now he had to find his way to a fancy restaurant somewhere in Los Angeles. And for the first time in his life, the need arose to buy clothes for the occasion. He had saved a tidy sum of money and decided that today he was going to splurge.

He asked one of the grips where he could buy nice clothes and requested directions to the Brown Derby, which was located seven or eight miles from the studio.

At the men's clothing store, less than a half mile from the studio, Scruffy tried on a pair of wing tip oxfords but decided they were not for him and settled on a pair of leather sandals, brown checkered woven trousers with a pleat down the center, and a floral yellow short-sleeve shirt with a pair of matching patch pockets, and he tied the entire ensemble together with red suspenders.

Back at his living quarters, Scruffy took a long hot shower, trimmed his thicket of hair with scissors, shaved his scant chin whiskers and peach fuzz above his upper lip, and got himself dressed in his new duds. He looked in the mirror hanging over his dresser and took in his new self.

"Not bad," he said aloud, "not bad at all." Before him was a lived-in face, weathered and yet robust, with symmetry in the lively blue eyes, strong nose, and prominent chin, the high cheeks flushed with color. It was a fine-looking face—not outrageously handsome like Errol Flynn's, but it would do.

Scruffy and Rusty headed back to the studio, where Scruffy flagged down a taxi—a first. He had thought about walking or figuring out where to catch the trolley but had decided that tonight was special.

When the taxi turned a corner and they came up Wilshire Boulevard, he spotted a dome structure with a steel frame supporting a giant version of a brown derby, its perimeter aglow, as was its name scrolled across the crown. In front of the restaurant, limousines were dropping people off, the men in expensive suits and the women in long gowns.

At the entrance, a well-groomed large dog with a long snout and long white hair was leashed to a railing and sitting on a blanket. Rusty exchanged sniffs with this elegant canine and returned to Scruffy's side.

Inside, a man dressed in a tuxedo was standing behind the reception stand. He eyed Rusty warily and said, "Sir, I am afraid dogs are not permitted." His accent was somewhat similar to Mr. Curtiz's, but he had more of a wheeze, as though he were speaking through his nose.

"My little dog and I were invited to the *Captain Blood* wrap party," Scruffy said as he offered a hand toward Rusty. "And both of us were on the set every day of filming."

The man had the look of composed satisfaction as though he handled problems such as this all the time. He lifted his shoulders and raised his hands, palms up. "Why, even Miss de Havilland knows to keep Borzoi outside on a leash." He lifted his brow, his eyes saying, "Are you with me?"

"Pierre, my so excellent maître d'." There stood the strapping Errol Flynn in all his swashbuckling glory, dressed in a black tuxedo. "Might we make an exception for this darling little dog? I will take full and complete responsibility."

Errol wrapped his arm over the maître d's shoulder. "What do you say, *mon ami?*"

Pierre glanced at Errol, who was smiling his most roguish of smiles, the gorgeous teeth seemingly glistening.

"Ah, for you, Mr. Flynn, but of course." He glanced down at Rusty and then lifted his gaze to Scruffy and, with a little forward movement of his fingers, ushered them in.

The Brown Derby had a comfortable elegance about it, much like Errol Flynn. There were waitresses scooting about dressed in short bell-shaped starched white skirts, every one of the young women beautiful—one of whom Scruffy had seen on the studio lot—and there were waiters in crisp tuxedos, confidently taking orders.

Situated around the perimeter of the space were semicircular brown leather banquettes, and against a back wall was a large fireplace, over which was a wooden mantel with old-fashioned pots and kettles. And the finishing touch was the caricatures of famous Hollywood folk taking up the walls.

Errol wrapped his arm around Scruffy's shoulder and leaned in to him. "So what do you think of my favorite watering hole?"

"It is the likes of which I have never seen," Scruffy said as Errol led him to the rear of the restaurant, his arm firmly gripping Scruffy's shoulder as though they were old mates, passing booths filled with crew members who all seemed to be having a grand time, laughing and talking over each other. "Scruffy," one of his fellow grips said in a slurred voice, "Looks like you got some catching up to do." He lifted a martini glass to Scruffy.

At the bar, Errol asked Scruffy what he was drinking.

"I would like a shot of whiskey, a draft beer, and a sarsaparilla for Wonder Dog."

Errol slid a look at Scruffy, his eyes shining his approval. "I like the way your mind works, Scruffy Lomax."

CHAPTER 47

AFTER A FEW ROUNDS OF drinks at the bar, Errol and Scruffy were each surprised to discover that the other had prospected for gold. "I sailed to New Guinea in 1927. Do you know of New Guinea, Scruffy?" Errol inquired.

"Yes, it is an island off Australia."

"Exactly," Errol said as he waved hello to a cast member. He went on to tell of finding no gold and getting terribly ill. "I returned to Australia and licked my wounds."

"You are Australian?" Scruffy said

"Yes, but the studio is passing me off as an Irishman with an English background." He threw down his whiskey, lifted his glass to the bartender and held it until he got his attention, and then said to Scruffy, "It is all a game, my friend, here in this pretend land."

Scruffy went on to tell Errol his most intimate life details, such as the marriage in Mexico and loss of wife and child that he had nearly abandoned, and his affair with Marne. He had never told anyone these sort of things, but Errol Flynn had a way about him that indicated he never passed judgment.

And Errol told Scruffy of being a thief as a youth. "I had to leave the country, for the authorities were after me, and I ended up in England. It appears we both have a bit of the rogue coursing our veins."

There was a long buffet table set up with an array of fancy food. One dish was a recipe from Mr. Curtiz's mother, Veal Paprika, which was the most delicious thing Scruffy had ever eaten.

After dinner, Mr. Curtiz asked for everyone's attention and gave a splendid speech that he ended by saying, "Human and fundamental problems of real people are the basis of all good drama." He raised a finger for emphasis. "And I believe that in *Captain Blood* we have made such a film."

After Mr. Curtiz's speech, the party really got going, with Errol hobnobbing his way around the restaurant, his charisma and good cheer lifting the spirit of the entire room. Scruffy thought it his best performance to date.

Past midnight, people began departing, and Errol returned to the bar. He patted Rusty on the neck. "Wonder Dog, how are tricks?"

Rusty sat up on his haunches, brought his front paws into his chest, and rotated around in a full circle. He then gave Errol an exaggerated wink of his glass eye.

"Ha ha ha!" Errol shouted gleefully. "By God, you *are* a wonder dog."

The night ended with Scruffy striking up a conversation with the waitress he had seen around the studio. Her name was Eva, and she was a gorgeous blonde with the physical assets necessary to be a starlet: a radiant face, generous breasts, and long, perfectly formed legs. She was from Des Moines and had studied theatre in high school. "And I decided to come out here and seek my fortune."

After a bit more chitchat, he asked her whether he could escort her home.

She gave him a quick up and down and said in a teasing tone, "Are you a gentleman?"

"Not if I can help it," Scruffy replied.

She smiled, revealing a row of teeth as white as ivory. "I was hoping that would be your reply," she said, her eyes glinting sexual hanky-panky.

They ended up taking a taxi back to Eva's place and sharing a night of wanton pleasure.

Scruffy saw Eva from time to time for a couple of months before she told him that she was heading back to Des Moines to get married.

"What—marriage? Des Moines?" Scruffy said as he lay in bed next to her, her head resting on his shoulder.

"My high school beau has inherited a tidy sum of money, and I have finally agreed to come home and marry him." She cocked her elbow, resting her chin in her palm, her tantalizing eyes on Scruffy. "Hollywood was something I needed to get out of my system. I never wanted to say what if.

Back at the studio, Scruffy worked with his team of grips for the next year, and then Mr. Curtiz requested him as errand boy for the filming of *The Charge of the Light Brigade*—a historical adventure set during the Crimean War, starring none other than Errol Flynn and Olivia de Havilland.

As Scruffy had predicted, Errol had become a huge star from his role as *Captain Blood*.

During the first day on the set, Errol greeted Scruffy like a long-lost friend, "Old chap, how has my fellow rogue been?"

Olivia, upon spotting Rusty, said, "Oh, what a pleasant surprise. My little wonder dog has returned." She patted her knees, and Rusty came scooting over and hopped right up on her lap.

There was another young and aspiring actor in the film, David Niven, who soon became fast friends with Errol. They were a pair together, laughing in soft voices as they hashed over some carousing escapade or another from the previous night.

Like Flynn, Niven had an upper-class manner, having all the charm and wiles of a man who had trained on the London stage.

During the last week of filming, Errol asked Scruffy if he had any experience as a bartender.

"Worked as a waiter in New Orleans and substituted for the bartender a couple of times—nothing to it," he said with a shrug.

Errol, still in his lancer's tunic with twisted gold shoulder cords, ran his finger over his pencil-thin mustache. "Would you be interested in preparing hors d'oeuvres and serving drinks for a poker game at a friend's house in Brentwood?"

"Yes."

Errol lifted his finger as though remembering one more thing. "Of course, you must bring the Wonder Dog," he said. "I have told all the chaps about him."

CHAPTER 48

A SHINY, SLEEK LIMOUSINE ARRIVED AT Scruffy's residence at seven o'clock sharp. The chauffeur, wearing a dark suit and black cap with a hard brim, opened the back door. "Mr. Lomax, I presume." The man was in his fifties and had the accent and air of a British butler.

"Yes," Scruffy said. "And you would be ...?"

"Jeeves, sir, at your service."

I have come a long way from riding the rails, Scruffy thought.

There was a glass partition separating the front and rear seats. Scruffy slid the glass open and said to Jeeves, "Is this not a Pullman limousine?"

"Yes sir," Jeeves said. "I see, sir, that you are an aficionado of luxury vehicles."

"No," Scruffy said as they turned up a two-lane road, exiting the San Fernando Valley and heading up into the Santa Monica Hills, "I work at Warner Brothers Studios, and I helped rig up the interior of one for a movie shoot."

"Ah," Jeeves said. "That must be the most interesting work."

"No argument there, Jeeves," Scruffy said, sitting back in his cushy leather seat as the car effortlessly and smoothly climbed up into the hills and back down toward Beverly Hills and beyond.

Just north of Sunset Boulevard, they entered the exclusive, leafy neighborhood of Brentwood. Jeeves turned on to Bundy Drive, where they arrived at a long driveway guarded by high hedges.

At the end of the driveway, Scruffy was dropped off in front of a house with a steeply pitched gable roof, adorned by a stone facade framed by decorative timber and an elaborate masonry chimney topped by a chimney pot.

At the heavy wooden front door, above a lion's head knocker, were sketched three words below two heraldic unicorns: "Useless. Insignificant. Poetic."

He banged the door knocker—no answer. An uproar of laughter coming from around the side of the house drew Scruffy to a terrace overlooking a heart-shaped pool. There was a patio door at the rear of the home, and inside a table of men sat playing cards. He tapped on the door, and no one paid him a bit of attention.

Errol sat with his back to the door, his head titled back in his classic laugh. Also at the table were David Niven and a couple of men Scruffy did not know, and two more who were famous actors whose movies Scruffy had attended over the last year.

On opening the door, Scruffy received a strong whiff of cigar smoke.

"Balderdash," said a portly man wearing a white shirt, red suspenders, and a checkered bow tie. He threw down his cards, stood, and eyeballed Scruffy, who recognized the famous comedic actor W. C. Fields.

W. C. twisted his face into a look of aggravated surprise and pointed an accusatory finger at Scruffy. He announced in his grating, gravelly voice, "Robb ... eeer!"

All eyes turned to Scruffy, who picked up Rusty as if holding a gun and said, "Your money or your life, gents!"

The table broke out in a rumble of laughter, with Errol standing and rushing to greet Scruffy with a slap on the shoulder. "Gentlemen ... and I use that term so very loosely ... may I introduce to you our tender of refreshments for the evening and a fellow scoundrel, Master Scruffy Lomax." Errol lifted his finger. "And lest I forget his loyal partner in scoundrelism, Rusty the One-Eyed Wonder Dog."

"And where did you find such an appropriate flair man," said John Barrymore, the most famous and brilliant of actors, who, along with W. C. Fields, was at least a generation older than the other men.

"Why, on the set at Warner Brothers," Errol said as he led Scruffy to the bar at the rear of the room, which looked like an exclusive tavern. It had a hand-carved backbar with three plate glass mirrors ensconced in arches, high-back stools with leather seats, and paneled redwood walls that provided an elegant, homey feel. And the octagon-shaped poker table was made of red oak with inlaid chip and drink holders, and a timber base. It had all the trappings of a gentleman's saloon.

"Scruffy, here we are," Errol said as he placed a hand on the bar and turned to the poker table. "May I introduce you to my compadres in mischief and low-level crimes. I give you, ta-da!" He gave a slight bow and hand introduction. "The Bundy Drive Boys."

And so it began. Scruffy tended to the thirst and hunger of the Bundy Drive Boys—a collection of seven or so regulars whose attendance varied based on the whims of martial or social obligations, shoots on location, or some sort of trouble one of the members got himself into, usually involving alcohol and the authorities.

The owner of the home was John Decker, a portrait artist who also did caricatures, one of which—of W. C. as Queen Victoria—hung on the wall at Chasen's, a new restaurant in West Hollywood. Decker was an older version of David Niven and Errol, but without the dashing looks, though what he lacked in physical attributes he made up for as a raconteur.

"Gentlemen," Decker said toward the end of one ribald evening, standing with martini raised, "I shall always consider myself a Bohemian rogue who sleeps under the sun and lives beneath the moon." And another time, he stated, "We shall live with our dreams until regret comes a-knocking and even then refuse to acknowledge the bloody whore's presence."

"Here ye, hear ye," said the others, fists pounding table, glasses raised.

These poker games did not end until the wee hours, and getting to the studio with little or no sleep made for a long day, but Scruffy would not have missed a Bundy Drive event for anything. He so enjoyed the carefree, highbrow inebriation and the sharp repartee, all of which was given as well as it was taken.

For the next four years, Scruffy continued serving as "flair man" to the Bundy Drive Boys and worked his way up the ladder at Warner Brothers to key grip. He also moved out of his small living quarters to a more spacious apartment in Burbank.

Part of Scruffy was getting itchy to hit the road, but the pull of working at a movie studio, even with all its craziness amid the over-the-top, egocentric personalities, had such a glamorous appeal, owing to the beautiful women, some of whom Scruffy had dated; the excitement of contributing to the making of a movie; and those nights at Bundy Drive, which Scruffy found addictive.

Scruffy had even begun to join into the banter with bon mots such as "If John Barrymore had known he was going to live this long, he would have taken better care of himself." That broke up the Bundy Drive Boys, none more so than Barrymore, who laughed so hard Errol had to pound him on the back.

But something else had dissuaded Scruffy from hitting the road: Rusty was beginning to show his age. Wonder Dog had been with Scruffy for over fifteen years and was well over one hundred in dog years. Rusty did not move with as much vigor as he once had, his movements slow and careful, like those of a little old man winding down. Taking him on the road would not be good a thing.

CHAPTER 49

December 7, 1941

SCRUFFY HEADED HOME AFTER A short day on the set. He had led his team of grips in filming *Captain of the Clouds*, directed by Michael Curtiz, who had insisted that Scruffy and his crew work this production. It had been a satisfying job, with Mr. Curtiz as particular and demanding as usual, but Scruffy had a real understanding of what was needed before each day of filming and worked closely with the camera crew to have cameras mounted to a dolly, crane, or even the top of a ladder. And his team had done a fine job in building the sets, often under the critical eye of Mr. Curtiz.

Later this evening, there was going to be a wrap party at the Brown Derby that Scruffy was looking forward to. But with everything going so right, there was one unsolvable off-kilter issue—Rusty. Wonder Dog could no longer make it to the set; he could barely walk at this point.

A vet that a friend at the studio had recommended had told Scruffy, "There is nothing that can be done. This is a very old dog that Father Time is catching up with."

The vet had gone on to tell Scruffy to make Rusty as comfortable as possible and to expect the end anytime now. Before leaving for work in the morning, Scruffy would take Rusty outside to relieve himself, but lately Scruffy had been coming home to find Rusty lying on a urine-soaked blanket that he had rested on during the day.

When Scruffy had left for work that morning, Rusty had struggled to get up to all fours, with a look that Scruffy had never seen from his little dog before: his mouth closed tightly in a downward slant, his graying muzzle only contributing to the melancholy.

Scruffy knew that the humane thing to do was put down his Wonder Dog, but God help him, he could not do it. Never. Ever.

When Scruffy got home, he found Rusty on his blanket in the corner of his bedroom, lying so very still. There was no sign of a puddle of urine, no sign of life.

Scruffy knew before he touched his dog's cold body that he was gone. Scruffy patted his little dog softly on the neck as tears streaked down his cheeks.

Scruffy borrowed a shovel from the janitor, wrapped Rusty in his blanket, and hailed a cab.

In a weedy patch along the side of the Union Pacific tracks near the freight yard, Scruffy began digging into the hard-shell earth. After an hour of work, he placed the blanket covering Rusty in the hole. As he began shoveling the dirt back over the hole, the blare of a train whistle caused Scruffy to stop. Coming toward him in the distance was a black speck that grew clearer. It was a massive steam engine in all its glory, whizzing past like a blast of wind. How appropriate.

Scruffy stood over the covered hole that had a hump from the loose dirt. Over time it would settle back, and over time Rusty's body would return to the good earth from which he came.

Scruffy thought about skipping the wrap party but decided he needed to go—not just as a courtesy to Mr. Curtiz but also for himself. He needed to be in the company of people—friends he had developed over the years in this land of make-believe.

Scruffy dressed in his typical wrap party outfit, the one that consisted of leather sandals, red suspenders, and the floral shirt he had purchased for *Captain Blood*. Why, if he had worn anything else, his fellow grips would not have had a chance to razz him. "A wrap party is not a wrap party without the Scruffy ensemble," one grip had commented.

When Scruffy arrived at the Brown Derby, he immediately knew something was wrong. There was a buzz coming from people milling outside the restaurant.

"The Japs have bombed Pearl Harbor," one man said in a raised, angry voice.

"It will be war," added another man, whom Scruffy recognized as one of the film's producers.

Scruffy turned and walked away, his mind set on what his next move would be.

CHAPTER 50

THE NEXT MORNING, SCRUFFY ROSE early but did not go to the studio. Instead he called in to say he would be late and caught a bus to the Marine Corp recruiting office in Los Angeles. Last year he had registered for the military draft, so he felt enlisting should not be a problem. He had heard on the way over that war had been declared on Japan.

After signing up, he was told that he would receive a notice for a physical in the next two weeks. "You are a little older than we like," the recruiting sergeant said, "but you look fit enough to handle the rigors of being a marine."

Scruffy returned to work, but he only had one thing on his mind—fighting for his country to defend this great land that had afforded him the freedom to live as he pleased. That was something Scruffy Lomax took to the core of his being.

Three weeks later, Scruffy received a letter listing a date and time when he was to report to the recruiting depot, where they would take a bus to the Marine Corp depot in San Diego for a physical exam.

On the bus ride down, thirty-six-year-old Scruffy was by far the oldest man on board. Most looked like teenagers, too young for what surely lay ahead.

After passing through one line after another, showing identification, and filling out forms, Scruffy and his fellow bus riders stripped down to their underwear. A doctor approached Scruffy and, after checking him over with a stethoscope, had Scruffy come over to the side and sit in a chair.

"Lift your foot," the doctor said.

As the doctor examined Scruffy's foot, he make a strange noise like a disapproving hum. "How old are you?"

"Thirty-six," Scruffy said as a sinking feeling came over him.

"Stand up, please," the doctor said with a lift of his hand.

The doctor ran his hand over the lower half of one of Scruffy's legs and then the other.

He called another doctor over to have a look. "Genum varum, all right" the second doctor said.

"Plus he has flat feet and is thirty-six."

"What is going on?" Scruffy said.

The first doctor nodded a thank-you to his colleague. "You have a modest case of bow legs—genum varum—and flat feet. Combine that with your advanced age, and I am sorry to inform you that you are unfit for military service."

By the time Scruffy got back to his place, it was early evening. He plopped down on his bed and laced his fingers behind his neck, staring at the ceiling. He had argued with everyone he could find at his physical, but it was to no avail. He also was informed by a sergeant back at the recruiting station, "If the Marine Corp will not take you, no other branch will either."

He felt they would have taken the seventeen-year-old version of himself—bow legs, flat feet, and all. But Scruffy Lomax was now a middle-aged man who had been rejected for military service in a time of war, having lived a full and challenging life—a life that from now on would be different.

It would be hard to match the first half of this life: the people, the adventures, the newness of it all. He had seen a lot of things and done a few himself.

He had lived a hobo's life and everything on up, including hobnobbing with Hollywood royalty. Along the way, he had accepted his faults, which he told himself centered on his inability to establish roots. But was that it? Or was it part of his weakness as a man? *Just might take the rest of my life to figure myself out*, he thought to himself.

But he saw faults in everyone he had encountered in this life, and the more talented and gifted the person, the greater the flaws. The Bundy Drive Boys were an appealing, witty group of raconteurs. But where would they be in the coming years? They lived hard lives of late nights and alcohol. In the few years he had known them, they seemed to have aged in dog years. And as much fun as they were to be around, Scruffy had heard enough in their private conversations to realize that these marvelously talented men did not always treat the people closest to them all that well. The only ones they were really loyal to were themselves—the Bundy Drive Boys.

Even so, he would not have missed being in their company for anything. When among them, he reveled on a higher plane of great wit, charm, and charisma. They were intoxicating.

After two weeks at work, with his heart no longer in it, Scruffy came to a decision. America did not want him to fight, but he still wanted America. There was only one thing for him to do.

The freight yard was quiet, the sun just peeking over the horizon. There were rows and rows of boxcars sitting still. But that was not what Scruffy was looking for. Around the back of a storage shed, there it was—a handcar.

He thought back to the beginning of this adventure and the places he had promised himself he would see: Yellowstone, Yosemite, and the Grand Canyon. *Those would be new and interesting experiences*, Scruffy thought.

But for right now he was not sure where he would go other than wherever the tracks took him—that, in a way, was a new and interesting experience, which was what his life had been since leaving Yakima.

Once again, Scruffy felt the thrill of the rail, the freedom and independence of going wherever the spirit took him. He did not feel young again, but he experienced an invigorating charge as he pushed the handcar off the side track and began pumping the handle on his way out of the freight yard, once again feeling the wind in his face, as he wondered what adventures were yet to come in the life and times of Scruffy Lomax.

Printed in the United States
By Bookmasters